It would all come down to timing

There were perhaps a dozen people in the hotel lobby, counting various employees. If Bolan had to take down the shooter in full view of an audience, this was the best place to do it, rather than during a protracted running battle through the streets.

The Executioner watched the young Colombian half rising from his chair, his hand reaching underneath the roomy jacket for his weapon. From ten feet out, Bolan's Spectre hammered him with half a dozen rounds, sending him somersaulting across the chair and out of sight.

Bolan kept walking, trailed by screams, until he reached the sidewalk. The doorman had his back turned, his nose in a corner, staring at the wall. He didn't turn around, intent on being deaf, dumb and blind until the gringo with the cold eyes had a chance to disappear.

MACK BOLAN ®
The Executioner

DON PENDLETON'S
EXECUTIONER®
THE
DIRTY MISSION

A GOLD EAGLE BOOK FROM
WORLDWIDE®

TORONTO • NEW YORK • LONDON
AMSTERDAM • PARIS • SYDNEY • HAMBURG
STOCKHOLM • ATHENS • TOKYO • MILAN
MADRID • WARSAW • BUDAPEST • AUCKLAND

First edition December 2001
ISBN 0-373-64277-6

Special thanks and acknowledgment to
Mike Newton for his contribution to this work.

DIRTY MISSION

Neither a man nor a crowd nor a nation can be trusted
to act humanely or to think sanely under the influence of
a great fear.

—Bertrand Russell

Any device whatever by which one frees himself from
the fear of others is a natural good.

—Epicurus

It's time to give the terrorists and those who sponsor
them a taste of fear and find out how they measure up.

—Mack Bolan

For the innocent victims
of Colombia's long civil war.

Prologue

Miami

The gringos sometimes said that all Latinos looked alike, and now, by God, Francisco Guzman had begun to see their point. He wasn't racist—he was Latino, and dark-skinned at that—but after weeks of glancing nervously behind him every time he made a move in public, watching for the men who would be sent to find him, Guzman saw the faces run together in his mind, their features merging, blurring, growing indistinct.

And there were moments when he wondered if his own myopia would get him killed.

Miami was supposed to be a refuge for his people, as it had been for more than nearly half a century. The city—once the South's most liberal and cosmopolitan—had been transformed since the late 1950s into a kind of Hispanic oasis. It was Rio, Bogotá, Havana and San Juan all rolled into one.

And still, Guzman didn't feel safe.

How would he know the killers when they came for him? Would there be time for him to run, or would they hide and cut him down from ambush? Maybe pull up next to him in traffic with their automatic weapons or perhaps attach explosives to the starter of his car?

The Colombian was frightened, but he worried more about his wife and children than about himself. How would Amalia cope with life in this strange country after he was gone? How would she raise Elena and Bartolo on her own? Would she forget him in the end and find herself another man?

It struck Guzman that he had already adopted a defeatist attitude, conceding victory—his death, in fact—to enemies whom he had never seen. There was a chance, he told himself, that they would never find him. They might never even look for him at all.

But that was wrong. Guzman knew it in his heart.

He had received word from Monteria, from men he trusted, that the hunt was under way. Colombian exiles who dared to speak or write about the "special circumstances" in their homeland, criticizing those who made the rules and called the shots, were being tracked and scoured from the earth. It would take time, of course. There was still so much killing to finish at home that only a certain number of assassins could be spared for hunting those who slipped away.

It stood to reason, though, that they would start the search where targets were most numerous. Miami seemed a poor choice for a sanctuary now, with that in mind. Of all his countrymen who had been driven from their homeland by violence during the past three decades, how many had settled here? How many in Los Angeles? Dallas-Fort Worth? New York?

Why were they all so damned predictable?

Guzman had trusted the time-honored theory of safety in numbers, believing that his chances of survival were enhanced by settling in a place where he wouldn't stand out, where others shared his passion and his memories of fleeing for their lives. How would he have concealed himself, his precious family, in Idaho, Kansas or Illinois?

They had been safe. Guzman was confident of that, but he had thrown it all away. A stupid letter to the newspaper, which he had felt compelled to answer, and the rest was history. He had been caught up in the moment, heralded as a spokesman for his people, drawn almost against his will into the fierce debate about his homeland and the mayhem that had racked it for so many years.

That was a lie, of course. Guzman hadn't done anything against his will, although his better judgment had suggested that he should decline the invitations to speak out in public, think about his family and keep his feelings to himself. It should have been enough simply to get away, but somehow it wasn't.

And now the urge to be a man once more and do something had placed his life at risk.

His wife had been part of it, Guzman thought, although he didn't mean to blame her for the danger they now shared—the threat of which she still knew nothing, since he hadn't spoken to her of the warnings sent from home. She had been proud of him when he broke silence. He had seen it in her eyes and in her attitude, had felt it in her touch, the ardor of their coupling. She had made him feel like more than a pathetic refugee whose first and last resort had been to run and hide from trouble in his homeland.

But what would come of all that pride and passion now, with hunters on their way to settle ancient scores?

Guzman had a pistol in his briefcase, purchased from a Cuban on the street who asked no questions, made no background checks, observed no mandatory waiting periods and only dealt in cash. It was a relatively small gun, semiautomatic, chosen on the basis of simplicity. Guzman had practiced with it at a local firing range until he was convinced that he could slay a paper target, but he drew small comfort from the weapon otherwise. The men who would be sent for him—assuming they were sent at all—would be assassins with experience and training, either from the military or in one of the guerrilla camps that flourished in his homeland. He would stand no realistic chance against such men unless they made some epic blunder, maybe let him get behind them with his gun, perhaps while they were drunk. Or, better yet, while they were sleeping.

He wasn't a soldier, had no martial skills beyond the bare ability to aim his newly purchased gun and squeeze the trigger without flinching. The paper targets he had practiced on didn't return fire, though; they didn't duck and hide, or creep into his house at midnight through a window jimmied open while his family slept.

Guzman thought again about the new security system he planned to install in the house. The installers were due on Saturday, but Guzman wondered if he could offer them some extra money to speed things up. His wife had been troubled when he mentioned it the first time, but Guzman had explained his new preoccupation with a reference to the rising number of break-ins. The new alarm system was for Amalia's safety and that of the children, he had told her.

And so it was, though burglars were the furthest thing from Guzman's mind.

With the alarms, at least, he thought that he might have some warning if the hunters came for him. There might be time for him to reach his pistol, maybe hold the men at bay until police arrived with their superior firepower.

He had considered visiting police headquarters when the first warning arrived, but trusting the authorities wasn't a habit learned in Colombia. There, a badge or uniform was normally another kind of threat, the individual behind it typically in league with those Guzman would count among his enemies. Corruption and fanaticism made the army and police as much a risk to public safety as were the guerrillas and the narcotraffickers who operated on the wrong side of the law.

And was it any different in the United States?

He would have liked to think so, but Guzman wasn't convinced. It seemed that each new day brought some report of a policeman caught with drugs or stolen money, charged with violating someone's civil rights. The victims too often were persons of color; the source of the money and drugs, almost inevitably, was the same pervasive underworld that seemed to thrive wherever Guzman looked these days.

It was a short walk from his office to his home, a mere six blocks beneath a nearly cloudless sky, with sunshine beaming down and children playing in the streets. He drove to work on rainy days, but otherwise preferred the exercise, and told himself that he might be a more elusive target on his own two feet than trapped inside a car. When Guzman reached Máximo Góaomez Park, he saw the old men playing dominoes and smoking their cigars while others stood around and watched them, offering encouragement or criticism as the spirit moved. Some of them—most of them—were refugees themselves. He wondered whether they still dreamed of home or if they ever gave a thought to danger from the past arriving on their doorsteps like a creditor appearing to collect his balance due.

Crossing the driveway to his house, Guzman started to relax. There had been no ambush this time, and it would be twelve hours before he had to make the trek again, checking over his shoulder every block or so for furtive movement, watching out for anyone whose eyes might follow him a moment longer than was absolutely necessary.

Guzman had his key in hand as he approached the door, but never had a chance to use it. He was reaching for the dead bolt when he noticed that the door was open, just an inch or two. A cool draft from the air-conditioning inside raised goose bumps on his hand and wrist; fear made them bristle on the rest of Guzman's body like a rash.

He dropped the keys, restrained himself with sheer force of will from rushing through the open doorway. Kneeling on the porch, he set down his briefcase and snapped it open, found the pistol by blind touch and thumbed back its hammer. The safety wasn't on because he meant the weapon to be ever-ready for emergencies.

Like this.

Thus armed, he stepped around the open briefcase and nudged the door open with his shoulder, stepping across the threshold into a familiar place that now felt hopelessly alien. He prayed that one of the children had simply forgotten to close the door upon returning from school, but something in him knew that wasn't the case.

It would have been too simple and too merciful.

Guzman moved from room to silent room, his pistol braced in both hands as the range instructor had taught him, feeling like a foolish parody of a policeman from some television drama. He called out Amalia's name, then called the children when she didn't answer him.

Silence.

But there was something....

It took Guzman several moments to identify the smell, and when it came to him, his stomach lurched, preparing to expel the remnants of his frugal lunch. Too late, he recognized the smell of cordite from the firing range where he had learned to use his pistol.

It was gun smoke that he smelled inside the sanctuary of his home.

Why were there no police in evidence if gunshots had been fired? Despite suggestions in the media, the neighborhood wasn't so jaded that a violent crime in broad daylight would simply be ignored. If no report of gunshots had been made to the police, it was because no gunshots had been heard.

And that meant sound suppressors.

He found them in the living room, its very name a mockery. His wife was sprawled across the couch, Elena and Bartolo stretched out close beside her on the floor. One of Amalia's hands was draped across Elena's slender back, as if to shield her.

Guzman was barely conscious of the cartridge cases crunching underneath his shoes with every step. His mind was blank, his eyes locked open, unblinking, as he scanned the ruin of his life. The killers could have taken him without a struggle then, but they left the house of death, moved on perhaps in search of other targets.

Leaving him a message on the wall above the sofa, painted there in crimson that had dried to rusty brown.

It read: NEXT TIME.

Los Angeles

RAUL MENENDEZ KNEW death when he saw it, coming up behind him in the rearview mirror of his vintage Coupe de Ville.

The Cadillac was old but well maintained, which made it classic—that was English double-talk for costly—and the V-8 engine underneath the hood had been designed for speed when engineers were more concerned about performance on the highway than they were about the ozone layer.

All things considered, Menendez thought, he just might have a fighting chance to stay alive.

It helped that he had missed rush hour on the Harbor Freeway. Otherwise, the shooters could have parked their Crown Victoria sedan and walked up from behind to kill him where he sat. Granted, it would have made their getaway a trifle awkward, but police could travel no more quickly in a traffic jam than anybody else. The hit men could have fled on foot and vanished by the time the first squad car or motorcycle had arrived.

This way, Menendez thought, they had to earn their keep.

Menendez mulled the possibility that he might be mistaken, that the two—or was it three?—men in the Crown Victoria were innocent of any criminal intent. There was a chance they were policemen, he considered, since the Crown Vic was a favorite for unmarked cars that screamed Official Business. If they were cops, there should be flashing lights and sirens wailing when he left them in his dust.

If they weren't...

He took the chance, bore down on the accelerator, feeling the Cadillac respond to his touch like a Thoroughbred under the whip. There was a rumble underneath the pearl-gray hood, raw power shedding its restraints, as Menendez clamped his large hands on the padded steering wheel and veered around a slower-moving minivan.

Behind him, the Crown Vic accelerated instantly and changed lanes without signaling to stay on the Colombian's tail. There were no flashing lights, no siren. In a flash Menendez saw his worst fear realized and knew that this could be the last night of his life.

But he wasn't dead yet.

The men had been hunting him for years. He had survived

a near-miss out in Tucson when a hasty triggerman had tried to take him in a shopping mall but wounded several by-standers instead. In San Diego they had tried a car bomb, but the mechanism failed and the device was found by a mechanic when Menendez took his car in for a tune-up. They had laughed about it afterward, but only when the two of them had put away enough tequila to suppress the shock.

This night, the hunters meant to do it properly.

Menendez powered north, passing on his left the sprawl of Exposition Park that included the L.A. Memorial Sports Arena and L.A. Memorial Coliseum. Memorial to what? he asked himself, distracted for a fraction of a heartbeat from the life-or-death pursuit in which he was the prey.

It almost made Menendez laugh, until he thought about the Colt revolver in the Caddy's glove compartment. Damn! He should have gone for it first thing instead of waiting.

Menendez checked the rearview mirror, flicked a glance at the speedometer, then took a chance and made the stretch. He had to lean across to reach the glove compartment, steer-ing with his left hand, groping with his right. A wad of crum-pled maps and credit-card receipts spilled out across the seat and floorboards as he rummaged for the pistol.

He felt it, hooked his pinky through the cool, smooth trigger guard, drew back his hand—and dropped it with a muffled thud,

"Shit!"

There was no way he could reach the weapon now, or even locate it without a major risk of cracking up the car. At this speed, eighty-five and climbing, a mistake could leave the wreckage and his body scattered over half a mile of freeway, traffic grinding him to pulp before the ambulance arrived.

Later, perhaps. If he couldn't outrun them. If he had to stop and fight.

Passing the University of Southern California campus on his left, Menendez thought about the students in their dormi-tories, drinking beer and having sex, the greatest worry in their lives involving what to wear the next day or the notes they had forgotten for some class. What did they know of life and death?

A flare of high beams in the Caddy's rearview snapped his mind back to the hunters as they closed the gap, running up close enough behind him to kiss bumpers in the center lane. Menendez cursed and floored the gas pedal, vehicles blurring around him as he cranked it up to ninety, pushing ninety-five.

Where were the traffic cops? Menendez would have welcomed them right now, but they were nowhere to be found.

After another mile or so, the Harbor Freeway veered to the northeast, angling toward Dodger Stadium and Elysian Park, beyond which it became the Pasadena Freeway and continued on through affluent suburbs. Menendez didn't plan to follow it that far. In fact, he was already planning where and how to leave the freeway, trusting that the city's maze of surface streets would help him lose the men who meant to kill him.

Menendez took the first off-ramp beyond the Los Angeles Convention Center, veering across three lanes in a kamikaze mode that left tires smoking, horns blaring in his wake. The best scenario he could imagine would have taken out the chase car in a flaming crash, but his pursuers had more skill and speed than the Colombian gave them credit for. The chase car had a close shave with a bright red Miata, but blew past the convertible and held its course. Along the way, there was a bright flash from a window on the Crown Vic's passenger side and Menendez heard something slap against the Caddy's bumper.

"Sons of bitches!"

There was nothing for it but to slow down on the off-ramp, otherwise, he would have scraped the Caddy down to primer gray along the guardrail and might well have lost control, flipping the car before he even had a decent chance to shake the hunters. As it was, they gained on him and nearly canceled out the lead he had attained by virtue of surprise short moments earlier.

So be it. It was all or nothing now.

He had a clear shot on the off-ramp, high beams burning up the night behind him. At the bottom of the ramp a red light ordered him to stop. Menendez ignored it, leaning on the Caddy's horn as he blew through the intersection, as if noise alone would save him from a lethal head-on crash.

There was no crash, despite the sound of new horns shrilling at him. Behind him, tiny in the rearview mirror, he saw the chase car jump the light and fishtail through the intersection. Muzzle-flashes from the driver's side weren't directed at his Coupe de Ville this time, but rather toward a high-rise pickup truck that nearly bashed the Crown Victoria. Before he tore his eyes away to watch the road ahead, Menendez saw the pickup swerve and jump the curb.

The pickup's driver bought him time, and the Colombian used the extra moments to his best advantage. Racing through another light as it turned yellow, he weaved in and out of slower traffic, answering the horn blasts with his own. Behind him, he could see the chase car following, too far away to risk a shot but gaining all the time.

Menendez stamped the accelerator to the floor, both hands white-knuckled on the steering wheel. A yellow taxi rushed to meet him at the intersection, Menendez cranking on the Caddy's steering wheel to avoid the collision, his rear end whipping around to slam the cab's left-front fender in passing. Shaken by the impact, he compensated by accelerating, leaving the taxi spinning in the middle of the intersection, with the Crown Vic coming through.

The two cars came together broadside, grating metal, seeming locked in apposition for a moment, then the Crown Vic shuddered, tore free and sped off in pursuit of the Cadillac. There was another muzzle-flash as Menendez turned right, still more as he swung left again. One of the incoming rounds took out a fist-sized chunk of his rear window, spraying pebbled safety glass across both seats.

Menendez didn't know where he was going now, driving on instinct, feeling panic like the clammy fingers of a dead hand clamped around his neck. A dark alley yawned, coming up on his right, and he cranked the steering wheel hard left, then back to the right as he swung the Coupe de Ville into the turn. He killed the lights, in case the hunters hadn't seen him make the turn, to give himself an extra margin of security.

It was going to be close, the Caddy seeming almost as wide as the alley's mouth from where Menendez sat, but it fit, tires crunching over gravel and collected trash as he accelerated down the narrow straightaway.

And when he hit the Dumpster garbage bin it was a complete surprise.

The impact rocked him and sent a stab of pain down his spine. Whiplash, for Mary's sake! Just what he needed now. The Caddy's engine growled, then sputtered before it died.

There was no point in trying it again, because the Dumpster garbage bin had him blocked. Menendez checked his rearview mirror, saw no headlights bearing down on him, no shadow-bulk of a pursuit vehicle in the alley. Had he foxed them?

Hissing at the pain, he threw himself across the front seat and fumbled around the floor until he found the Colt and gripped it in his fist. Thus armed, he tried the driver's door and opened it a foot or so before it jammed against the brick wall of a building to his left.

The panicky feeling returned as Menendez slid across the seat, glass rolling underneath his backside like marbles, to try the other door. It opened slightly farther, maybe eighteen inches, then collided with another wall. Menendez got one leg out through the narrow opening, but he could never hope to clear it with his bulky torso. Adding insult to the injury, he scraped his shin as he withdrew the leg and felt blood seeping through his high-topped cotton sock.

Now what?

He had two choices, front or back, and if he had to guess Menendez would have said the hunters were more likely to be waiting somewhere at his back, in the direction he had come from. Having missed him in the alley, they would probably retrace their route and try to find where he had lost them.

To the front, then.

When he tried to kick out the windshield, it felt as if his

ankle bone were shattered. Sprained, at least. In desperation, Menendez raised the Colt and aimed it at the windshield, squeezing off one shot and then another, with the points of impact spaced a foot or so apart.

His bullets didn't take out the windshield completely, but they weakened it enough so that when Menendez awkwardly resumed his kicking he was able to produce a man-sized hole above the dashboard. Wriggling headfirst through it, with the warm gun clenched between his aching teeth, he prayed that those who hunted him hadn't been near enough to hear the shots.

It seemed to take forever, but at last he slithered off the Caddy's crumpled hood, rebounded from the garbage bin and landed in a heap on filthy pavement. Struggling to his feet, brushing his ruined suit from force of habit, the Colombian started hobbling toward the far end of the alley and the lights that beckoned him.

He almost made it.

Half a dozen paces from the sidewalk, he stopped short as the Crown Vic rolled up to block his path. Both windows on the passenger side were down, two grim-faced hit men leaning out with automatic weapons in their hands.

It was a soldier's truism that no one ever heard the shot that took his life. In Menendez's case, he saw the muzzle-flashes winking at him but there was no sound to speak of, since the guns were fitted with heavy-duty sound suppressors.

Menendez felt the bullets, true, but only for a moment, as he toppled over backward and the swirling darkness carried him away.

New York City

"I DON'T CARE if we couldn't get the full half hour," Dr. Mateo Espinosa said. "They'll listen, that's what matters. I can always edit. Fifteen minutes is enough."

It was a great deal more than he had counted on, in fact. How many ordinary men were granted fifteen minutes—even fifteen seconds—of their lives to speak before the General Assembly of the great United Nations?

There were some, of course, who would have said Espinosa was no ordinary man. For one thing, he was a physician—and a heart surgeon, at that. He had been moderately famous in his homeland for the skill with which he healed his patients, and in later life for the audacity with which he spoke against abuses practiced by some organs of the state. It was the latter action, rather than his medical technique, which had resulted in his exile to America. Now, after two years working at a clinic for the poor and homeless, writing editorials and making speeches in his spare time for the International Consultancy on Human Rights, he had a chance to tell the world at large about the burden that he carried on his soul.

How long had he been waiting for this moment?

Looking back, it seemed like half his life.

"There won't be time to show the slides," Jorge Aguedo said. He served as Espinosa's combination bodyguard and personal assistant, brooding over both jobs to the point where he seemed almost clinically depressed.

"It makes no difference, Jorge. We'll use the time they give us to the best of our ability, and show the slides to someone else."

Espinosa didn't really wish to see the slides again, himself. How many shattered bodies, sightless eyes and gutted homes could any man observe before they all began to look alike? That was the secret weapon of the modern tyrant, he believed. Where once upon a time a grainy newsreel might have captured bodies rotting in the courtyard of a Nazi prison camp and stunned the world, today the web of television hammered everyone with nonstop images of hurricanes and forest fires, explosions, train wrecks, riots, genocide—all beamed into boardrooms and living rooms around the clock. The human race had been desensitized to suffering by mass exposure to the pain of millions, sandwiched in between slick advertisements for cosmetics, cars and clothing.

Why bother, then? Why even tell the story one more time?

Because he couldn't help himself. He was compelled to

speak and write about the agony Colombia suffered under cruel and venal men, until such time as things had changed or he ran out of breath. If anyone had asked Espinosa which event he thought would happen first, he couldn't have replied with any certainty.

This day, though, he would strike a blow against the savages.

This day he had a chance to speak the truth before a global audience.

But would they listen? Would they hear him?

Dr. Espinosa knew the grim reality of Third World politics. Civil wars and insurrections raged around the world. Slavery was still alive and well on several continents. Women and children still had fewer rights than men under the thumb of too many regimes.

When he addressed the UN General Assembly that afternoon, Espinosa knew he would be speaking to the handpicked representatives of the same men who clung to power by committing vicious crimes against their captive peoples every day. Why would they care about what happened in Colombia? Was he a fool for clinging to the slender reed of hope?

"It's time," Aguedo informed him. "We should go before the traffic gets too bad."

"Of course."

It was a two-mile drive to the United Nations building. Most days it was quicker to walk than to drive at this hour, but Espinosa required the extra security and mobility of an automobile. It wouldn't do for him to be caught out on foot by the hired assassins.

So far, they had failed in their mission.

Tomorrow...who could say?

Espinosa and Aguedo had the elevator to themselves for the long ride down from the seventeenth floor to the office building's underground garage. Aguedo's car was parked a few steps from the elevator. Aguedo opened the passenger's door for his friend and closed it again when Espinosa was comfortably seated. Circling around the Nissan Maxima, he slid into the driver's seat and turned the ignition key, bringing the engine to life.

The first, faint popping sound didn't alarm Espinosa. It was only when he saw the tiny tongues of flame dancing inside the dashboard air-conditioner vents that he realized they were in deadly peril.

"Jorge—"

Too late.

The shock wave of the powerful explosion shattered windows on another eighty vehicles in the garage, the spreading pool of gasoline from the Nissan igniting half a dozen other cars before the built-in sprinklers opened up and drenched the **smoky cave**. It was another seven minutes before the first fire engine reached the scene.

But it didn't matter.

1

San Francisco

A large urban hospital mirrored the city it served. It was a world of sorts unto itself, humming around the clock. The ER was the combat zone, where desperate people bled and often died. Maternity was filled with promise, while the ICU was hushed and reverent. If the hospital was large enough, there may be one or even several chapels, with a morgue downstairs to store the dead.

Because the hospital was like a city, it attracted inhabitants and visitors of every sort. Most of them were distinctly average; a few were known to shine among their fellow human beings.

And a few of them were evil, without conscience or remorse.

Mack Bolan left his rented Jeep Grand Cherokee on level three of San Francisco General Hospital's attached parking garage. He left his ticket on the dashboard, knowing in advance that there would be no opportunity for him to have it validated at the nurses' station.

If his plan worked out, the nurses and the other staff of SF General would never know he had been on the premises.

There were no signs in the garage admonishing arrivals to be quiet, but the tall man dressed in black was mindful of his place. The only weapons that he carried were a razor-edged stiletto with a six-inch blade and a Beretta 93-R pistol fitted with a custom sound suppressor. The pistol hung beneath his left arm in a Galco fast-draw rig, spare magazines in leather pouches slung below his right arm; the stiletto occupied a sheath on Bolan's belt, concealed beneath his jacket.

Those he hunted would be better armed, but they wouldn't expect to find him there. The man known as the Executioner cherished the advantage of surprise.

The targets were Colombian assassins. Three men, maybe more. The coke-addicted orderly who had accepted their blood money to betray one of his patients, then experienced a trembling change of heart could vouch for three hit men. Survival instincts told Bolan to be prepared for more.

He knew the shooters were supposed to strike this night, because the bought-and-paid-for orderly had been alerted to desert his post at half-past midnight, if he cared to see the sun come up. Thus forewarned, the orderly had called the FBI in hopes of picking up a bonus on the side. By pure dumb luck, the G-man he had spoken to was wired to Hal Brognola, the director of the Sensitive Operations Group.

The rest was history—or would be, in another thirty minutes, give or take.

There was a certain irony implicit in the fact that the assassins meant to kill a dying man. Their target had been battling terminal cirrhosis for the past twelve months and had perhaps a week of pseudo-life remaining, hooked up to machines, but those who paid to have him killed wouldn't allow the man to die in what some might have labeled peace.

They had a message to deliver, and the target's life was secondary to the broadcast of that message. The assassins had been told to beat the Reaper, do their job and make it plain to any witnesses that there could be no sanctuary from the long arm of revenge. If they should fail for any reason, if the target happened to expire of normal causes, the assassins would receive no pay for the assignment.

And there might be worse in store for them at home, when they returned.

Bolan entered the hospital, passing an unattended Information desk. A plastic sign said Back in 15 Minutes, but he didn't plan to wait. He knew his way to the Intensive Care

Unit from scouting out the hospital that afternoon, a daylight run on which he carried roses and an empty box that might have harbored chocolates under other circumstances. There was no great mystery about the SF General layout; it was user-friendly to a fault, with posted signs and arrows, the instructions offered up in English, Spanish, Cantonese, and Braille. Bolan took his time, examining alternate routes, checking out the service stairs and elevators, marking utility closets and the doors that opened for Employees Only.

He was ready, now, to meet his adversaries on the grave-yard shift.

Ideally, Bolan would have met them on the street or in the hospital's garage, away from sleeping patients and the night employees who were more or less divided between cleaning personnel and medical staff. A firefight in the midst of heal-ers and their charges was the last thing the soldier wanted, but he had no realistic hope of knowing where the shooters would make entry to the hospital, which stairwell, corridor or ele-vator they would choose.

He knew only with certainty where they were going, and he had to meet them there.

Intensive Care was staffed around the clock, but only a skeleton crew remained after visiting hours. The crash carts and defibrolators stood ready for any emergency, but it would take a Code Blue to roust out a full complement of troops. Two nurses watched the ward from midnight until dawn, prepared to hit the panic button at the first sign of a patient's vitals shut-ting down.

No crisis was in progress when the Executioner arrived. The ICU was nearly silent, lights dimmed slightly in the cor-ridor outside. One of the nurses was checking on the seven patients currently in residence while her companion occupied a desk and dealt with paperwork. Bolan stood back from their line of sight, remaining in the shadows while he waited for the hunters to appear. An orderly passed him once, moving with muffled squeaks on rubber soles, failing to notice Bolan in the shadowed doorway to his left. The soldier wondered whether this one was the turncoat, but he caught no nervous vibe, saw nothing to suggest awareness of disaster poised to strike the nurses and the patients in their care.

Bolan had no idea if the intruders he was waiting for would try to take out everyone they found in ICU, but he assumed the nurses would be first to go, since they were on alert and would be sure to see the shooters.

But they would have to go through Bolan first, and he wasn't about to let them get that far.

"ALL READY, then?" Ernesto Calderon inquired of his companions.

"Yes," Basilio Ruiz replied.

"Ready," Filipe Vega said.

The three of them were standing at the bottom of a service stairwell at the southeast corner of the hospital. Outside, Ramon Agnar was circling the large facility in a stolen Mercury Cougar, constantly in motion, like a shark that had to keep swimming or else sink and drown. Because they weren't sure precisely what would happen after they took out their target, Calderon had told Agnar to watch the several exits from the hospital, keep moving, and be ready to evacuate them at a moment's notice when he saw them on the sidewalk.

Simple.

Calderon was fairly confident that they could carry off the job without attracting unwanted attention from the night-shift staffers in the hospital. It meant that certain bystanders would have to die, of course, but that was standard operational procedure for a team like his. Only a fool left witnesses to testify in court, and one who was so careless had no one beside himself to blame if he was sent to prison for his trouble.

The three men were armed with Cobray M-11 machine pistols, modified versions of the classic Ingram "room broom" chambered for 9 mm short rounds that made the weapons easier to handle, despite their cyclic fire rate of some 1,200 rounds per minute. Each machine pistol was fitted with a foot-long sound suppressor inside a heat-resistant sleeve, for maximum stealth and improved fire control. Together, the assassins could unload ninety-six rounds in a second and a half, reloading swiftly with the spare magazines that weighted their pockets if anyone was still alive in the hospital's Intensive Care Unit.

"Let's go," Calderon commanded, leading the way as they started their climb to the hospital's fourth floor, eight flights above. He had the short, sturdy legs of a mountain-born peasant, but years of chain-smoking had weakened his lungs, and Calderon was breathing heavily before they were halfway to their destination, vowing for the thousandth time that he would cut back on the harsh unfiltered cigarettes.

Behind him, the two younger men had an easier time of it, whispering between themselves, Vega laughing at some comment from Ruiz. Incensed by their behavior, no less by their youth, Calderon rounded on them when they reached the third-floor landing, snapping at them, "Shut up, you two!"

They blinked at him, surprised, but didn't answer back. He was the leader here, with more kills to his credit than the two of them combined, and they weren't about to cross him in the middle of a mission. Both men knew their leader would as soon take down an insubordinate employee as he would the target he was sent to kill. It made no difference to Calderon if he spilled blood from one victim or five. Since neither of them carried any ID and they were unknown to the American authorities, it would mean nothing if Calderon left an extra body in the hospital.

When he was satisfied that he had made his point, Calderon turned his back on the young shooters and resumed his climb. The momentary flush of anger seemed to help him with his breathing, the adrenaline supporting him as he fairly jogged up the last two flights of stairs. Despite the speed with which he moved, Calderon made no noise. Like Vega and Ruiz, he wore the latest, most expensive of American athletic shoes, their cushioned soles muting the sound of footsteps, while providing extra speed if necessary, for a hasty getaway.

At last they reached the fourth-floor landing, where they

stood before a metal door emblazoned with the order To be Left Unlocked at all Times: Order of the Fire Marshal, SFFD. Calderon appreciated the convenience. If the fire marshal had ordered that the door be locked at all times, he would have been forced to pick the lock—or possibly to blast it with his M-11. That, in turn, would almost certainly have sounded an alarm before he and his men could reach their target, and Calderon didn't look forward to a full-scale massacre if he could do his job the easy way.

Standing in the stairwell with its vaguely antiseptic odor, Calderon wished that he had brought along a smoke grenade or two to aid in their escape if things went badly. The threat of fire raging through a hospital, even if illusory, would have created chaos enough to disguise a small army's retreat.

No matter, he told himself. If it came to that, gunfire would do the same trick well enough.

Calderon gripped the doorknob, felt cool metal through the latex glove he wore to eliminate fingerprints. He hesitated for a fraction of a second, half expecting the door to be locked in defiance of posted orders, but it turned easily in his hand. He cracked the door, peered through into a silent corridor, then took the risk and stuck his head around the corner.

Nothing.

He stepped through into the hallway, followed by Vega and Ruiz. The last man through took care to easy the door shut, not to let it slam. Calderon experienced a moment of disorientation, resolved as he focused on the square sign posted directly opposite the doorway. Arrows aimed in both directions, pointing the way to Intensive Care, Oncology, Osteopathy, Urology and Gynecology.

Americans were so considerate.

Calderon and his shadows turned to the left, following the pointer toward ICU. Along the way, more signs were hung to reassure them that they hadn't deviated from their course by accident. They carried their weapons in opaque plastic shopping bags, presenting the image of three men who had missed visiting hours but were still determined to proceed.

And so they were.

A sign outside Intensive Care told them that access was restricted and that visitation was permitted by appointment only. These were patients on the edge of death, not merely ill or injured. Even relatives and loved ones could be excluded from the bedsides of these sufferers if a physician ordered it.

Calderon peered through the slightly tinted glass and found that he couldn't observe the patients in their beds from where he stood. The layout was designed for privacy, he thought. Who wanted peasant passersby to stand and gawk while doctors labored with their needles and electrodes, trying to preserve a fragile life or making the decision to forbear?

To reach the target Calderon knew they would have to go inside, confront the nurses, kill them first. The rest would be a simple matter of mechanics.

So be it.

Calderon half turned to issue final orders, and he was astounded when Vega spit directly in his face. The thick, warm fluid stung his eyes and nearly staggered him, his left arm raised to block another shower, swiping at the mess, while with his right he shook the M-11 from its plastic bag. Vega would be dead before he hit the polished floor.

Two bits of information penetrated Calderon's blind rage before he opened fire. First, in a bleary flash, he noticed that the spittle on his sleeve was bright crimson, the color of blood. And second, he discovered that Filipe Vega was already dead.

The shot had obviously come in from behind Vega, taken out a portion of his sallow face when it burst free, and dropped him at Calderon's feet. Ruiz had seen the danger first, crouching, sweeping the silent corridor for targets, hand and gun still swaddled in the shopping bag. Calderon could see nothing, no one, but the bullet that had dropped Vega had to have come from somewhere.

And another followed it a moment later, slamming hard into Ernesto Calderon's broad chest.

THE FIRST SHOT had been easy, with the three killers off guard and focused on the residents of ICU. Bolan had the 93-R set for 3-round-burst mode, to minimize the risk of a near-miss. It was already hazardous enough, aiming in the direction of Intensive Care, and he didn't want to compound the risk to innocents.

The first gunner took it like a man—or, more precisely, like a target on a firing range. The bullet drilled his skull and spattered blood in his companion's face, startling and briefly blinding him. That left one shooter who had seen it happen, more or less, and who seemed ready to defend himself.

Bolan didn't know what kind of weapons they had hidden in the plastic shopping bags, except to hear the first one clatter, slipping through dead fingers to the floor, but size was a consideration, and he knew the kind of hardware favored by Colombians. He wasted no time, then, on squeezing off a second round that took the blood-sprayed shooter high on the left side of his chest and punched him backward.

A burst of automatic fire blazed from the falling gunner's shopping bag, muffled by a suppressor, contact muzzle-flashes melting the thin plastic instantly. A stream of bullets chewed its way across the wall to Bolan's left, then ripped through ceiling panels, shattered some of the fluorescent lights, glass and acoustic fiberboard cascading down.

The third shooter had Bolan marked, firing a hasty burst that missed its mark but still came close enough to ruffle Bolan's hair. The Executioner hit the floor, sliding, and squeezed off a shot, and saw his bullet pluck at the Colombian's coat sleeve. If he drew blood, it wasn't adequate to slow the shooter or make him turn and run.

Another burst sheared through the gaping bottom of the gunman's shopping bag, slugs gouging divots in the vinyl floor to Bolan's right. He heard the impact and the whine of ricochets. At least one of the bullets shattered on concrete, its fragments stinging Bolan's ribs and flank. There would be tweezer work to do when he was clear of this.

Assuming he survived.

The stocky gunner ducked and weaved, still firing, trying for the kill. Bolan returned fire, but his next round was a clean miss as the target bobbed his head and shimmied out of line, the move resembling some kind of demented dance step.

Tracking, he tried to frame another shot, but the Colombian chose that moment to fire the remainder of his magazine. Bolan could see the bullets striking, eating up the floor, as he hitched in a breath and flung himself away to his left, rolling beyond the shooter's line of fire.

It was close, even so, new fragments biting at him through his clothing. Bolan felt the warm-slick blood sliding between his flesh and fabric, but the cuts were superficial, none of them debilitating. By the time he got his bearings, realizing that his adversary hadn't scored a major hit, the Colombian was off and running down the hallway, toward the exit for the service stairs.

Bolan was on his feet before the thought was fully realized. He had a glimpse of nurses crouched behind the desk in ICU, peering over the top for a fearful glimpse of the action. Moving on a tangent, so that they would only see his face in profile, Bolan passed the fallen gunners, noting that the second one to fall was still alive and squirming, trying to remove his weapon from its tangled plastic bag in order to reload. A close-range bullet to the forehead took him out and made the frightened nurses drop back out of sight.

Bolan pursued the vanished shooter, found the door that served the stairwell hissing slowly shut on its sluggish air piston. He shouldered it open and covered the landing, glancing briefly upstairs to his left before he heard the clatter of descending footsteps putting space between him and his quarry.

Down, then.

Bolan took the concrete steps two and three at a time, flexed knees absorbing the impact. He slowed at each landing in turn, to listen and prepare himself for another burst of gunfire, but his human prey was making tracks, more intent on clearing the premises than covering his tracks. It took some risk out of the chase, but Bolan's combat instinct still reminded him that he was dealing with a killer who was armed and reasonably skilled.

The really tough part would be taking him alive.

That was the plan, at least, though Bolan knew he might be forced to let it go and settle for a kill if he wasn't presented with an opportunity to bag the shooter. It would be a disappointment, granted, but he wouldn't sacrifice himself to gain a prisoner.

Below he heard a shuffling, stumbling noise immediately followed by a bitter curse in Spanish. Something clattered on the steps, a harsh metallic sound that Bolan took to be the shooter's weapon tumbling from his grasp.

How far below? He had already reached the second floor, which meant his quarry had to be very near the service exit. If he made it to the street...

Bolan took his shot, vaulting the slick metal banister, feeling the giddiness of vertigo as he cleared both railings and dropped toward the last flight of stairs. Beneath him, the Colombian was down on one knee, snarling back over his shoulder as he lunged for his fallen machine pistol. Bolan landed a yard or so behind the smaller man, let gravity and momentum pitch him forward in a flying tackle. He swung the Beretta right-handed and was rewarded with the *thunk* of solid impact against his adversary's skull.

The Colombian folded, slumping forward under Bolan's weight, his forehead cracking hard against the floor to snuff out any latent spark of consciousness. Bolan lay still for a moment, on top of his captive, waiting for the struggle to resume, but there was no resistance left. Aware of scrapes and bruises now, to complement the shrapnel cuts and stings, he scrambled to his feet and stood above his assailant.

"Time to take a ride," he said, expecting no reply.

BASILIO RUIZ awoke to pain, with thunder hammering between his ears and nausea churning his stomach. It was always so when he came back from being knocked unconscious, a reaction lingering from childhood days when he was beaten senseless by his drunken father. Normally, these days, Ruiz made sure that he wasn't the one who took the fall when there was rough contact, but something had gone wrong this time.

He tried to shift himself before the nausea won out and spilled his dinner, but too late he found himself immobilized, bound tightly to a chair. There was no stopping the explosion from within, and he suffered the humiliation of his own vomit soaking through his shirt and slacks.

Another spasm and the moment passed, leaving the headache as its only legacy. Ruiz could function with a headache; it wasn't a problem. No, the problem was that he had somehow been disarmed and incapacitated, turned into a prisoner whose arms, torso and legs were wrapped in what appeared to be silver tape. The more he strained against those bonds, it seemed, the more restrictive they became, until his hands and feet were on the verge of going numb.

Ruiz remembered stumbling on the stairs while fleeing from the hospital. A tall, dark man had sprung upon him from above and clubbed him. Vega had been killed, and probably Calderon, too. There had been pistol shots behind Ruiz, as he ran for his life.

But why had he survived? Where was he? Who were his captors, and what did they want?

The questions crowding in upon him only made his headache worse. The Colombian attempted to dismiss them, tried to keep his cool, but it wasn't an easy task. Though seldom in command, he was accustomed to control—of his victims and his women, at the very least. Machismo called for him to put a bold face on the worst of circumstances, even when he found himself tied up and helpless, vomit reeking in his lap.

"You're back," a male voice said from somewhere on his blind side. "I was just about to wake you."

Slow footsteps moved around from Ruiz's left until a tall man stood before him. Raising his chin despite the pain in his head, the Colombian squinted against the overhead lights and focused on a familiar face. This was the man who had pursued him in the hospital stairwell, clubbing him unconscious.

Ruiz didn't respond to his captor. There might still be something to gain from feigning ignorance of English. He used the moment to examine his surroundings, but he could make nothing of the bleak decor. It might have been a storage shed or small garage with a concrete floor underfoot, a wooden workbench to his left, and little else of note within his line of sight.

"I heard you talking at the hospital," the stranger said, "so don't waste time pretending you can't understand me. You came in with certain information and your life. It's time to think about which of the two you want to take away from here. You can't keep both."

Ruiz felt a scowl tugging down the corners of his mouth. They had been talking at the hospital, though he couldn't recall exactly when or what was said. He wondered for a moment if the gringo could be bluffing, thought of pleading ignorance in Spanish for the hell of it, but finally decided it wouldn't be worth the trouble.

Still, a man had to have his pride.

"I don't know who you are," he told the gringo. "I don't have any information."

"Fair enough," the stranger said. He didn't seem upset. "I know exactly where you're coming from. Your friends are dead, back at the hospital. You walk, somebody wants to know why fortune smiled on you. Right off the top, I can't imagine any answer they'd accept."

"I don't know what you mean," Ruiz replied.

"You want to play games, we can play all night," Bolan said. "I don't think you'll enjoy the game I have in mind. Or, on the other hand, we might just talk. I'll start. You and your two dead friends were sent to kill a man named Hector Garavito in the ICU at San Francisco General. Your contact sold you out. You blew it. Here you are, and here you stay—whatever's left of you, as time goes by—until I find out what I need to know. Does any of this ring a bell?"

"I don't—"

"Know what I mean. Gotcha." Incredibly, the gringo stranger smiled. The flash of teeth was more unsettling to Ruiz than if the man had screamed and cursed him, even struck him in the face.

This one was bad.

"Let's see if I can clear that logjam in your head," Bolan offered. "I don't care about your name or your life history. I don't care how you got here from Colombia. That holds no interest for me whatsoever. Likewise, I don't care if you survive the night. Are we communicating, now?"

Ruiz didn't respond. His mind was racing, strangely unimpeded by the throbbing headache. He was wondering how Hector Garavito, dying in the hospital, had found such friends as this one to defend him in his final days.

"You aren't the FBI," he said.

"That's right. You're exactly right. No badge, no rules. Nobody knows about this place, or where you go from here. You're catching on."

The gringo was telling him that he could die, or maybe walk away if he decided to cooperate. In that case, there would be no going back to his associates. Ruiz would be a fugitive from men who made the dying last for days. But if he didn't speak...

"Suppose I don't say anything?" he inquired.

"Your call." Bolan disappeared from view, returning with a leather bag that clanked metallically on contact with the floor. He knelt beside it, rummaging inside, extracting shiny tools. Pliers. Wire cutters. Something like an awl. A folding knife with many blades.

"I don't know much." Ruiz was humbled by the tremor in his voice.

"Just do your best."

New York City

One day before the firefight at San Francisco General Hospital, the Executioner had gone out for a stroll in Central Park. The Rambles offered shade and an illusionary sense of privacy as Bolan dawdled by The Lake—so named, with typical Manhattan arrogance, as if it were the only one on Earth. He feared no evil in this place that was a trysting spot for some, a hunting ground for others. Bolan spared no thought for what would happen if a roving predator should pass by and mistake him for an easy mark.

Been there. Done that.

The last time he had fought in Central Park it had been Hell on Earth for some—and he had died, with some assistance from the clever minds in Washington. Mack Samuel Bolan was officially deceased, his dusty file eviscerated, the slate wiped clean with blood.

And yet...

The more things changed, the more they stayed the same.

He heard his twelve o'clock contact approaching on his blind side, from the east. The heavy footsteps shuffled slightly. Not an old man's tread, perhaps a signal of preoccupation or a hint of weariness. There was no jet lag, flying to New York from Washington, but with the various obligatory preparations and distractions he wouldn't have been surprised to see his contact showing earmarks of fatigue.

In fact, when Bolan turned to greet the new arrival, Hal Brognola was alert enough, though possibly preoccupied with his surroundings.

"This place always creeps me out," the big Fed stated by way of salutation as the two of them shook hands. "I see it, I always flash back to *Cruising,* with Al Pacino."

Bolan smiled. "I thought the two of you were just good friends."

"Smart-ass. I take off half a day to fly up here, and this is what I get? You cast aspersions on my manlihood?"

"Who would believe it if I did?" Bolan replied. "Your reputation precedes you."

"That's the trouble," Brognola groused. "It puts all the cute ones to sleep before I can use my best pickup lines."

The greeting ritual complete, Bolan proceeded to shift gears. "You mentioned the Colombians," he said.

It was a reference to their conversation of the night before. Bolan had checked in with the ultracovert team at Stony Man Farm and had been shunted to Brognola's private line at home. Despite the scrambler, the big Fed had kept the details to himself, referring vaguely to "a Colombian problem" as he requested the meet. Bolan, already in New York on other business, had agreed to meeting by The Lake at noon, with an alternative location at Bethesda Fountain, two o'clock, if Brognola was late departing out of Washington.

"It isn't dope this time," Brognola said. "At least, it isn't all dope."

"I'm listening," the Executioner replied.

"You keep track of the trouble in Colombia?"

"I watch the news," Bolan said. "They've got narcoterrorism and political unrest. Their crime rate's through the roof."

"Uh-huh." Brognola frowned.

"So, tell me."

"You're familiar with La Violencia, I take it, after World War II?" the big Fed forged ahead without waiting for an answer. "They'll never get a final body count on what went down back then, between 1946-1958. The ballpark estimates refer to hundreds of thousands killed by bandits, insurrectionists, the army and secret police. You couldn't tell the shooters apart without a scorecard."

"Sounds familiar," Bolan said.

"The point is, things cooled down and for a while they weren't so bad—by South American standards, at least. Then comes the 1980s, and it all went back into the crapper. On the one hand, there's the whole cocaine explosion taking off like no one ever saw before, with Colombia right in the thick of it. They grow about sixty percent of the world's coke supply, and American's snort eighty-odd percent of it each year. Between the paying customers and certain elements of the intelligence establishment, we fund the very dealers and the narcoterrorists that Justice and the DEA keep trying to eradicate."

Bolan said nothing. He was painfully familiar with the facts Brognola had recited, having been engaged firsthand in some of the campaigns that marked the progress of the so-called War on Drugs. It was an intermittent and erratic war at best, disorganized to the extent that it could sometimes make the war in Vietnam seem orderly and sane by comparison.

"So, anyway," Brognola said, "as if the drugs weren't bad enough, around the same time the coke traffic was warming up—1982–1983, around in there—another insurrection starts, and it's been rolling ever since. You've got leftist guerrillas waging war against the government and skirmishing with right-wing death squads that are almost certainly connected to the military, maybe even back to Washington. You've got the drug cartels assassinating anyone who mentions extradition or trespasses on their turf. And just to top it off, you've got a whole subclass of outlaws cashing in on the confusion anyway they can—armed robberies, extortion, kidnapping, you name it."

Bolan didn't have to name it. He had seen it all before.

"So, where do I fit in?" he asked.

"This time around," Brognola said, "the State Department calculates some thirty-five or forty thousand people have

been killed down there, and it's still rolling in high gear. Another million and a half are homeless for one reason or another. They've either been threatened and driven away, or
their homes were destroyed in the fighting. Add a twenty-one-
percent national unemployment rate on top of that, and you're
looking at a king-sized refugee problem."

"Many of them coming here?"

"A fair percentage," the big Fed replied. "More of them grav-
itate to Bogotá or Cali, living on the streets, but the ones we do
get are among the more affluent and respected. Also, the most
vocal. They've established newspapers, a public speaker's group.
They won't shut up about the trouble going on back home."

"Why should they?"

"Right. Exactly." Bolan's oldest living friend was frowning now. "The trouble is, somebody wants to shut them up for
good. Within the past eight months, we've had at least eleven
exiles murdered in the States, from California to New York.
None of them were involved in drugs, as far as DEA can tell,
but all of them had spoken out at some point on the violence
in Colombia and the official negligence that lets it carry on."

"Political assassinations?" Bolan asked.

"They have to be," Brognola said. "We've got eleven,
maybe more we have heard about, some bodies no one's
found. It smells."

"The FBI's been looking into it." Bolan's tone made it a
statement, not a question.

"Sure, they have," Brognola said. "They've dotted all the
i's and crossed the *t*'s, turned in their usual reports. The file
is code-named COLKILL, if it matters."

Bolan almost grimaced at the FBI's fondness for abbrevi-
ations. COLKILL doubtless stood for something like Colombian killings, the same way Bureau filing clerks had come
up with such gems as UNABOMB or BRILAB, for bribery
committed by a certain labor union. He wondered how his
own file had been labeled in the bad old days, but didn't have
the heart to ask.

"You think the Bureau's fumbling it."

Brognola shrugged resignedly. He had been FBI himself, back in the days when he was hunting Bolan, before they cast their lot together in a wider war. Brognola felt a sense of loyalty toward the Bureau, but he never tried to camouflage its foibles either. Get him started, and he was among the first to recite J. Edgar Hoover's faults, ranging from notorious blind spots on civil rights and organized crime to escalating megalomania in the old man's final years. The big Fed knew where most of the FBI's bodies were buried, and while he made no apology for the Bureau bending certain rules to nail its targets, he had been known to flay badge-heavy agents who threw their weight around for the hell of it. In short, Brognola saw the FBI for what it was, warts and all, and he wasn't above using the Stony Man team to circumvent federal stumbling blocks.

"Fumbling's too strong a word," he said to Bolan. "They've checked out the killings, connected all the dots, but they can't bag the shooters without evidence. From the dispersal and the timing of the hits, we're looking for at least two teams. So far, they've left behind one stolen car, a few generic footprints and a lot of smoking brass. No fingerprints on anything, no DNA, no witnesses worth mentioning. They go in hard and fast, take down their mark and split. The only pattern visible is choice of targets. They go here and there, no geographic angle working east-to-west or anything like that."

"No misses yet?" the Executioner inquired.

"There was a thing three weeks ago, down in Miami," Brognola replied. "The target should have been a fellow named Francisco Guzman. He's been in the States a while, but took his time before he started speaking out against the violence at home."

"You said he should have been the target."

"Right. You'd think so, anyway," Brognola said. "He's reasonably open, out there in the public eye, no bodyguards. From what I understand, he walks to work most days—or used to, anyway. On April 17 he came home to a slaughterhouse. The shooters dropped his wife and their two children. One of them got cute and wrote 'Next Time' across the wall, in blood. Sick bastards."

Bolan had seen worse—much worse, in fact, during the course of his long-running wars—but he could feel the muscles in his jaw and shoulders clenching as Brognola spoke. Murder was one thing, in the world he occupied. Most of the targets saw or sensed it coming and prepared themselves to some extent. A social activist with mortal enemies was generally conscious of the risks involved in any course of action he or she pursued.

It took a special kind of savage, though, to kill a target's soul by taking out his wife and children, scrawling threats around the murder scene in precious blood.

That kind of human animal cried out for personal attention from the Executioner.

"No leads, you said."

"None from the hits that have gone down so far," Brognola answered. "As it happens, though, we may have something on the next one up."

"Tell me."

"Let's take a walk."

And while they made a circuit of The Lake in Central Park, Brognola had explained about the coke-addicted orderly at San Francisco General, the cold-cash offer he had readily accepted prior to having second thoughts. The big Fed had recounted how a contact in the Bureau's San Francisco field office had made the call to Washington, potentially endangering his own career by going outside channels. He had known, going in, that the best the FBI could do was bag the shooters—if they even managed that—and try to make them spill their guts. In any case, if full confessions were obtained and they named sponsors in Colombia, the odds against indictment and successful extradition to the States were still extreme.

It would require a longer, stronger arm to reach out for the men behind the guns. An arm like Brognola's, stretching from Stony Man Farm, with Bolan as the deadly fist.

"If you want to try it," the big Fed had told him, winding down his story of the patient in Intensive Care and those who

meant to terminate his already foreshortened days, "you've
got something like sixteen hours, door to door."

"So, did you bring the airline tickets with you?" Bolan
asked. "Or do I have to pick them up myself?"

IT WAS A FULL day later, and everything had changed. One death
sentence on Hector Garavito had been lifted, thanks to Bolan,
but the other was immutable, beyond the reach of any human
agency. He might have days or hours left, but he would make
the final passage with a team of bodyguards to see him through.

That was the easy part.

The rest would take a bit more work.

Bolan's interrogation of the shooter from the hospital had
gleaned sufficient information for him to proceed, but he had
come up short on answers to the larger questions he would have
to deal with somewhere down the road. He knew the name of
a contractor, operating out of Bogotá, who had arranged the
hit on Garavito and a couple more besides. There was a victim
in Los Angeles and yet another farther south, in San Diego, who
would also be avenged. Quite possibly, he thought, the man in
Bogotá had been responsible for most or all of the assassinations on Brognola's list. Regardless of the final stats, he would
be a potential source of other names, connections, targets.

It would have to do.

Bolan had two more names, as well, but these were friendlies, both associated with the International Consultancy on
Human Rights. They had been working overtime with
refugees and other victims of the terror in Colombia, Brognola's notion being that they should have access to more
names, addresses, information on the men behind the blood-
letting. Perhaps, if no one in the government would listen or
respond to their complaints, the do-gooders might share their
information with a sympathetic visitor from the United States.

Or, maybe not.

It would be touch-and-go on that end, Bolan understood,
because the ICHR's people were committed to a cease-fire
all around. They had no ax to grind with one side or the other.

What they wanted was an end to murder, maiming, torture—all of it. They were unlikely to assist an executioner who came to them in search of targets, but there was no rule that said Bolan had to share his plans up front.

He was a gentleman in some things, but he still knew how to lie. And sometimes, in a soldier's mind, the ends did justify the means.

His captive from the San Francisco hospital, for instance.

Bolan had encouraged the assassin to believe that he would be released, perhaps into protective custody, if he cooperated and made full disclosure of his knowledge on the Garavito contract, plus associated crimes. One look at Bolan's tool kit, with the implements spread out around his feet, and the shooter had started to babble. There had been no need to break a sweat, much less his skin. The self-styled hardman had apparently been anxious to avoid experiencing any great discomfort.

When they were done he had a choice to make. It would be possible, he knew, to make a call and put the wheels in motion for his captive to be placed in federal custody as a protected witness. Brognola could set it up as he had done for other helpful thugs, perhaps a thousand times before. It would be simple, quick and clean.

But there were problems with the handoff, too. For one thing, Bolan had no guarantee that his cooperative prisoner might not experience a sudden change of heart. Perspectives change, and one fear might replace another in the long run. It was possible that the Colombian would reconsider his arrangement with the Feds, demand a lawyer and attempt to save himself by setting off alarms along the Colombian pipeline, all the way from San Francisco down to Bogotá. Bolan couldn't afford to have that happen when his life was riding on the line.

It was, at last, a relatively simple choice.

One shot behind the ear, and he was finished with the gunman, all of his accumulated sins erased in one bright splash of crimson. Garbage bags and Lysol made the cleanup easy, mopping down concrete to clear the stains. He left the body in a rental car at San Francisco International Airport. By the time it was discovered, days or weeks later, identification would be problematic at best. Even now, if an alert patrolman stumbled on the body overnight, it was unlikely that the dead Colombian would ever be identified. As far as linking him somehow to Stony Man, Bolan regarded it as physically impossible.

Bolan booked the flights himself. It was ten hours in the air, give or take, to cover some 5,600 miles between San Francisco and Bogotá, with layovers at Dallas-Fort Worth and in Mexico City. Call it half a day and change between departure from the city by the bay and his arrival at the heart of Colombia's combat zone. His enemies would have no warning. Even if there was a leak inside the International Consultancy on Human Rights, his contacts on the ground knew nothing of his mission or his true identity. They could do no more than report that yet another gringo visitor was coming to discuss the country's troubled past and present. What could such a tourist possibly achieve?

It was a question Bolan had to ask himself, as well.

He couldn't hope to change a country's mood or stamp out crime. With any luck, he might be able to eliminate some individual contenders in the conflict, maybe frighten others into backing off the course of ruin they had charted for themselves and those around them. Still, between the mayhem and political upheaval that had scarred the region, going back for nearly half a century, he had no realistic hope of changing many hearts or minds.

Which still worked out, because he was the Executioner, not a professor of philosophy. Bolan took the world as he found it, complete with predators and pitfalls, working overtime to smooth the way for those who sought to lead a peaceful and productive life, but who had trouble fighting for themselves.

One man could make a difference.

Somewhere on the globe, it happened every day.

Bolan knew he would have to travel light, in terms of weaponry. He packed up the Beretta 93-R with his clothing, checked the bag as cargo to avoid X-ray devices, and was un-armed as he walked to the departure gate. He had no reason to expect that he would be attacked in the airport or anywhere along his route, but he had balked at touching down unarmed in Bogotá. The pistol would provide a margin of security once Bolan had unpacked, and his first order of business on arrival in the battle-torn republic would be to acquire com-ponents for a mobile arsenal.

That was the good news in a combat zone: wherever in-nocents were being slaughtered left and right, there would be arms available for those with cash or strength enough to take them from their owners. Bolan would attempt to buy his hard-ware first, before resorting to some more flamboyant means. The bankroll in his suitcase was a mix of funds from Stony Man, transmitted via Brognola, and leftovers from the treas-ury of an illicit arms cartel he had destroyed in the Louisiana bayou country six weeks earlier. His needs were relatively simple on the road and money had a tendency to last, unless some special need arose—in which case, he had found that there was always more available.

The predators made up their own rules as they went along, but one was always fairly constant: they couldn't complain to the authorities if they, themselves, were victimized. A num-bers bank or a narcotics syndicate, a prostitution ring or kiddy porn distributor, an outlaw motorcycle gang with crank labs in the desert or a paramilitary hate group plotting war against society—the traits they shared in common were a certain ar-rogance that masked their weakness when it came to being taken down by larger, stronger predators.

Bolan considered ripping off the savages from time to time as an expected part of his ongoing war. It also meant that he wasn't beholden to the treasury at Stony Man to any great de-gree, on any given day. He logically and gratefully accepted aid on missions that he drew from Brognola, but there were also various occasions when he acted on his own, choosing a target in response to some perceived emergency. The big Fed and the team based in Virginia understood the difference, and they didn't interfere. Bolan, for his part, cherished a degree of independence that hadn't existed when he served the government in uniform.

Those days were gone. The Executioner had long since graduated to a higher plane, but it was still the same old war in many other ways. The faces of his allies and his adversaries changed, but there was little deviation in the stakes. The conflict between Good, however racked by human frailty it might be, and Evil, even when it wore a sweet, seductive face, would never really change. Not where it mattered, in the trenches, where combatants bled and died.

The battleground was shifting from the hallways of a San Francisco hospital to Bogotá, but it was still the same unending war.

And when the Executioner touched down, there would be hell to pay.

3

Bogotá

"Tell me again who this one is supposed to be. I still don't understand."

The statement came from Ciro Aguiar, his voice deliberately pitched below its normal level as a pair of soldiers armed with submachine guns sauntered past. His dark eyes followed them, and Regan Kelly felt the apprehension that her friend experienced each time he saw a uniform and gun. She had begun to feel a measure of that creeping paranoia for herself.

"I'm not exactly sure, myself," she answered honestly.

"It's dangerous," Nestor Gomez said, standing to her right. "For all we know, he could be CIA or something else. You know the U.S. State Department, Regan. They are not our friends."

"He's not a spook," she said with more assurance than she felt.

"How do you know that?" Aguiar asked her.

"I explained that," she replied. "My friend in Washington—"

"A friend in Washington." Aguiar was frowning as he interrupted her, shaking his head.

"A very close and trusted friend in Washington," Kelly amended, "who would never lie to me—"

"Of course," Aguiar retorted. "Who in all the capital of the United States would ever tell a lie or break a trust?"

She felt a sudden flash of anger at the man who had become her friend through mutual exposure to the heartbreak that was all too common in Colombia. "I don't need any civics lessons," she responded sharply. "I was a reporter for the *Post,* if you recall. I know damn well that people lie in Washington, Ciro, okay? I'm telling you that this one person wouldn't lie *to me.*"

"And you know this because...?"

"None of your business." Kelly glared at him. "As I was about to say before I was so rudely interrupted from the peanut gallery, my friend in Washington assures me that this person isn't CIA or DEA or anything like that. The phrase he used, if I recall, was 'unofficial but effective.'"

"How effective can he be," Gomez inquired, "without the power of the state behind him? Will he counsel us? Perhaps go home and write a long, sad story of the lowly but courageous peasants in Colombia?"

"He's not a journalist," Kelly replied.

"We only know what he is not." It seemed almost as if Gomez were talking to himself. "And still it is no help."

They sat together in three stiff, floor-mounted plastic chairs, set back from the bustle of the main concourse inside Bogotá's international airport. Loitering could be perilous here, and each of the three carried some prop—a newspaper, a paperback novel, a book of crossword puzzles—to suggest that he or she was here on lawful business, waiting for a plane.

In fact, that was the truth of it, but Kelly knew from personal experience that truth was seldom taken at face value in Colombia these days, and it could work against her if she offered it too freely. One remark could breed a thousand questions, like a nest of roaches growing in the dark and damp, plotting to overrun a home.

Kelly despised the cynicism that had grown inside her after fourteen months in Bogotá, working for the International Consultancy on Human Rights. It had been one thing, with the *Post,* when she was sent to cover criminal proceedings in D.C. No matter what the crime involved, no matter how much it depressed her, there had always been a sense that it was aberrant, outside the norm. In Bogotá and in the countryside, by contrast, she had quickly learned that violence, corruption and depravity appeared to be the norm. Even so-called reformers in the strife-torn nation's capital were darkly pessimistic, simply going through the motions. Most of them, she guessed, would soon adapt and find the path of least resistance. Those who didn't would be winnowed out by one means or another, fair or foul.

She had been venting when she told her friend in Washington—ex-lover, that was, if she ever felt like going to confession—all about the mayhem she had witnessed since arriving in Colombia, the grinding poverty that haunted homeless refugees and millions of the unemployed. She had expected nothing but a sympathetic ear, perhaps a platitude or two. She might have grasped an invitation to escape the carnage for a weekend, run away to Washington and bask in Western decadence, whatever came of it.

Instead, her ex-lover had suggested that there might be someone who could help. He had been purposefully obscure, verging on cryptic, but had taken Kelly's number with the promise of a callback either way. Three days later, when the conversation was a fading memory, he had called back to rouse her on the cusp of midnight and report that someone was en route to visit and survey the situation. There was no more to be said. Kelly should meet the visitor and use her own best judgment after that.

Intrigued—the old reporter's instinct kicking in—she had resolved to keep the date. Because her tenure in Colombia had taught her certain things about security precautions, she immediately drafted Ciro Aguiar, a working friend from the consultancy, to join her at the airport. Nestor Gomez was an afterthought whose status as a lawyer and a former prosecutor might just come in handy.

She could never be too careful these days, when she ventured out among the violence.

Such thoughts would have been foreign to her nature in the other life, the one that she had left behind to chase an altruistic impulse southward. What had she been thinking? Why had she remained after the first atrocity? The tenth? The hundredth? What did she hope to accomplish in an alien land where violence was the rule and most of the natives regarded her with frank suspicion?

Nothing, perhaps. And yet, she felt the need to try.

If she could only capture the attention of someone in authority, someone with the pull to influence Colombian officials and make them do their jobs more evenhandedly, without fear or favor. It might be a pipe dream, Kelly realized, but she would never know unless she made this one, last effort.

And supposing that she failed, as seemed entirely probable. What then? Would she give up and pack her things, retreat to the United States and find herself a nice safe job in journalism? Maybe turn her graduate degree toward teaching at some school where tenure was assured and life could fall into a bland but undemanding rut?

She almost shuddered at the thought, but Regan Kelly understood that she was running out of options in Colombia— and maybe in her life. She would be thirty-two-years old next time a birthday rolled around, and while that hardly made her ancient, she was mindful of the fact that "middle age" was relative. It came at fifty only if someone planned to live a hundred years or more, and who would ever bet the farm on that?

Kelly had never seen herself as the maternal sort. She heard no ticking from the biological clock in that respect, but she was conscious of a yearning to accomplish something in her life before it was too late. At one time, not so long ago, she had believed the International Consultancy on Human Rights would be the vehicle to that end, but reality had very nearly changed her mind by now.

"He should be here by now," Aguiar remarked.

Kelly attempted to be nonchalant as she glanced at her watch. They had refrained from walking down to the arrivals gate, as it had been requested. Now, she wondered if the flight from Mexico was late, or if—

A shadow fell across her face, and she glanced up into piercing blue eyes, set in a darkly handsome face. "You must be Regan Kelly," the stranger said, offering his hand. "I'm Mike Belasko. Will you walk me down to baggage claims?"

"HOW DID YOU know my name?" the redhead asked, as she unfolded from her chair, still gripping Mack Bolan's hand.

"I saw a photograph before I left," he said.

"A photograph?" She seemed confused.

"Your driver's license, I believe it was. Maybe a passport."

"God, I look like hell in both of those." She thought about it for another moment, adding, "You have access to that kind of thing?"

"Sometimes." He cocked a thumb in the direction of some nearby stairs. "My bag?"

"Oh, right. First, though," she told him, "this is Ciro Aguiar. We work together at the ICHR office here."

The man's handshake was firm, but it didn't test Bolan's strength. There was no challenge, only wariness behind the eyes and vestige of a smile.

"And this is Nestor Gomez," she continued, nodding toward the dark man on her right. "He used to be...in government."

"So, you're retired, then," Bolan said as they shook hands.

"Things change," Gomez replied.

"I've heard that said."

They moved together toward the stairs, Kelly at Bolan's side, the two men following a few steps back. There was no conversation as they found the baggage carousel and waited for his suitcase to appear, no more than casual discussion of the weather and his flight as they departed from the terminal and hiked across a hundred yards of asphalt to a parking lot, where Kelly led him to a ten-year-old Toyota minivan. They stowed his bag in back and Bolan took the shotgun seat, with Kelly at the wheel, Gomez and Aguiar behind them.

As they pulled out into midday traffic, Gomez was the first to speak. "I'm not clear," he said, "which agency of the United States regime you represent."

"Nestor..." The redhead glared at Gomez in the rearview mirror, as if warning him.

"Who said I represent the government?"

That drew a frowning glance from Kelly. Bolan didn't turn to face Gomez and Aguiar, but he could feel them watching him.

"We understood—" she began, then caught herself. "That is to say, *I* understood that you were being sent from Washington to see us."

Bolan shrugged. "I know some people there," he said. The rest came easily and was, perhaps, no more than half a lie. "I don't belong to any formal agency."

Kelly was concentrating on the traffic, but her frown had deepened. "I'm not sure I understand," she said, when it was clear that Bolan meant to offer no more information. "Just who are you, then?"

"I'm a consultant," he replied. "A troubleshooter, if you like."

The three of them considered that for something like a quarter mile. When Kelly spoke again, there was a sharp edge to her voice. "Jerome...that is, my friend in Washington...said someone would be coming who could help us here."

"You never know," Bolan replied. "I haven't heard your problem, yet."

"He didn't fill you in at all?"

"I've never spoken to Jerome," he said. "I wouldn't know him if he stepped in front of us right now."

"But, then—"

"Why don't you fill me in on what you need," he said, delaying any questions on his own part that would spook the redhead or her two companions, put them off before he had a chance to win their confidence. "You brief me, and I'll see what I can do."

"It's complicated," she replied.

"Take your time."

"Speaking of time," Gomez said, "I believe consultants work for hire. In this case—"

"It's already covered," Bolan said, half turning now to

meet the former government employee's gaze. "You won't be getting any bills."

His answer had preempted a reply from Kelly, but she flicked Gomez another rearview glower. Bolan noted that her small hands gripped the steering wheel with force enough to bleach her knuckles.

"Are we going far?" he asked of no one in particular. His mind was on the pistol in his suitcase, wishing he had found a men's room at the airport terminal to strap it on.

"Another couple miles," Kelly replied. "My place."

It seemed unlikely that the meet would turn into a trap, at least with these three on the other side, but Bolan had survived this long by covering the bases, taking every feasible precaution to protect himself before battle was joined.

"Are any of you under government surveillance?" he inquired, making the question sound entirely natural. "Feel like you're being followed? Hear clicks on the line when you make phone calls?"

There were many methods to eliminate those obvious techniques, but he was covering the basics, thinking that a little shakeup now might save a world of trouble later on. Of course, if it was already too late...

"We take care of ourselves," Kelly said, irritation audible in her reply.

"Watch out for tails when you're on errands to the airport, things like that?" he prodded, watching color rise in Kelly's cheeks.

"You think we're being followed?" the woman challenged him. "If you want me to, I can drive around the block a few times, see if anybody tags along."

"Don't bother," Bolan said. "You're either right, or it's too late."

It was apparent that she wanted him to spell out what he meant by that, but she wasn't about to ask and Bolan didn't volunteer. Commercial buildings were already giving way to residential streets as they rolled on, the traffic thinning out somewhat. He estimated they were forty minutes from the airport when she turned the minivan into an alley on the left, crept past a line of battered garbage cans and stopped outside a small garage approximately halfway down. On some unspoken cue, the door to Bolan's left-rear opened, Aguiar stepped out and went to open the garage. Kelly backed in, the Toyota's nose aimed toward the alley as if ready for a hasty getaway.

Bolan got out, retrieved his bag from the rear hatch, and waited while the wooden door to the garage was closed and padlocked. A simple wooden fence screened off a courtyard to their left and Bolan followed Kelly through the gate, with Aguiar and Gomez bringing up the rear. A dozen paces farther on she paused before a door and rattled keys until she found the one that fit the lock.

Glancing across her shoulder, she flashed the Executioner a smile that never reached her eyes. "Step into my parlor."

CIRO AGUIAR had visited Kelly's bungalow at least a dozen times, on business for the consultancy. They weren't lovers, though he wanted her intensely. It amused and saddened him, both feelings all at once, that she couldn't seem to see the yearning in his eyes or hear the tremor in his voice that seemed so obvious to him each time they spoke.

This night was different, though. There was a tension in the air, but it was hardly sexual. It was the stranger's fault of course. This tall American, with his attitude and his evasion of the simplest questions troubled Aguiar no end. He looked like trouble, moved like a professional athlete or someone who was used to sudden bursts of violent activity. His eyes were restless, searching everywhere for signs of danger, angles of attack.

He was no diplomat. Aguiar would willingly have bet his life on that.

A soldier, then? A spy? The fact that he denied direct affiliation with the U.S. government meant nothing. Would an agent of the CIA announce himself to strangers while he labored to manipulate them? Aguiar didn't believe the name this man had given them, but that was unimportant at the moment. He was more concerned about the stranger's mission, what it had to do with Kelly and himself, with the ICHR.

Perhaps he was a mercenary, Aguiar thought, then frowned at the absurdity. Soldiers of fortune were for hire, and who would pay this man to travel so far from his home? Not Kelly, certainly. Not the consultancy. No one of influence in the United States would care enough, and if they had, the ICHR's leadership would have rejected the attempt outright. The group was devoted to peace and justice. It wouldn't have thugs.

A journalist?

This time Aguiar almost smiled. He knew his share of combat-hardened correspondents, one or two of whom had killed in self-defense. But none of them had this one's eyes.

"If you don't mind," Bolan said, "I'd like to freshen up."

Kelly supplied directions to the bathroom and the tall man took his suitcase with him. Water ran, the toilet flushed. When he returned five minutes later, Aguiar could have sworn that he was different somehow. Was it simply attitude, a hint of relaxation in his new surroundings or...?

"We may as well get down to business, then," Bolan said, when they were seated around the table in Kelly's small dining room, steaming coffee mugs in front of them. "From what I understand, you work with refugees and other victims of the fighting. You take flak from both sides, left and right. The government is on your case for criticizing its official policy, and I suspect you may have problems with the narcotraffickers as well, from time to time. Is that about the size of it?"

"You have a talent for distilling problems," Kelly said.

"I take for granted that we don't have a lot of time to spare," Bolan said. "And since I'm new in town, the first thing that I need from you would be a rundown on the major players."

"Rundown?" Nestor Gomez echoed.

"Names, background, affiliations," Bolan stated. "Contact addresses, if you have them. For guerrillas in the field, some kind of general location for their base camps would be helpful. If you can't swing that, maybe the different groups have front men in the city, handling their business here."

Kelly had watched the man while he spoke, her own expression shifting rapidly from curiosity to disbelief, and on from there to something like amazement.

"What?" she blurted out. "You want to see these people? I mean, talk to them? Contact them?"

"I find the most direct approach is usually the best," Bolan said. "If there's no common ground, nothing to talk about, at least I'll know it going in. If that's the case, we can move on to other options."

"Other options?" Gomez asked.

"This I'd like to hear," Aguiar put in.

Bolan studied each of them in turn. His eyes dissected them, boring into their heads before he answered.

"Don't ask questions," he replied at last, "unless you're sure you want to hear the answers."

"I'm sure. I'm asking," Kelly responded.

"Right." Bolan tilted forward in his chair, hands clasped together on the tabletop. "I told you that I'm not a diplomat. I'm also not in Bogotá because you asked a friend in Washington for help. Your name was given to me as a contact of potential value, but I'd be here either way, whether you had agreed to meet with me or not."

"And why is that?" she challenged him.

"Over the past eight months or so," he said, "we've had eleven murders of Colombian exiles in the United States. Each one of those who died had spoken out against the troubles here—or else had relatives who did. They were assassinated. One team of assassins has been interdicted, but that won't resolve the problem. Those responsible can hire a hundred more hit men by noon tomorrow, if they haven't already. I'm here to check the operation at its source."

"So, you are from the CIA!" Gomez was almost smiling at the thought of vindication.

Bolan shook his head. "The Company has no brief for this

kind of thing. I don't expect you to believe me, and it doesn't matter either way. You either help me or you don't. If not, I'm on my way."

"Hold on a second," Kelly said. "I still don't follow—"

"He's a soldier," Aguiar interrupted her.

"Or an assassin," Gomez suggested.

Bolan eased back in his chair, made no reply. His eyes were fixed on Kelly's face, ignoring Aguiar and Gomez.

"So, it's true?" Kelly asked, pressing him. "You're here to fight?"

'I'm here to judge the situation and react accordingly."

"You don't know who we are at all," she answered with a kind of sadness in her voice. "We work to help people, not kill them."

"And so far you've managed to accomplish...what, again?" There was no mockery in Bolan's tone. He simply left the question lying on the table.

"You believe we're wasting time?" she asked.

"I understand one of your people in the field was killed ten days ago, near La Dorada. He was executed by a firing squad, the way I heard it. Maybe narcotrafficker did it, maybe soldiers. He's the second agent that you've lost this year, I think, the third within twelve months."

"We're not an army," Kelly said.

"Nobody's asking you to fight."

She glanced at Aguiar briefly but didn't solicit his opinion. "No," she said. "We won't be part of this."

"Okay, then," the American replied. "Can someone drop me at a rental office to pick up a car?"

THE RENTAL CAR was a two-year-old Volkswagen Passat with multiple dings on the bodywork and close to eighty thousand miles on the odometer. Bolan had checked beneath the hood and found it healthy. A test run reassured him that it could corner, brake, accelerate. It also had a fairly spacious trunk, which suited Bolan's purpose at his third stop in the city.

Regan Kelly had been silent for the most part on the drive to drop him at the auto rental agency. Only within the last few blocks had she begun to question him about his knowledge of indigenous Colombians, his stance on human rights—a sudden rush of queries that displayed more passion than organized thought. She had the urgency to be a leader, he decided, but for all that she had seen since traveling to Bogotá, she still maintained a touch of that idealism that was sometimes labeled "starry-eyed," more common on some college campuses than in the jungles or the streets.

He envied her, in that respect.

He also hoped it wouldn't get her killed.

The weapons dealer was Bolan's next stop. One of the guys from Stony Man Farm had turned him up and passed the name along for future reference. He called himself Guillermo Cruz, but Bolan didn't care what name the dealer used. He operated from the basement of a small repair shop in a neighborhood where shops and cheap apartments huddled side by side. One narrow flight of stairs, Cruz leading, and the well-stocked armory had been revealed.

On some of his excursions into foreign countries, Bolan took care to select weapons of European manufacture, thus averting any link to the United States if something was discarded in the heat of battle and recovered by his enemies. There were no such restrictions in the Western Hemisphere, where every nation but Cuba had been armed by the U.S. at one time or another, American arms and martial technology more common in most South American countries than adequate meals for the poor.

Bolan made his selections from the stock on hand. He chose an M-4 carbine version of the M-16 assault rifle as his lead weapon, a chunky M-203 40 mm grenade launcher mounted underneath the barrel. For better concealment and close-quarters work, he chose an Italian Spectre submachine gun, with its unique 50-round four-column box magazines. With long-range hits in mind, Bolan treated himself to a

M-24 sniper weapon system, a militarized version of the Remington 700 sniper rifle used for years by American troops. The Desert Eagle semiauto pistol was a sweet surprise, and while it was only a .357 Magnum, compared to Bolan's more familiar .44-caliber model, he took it anyway. Spare magazines and ammunition, a mixed assortment of 40 mm rounds, plus U.S. military frag and smoke grenades rounded off the Executioner's shopping list. There was a dumbwaiter to hoist his purchases upstairs, and Bolan brought his car around in back, loading the trunk in three quick trips while Cruz stood guard.

Renting a small apartment in the city proved to be no problem for a gringo visitor with cash in hand. He took it for a month, though he didn't intend to be in Bogotá longer than a week and knew that he might never occupy the premises at all. It would be handy if he needed somewhere to lie low, recuperate from wounds, or otherwise get off the streets.

Which only left the planning of his strikes.

It was a disappointment that he couldn't tap the brains of Regan Kelly and her friends for leads on targets, judging as he did that they had to know the major players on all sides, but he would live with it. He still had one lead from the shooter he had grilled in San Francisco, and if Bolan played his cards right it would point him toward others.

Improvise.

Adapt.

Prevail.

He was about to bring the war home in a way certain Colombians hadn't experienced before. The fat cats and the men in charge were accustomed to enjoying virtual immunity, hiding behind their walls of guns and money. Leaders of the rebel opposition had a somewhat tougher time of it, but they were used to watching peasants cringe in terror.

Both sides were about to get a rude surprise.

The Executioner was up and running.

And it was going to be one hell of a ride.

4

The contractor, one Saturnin Fermina, occupied the top floor of a midrange Bogotá apartment house. He wasn't rich enough, as yet, for an estate outside the city. Even mansions in the suburbs were beyond him at the moment, but he was by all accounts industrious and would be very wealthy soon.

Assuming he survived.

Arranging murder contracts in Colombia wasn't particularly difficult—or lucrative, for that matter, unless the target was a prominent official, businessman or something similar. Such men had friends, of course, and making war on them was hazardous. The real money, just now, was in promoting homicides abroad. It meant much better payoffs, plus expense accounts for travel and the like, with little risk that any of the targets or their allies would strike back.

From all appearances, it was a fairly pleasant life.

Bolan made one pass by Fermina's place in the VW, then came around the block again and parked, strolling back as if he owned the sidewalk. He was out of place and knew it— even with the hair and tan that could have passed for native at first glance, he was too tall, too muscular—but Bolan didn't let it trouble him. Four million people lived in Bogotá officially, not counting homeless peons, and a fair number of those were gringos, either North American or European.

If he couldn't pass, the next best thing was to be overlooked.

He had the Spectre submachine gun tucked away inside a cut-rate imitation leather briefcase, the Beretta 93-R slung be-

neath his arm in fast-draw leather. Going in with no idea of
the security his target had in place, Bolan was at a starting
disadvantage, but he hoped to make it up with sheer audacity.

There was a doorman in the lobby, but he took one look at
Bolan and decided not to ask whatever questions may have
sprung to mind. Discretion was the better part of valor for the
working classes in Colombia. Bolan didn't enjoy the way the
doorman turned away from him, eye shifting with a practiced
ease to focus on some unoffensive piece of furniture, but fear
would serve his purpose well enough.

He took the elevator up, noting that it required a special
key to reach the topmost floor. No problem. There was bound
to be another mode of access to and from the lower floors.

Bolan rode the elevator to the eighth floor, disembarking
into silence, with muted track lighting overhead. He assumed most of the tenants would be at work by this time,
maybe having power lunches or preparing for the afternoon's siesta. Glancing both directions as the elevator's
door hissed shut behind him, the soldier saw a door off to
his left that bore a sticker with a picture of a cartoon figure
climbing stairs.

Perfect.

A backward glance to verify that he hadn't picked up an
audience along the way, and Bolan slipped into the stairwell
and closed the door softly behind him.

Two flights up to nine. He took his time, slipping the single button open on his sport coat so that he could reach the
93-R in a hurry, should he have to. Moving cautiously, he still
couldn't suppress a grimace as his shoes made little rasping
noises, amplified within the echo chamber of the stairwell.

Would they hear him coming? Was there anyone upstairs at all?

It had occurred to Bolan that his quarry might not even be
at home. In that case, he would have a choice: to wait and
maybe search the place for any clues or come back later, try
again.

And if the contractor had bolted, seeking cover for whatever reason...what, then?

The Executioner would have to find another way.

He always did.

The door at the top of the staircase was identical to the one Bolan had used on eight, except that this one had a Spanish sign that read: Private. He ignored it, tried the knob and felt it yield enough to know it was unlocked.

Bolan stepped back from the door—no window, naturally, to let him glimpse whatever lay beyond—and set down his briefcase before he drew the sound suppressed Beretta. He was gambling now. For all he knew, there could be half a dozen soldiers waiting for him on the other side, but there could just as easily be none. All things considered, he would put his stealth this time, holding firepower in reserve.

He had the layout of the eighth floor memorized, but it meant nothing where the penthouse was concerned. He could be walking into anything from one great room to a maze of hallways and cubicles. Bolan knew he would simply have to play it by ear.

He shouldered through the doorway, following his pistol into a smaller copy of the lobby downstairs. To Bolan's left, positioned in the northeast corner of the room where he could cover both the elevator and the stairs, a gaunt-faced man in shirtsleeves with a double shoulder rig was rising from a bench against the wall, drawing both pistols as he stood.

They looked like matched Colt .45s, their finish worn from long, hard use, but they wouldn't be used this day. The 93-R, set for 3-round bursts, stuttered in Bolan's fist and splashed a crimson smear across the shooter's concave chest. He slumped back toward the bench but somehow missed it, sliding, his buttocks thumping on the carpet. He went no farther, braced upright, his head thrown back, eyes open, mouth agape as if to let his soul fly free.

Another moment ticked away as Bolan waited for the reinforcements to appear. There could be hidden cameras in the room, or some kind of listening device that would alert a team of backup gunners waiting in the penthouse. After counting off ninety seconds, he finally decided it was clear and fetched his briefcase from the stairwell.

He knelt before the briefcase, opened it and lifted out the SMG. It was already cocked, the Spectre's closed-bolt design and double-action trigger permitting the weapon to be carried safely with a live round in the chamber and the safety off. Bolan was on his feet an instant later, moving toward the only other door in sight.

There was no bell. Why would there be, when anyone arriving for a visit had to use a special elevator key and pass the outer guard to reach the door? Would it be locked, an extra nod to privacy despite the shooter in the lobby?

Bolan didn't know and didn't bother finding out.

He stepped in close, his right leg rising almost to his chest, and slammed his heel into the wood an inch or two above and to the left of the doorknob. It worked on the first try, wood splintering, a loud *twang* from the shattered latch before the door flew open and he crossed the threshold in a fighting crouch.

There was another guard, but Bolan caught him napping. He bolted upright from a long, low sofa roughly centered in a spacious living room. Unlike his dead friend in the lobby, this one wore no pistols, but there was an Uzi lying on the coffee table close at hand, a magazine spread under it to keep the gun from scratching the polished ebony.

The shooter cursed in Spanish, tried to reach his weapon, but the Spectre got him first. A short burst made the target shimmy, twitching backward, spraying stains across the sofa's fabric. He was dead before he settled on the cushions, one last shiver running through his body as synapses fired in vain.

Three doors faced Bolan from the far side of the living room, each leading off to different portions of the penthouse. One of them had to serve a dining room and kitchen, he imagined, while the others...

Bolan started searching and found his quarry hiding in the master bathroom, crouching in the shower as if frosted glass could hide or protect him from a burst of automatic fire. Bolan unleashed a quick half-dozen rounds that showered Saturnin Fermina with a rain of jagged shards, gashing his scalp and shoulders, hands and arms. It was a simple thing to reach in and twist the shiny little automatic from his fist, before he found the nerve to use it.

"You speak English?" Bolan asked him, levering the Spectre's muzzle underneath that bloody chin until the eyes met his.

"Yes! I do!"

"All right, then," Bolan said. "Let's have a little chat."

CALVINO ESCOBAR loved dining in the open air. He took meals on the patio behind his split-level house whenever possible, weather permitting. One of the young women who served him lingered close at hand, an ostrich feather poised to keep away the flies. The feather might find other uses, too, if Escobar decided on a more unorthodox dessert.

This afternoon he dined on veal, asparagus and potatoes, with a salad on the side and vintage claret in his glass. It was delicious, as it damned well should be for the salary his live-in chef was paid. Dessert, if Escobar decided to forgo the ostrich feather and the servant girl, would be his other favorite: chocolate mousse.

At fifty-three, a man of more than average wealth and influence, Escobar no longer felt the least bit foolish even when indulging the most outrageous whims and passions. He had struggled for the first half of his life to build an empire in this backward nation, had commanded men to kill and die on his behalf. He planned to spend the second half enjoying all the privileges that came with triumph, and he would apologize to no man for his gluttony.

Who has a better right to satisfy himself than one who had risked everything and had emerged victorious?

This was a time of hardship for the peasants of his homeland, but Escobar no longer ranked himself among the poor. He had been one of them at birth, but half a century and several dozen deaths had separated him by light-years from his altogether undistinguished roots. Some years ago, he had employed a top-line forger to upgrade his birth certificate, even as two corrupt policemen and a judge whose taste in females ran toward those below the age of puberty were used to purge the records of his legal indiscretions as a youth.

Escobar had thus become a brand-new man, entitled to the benefits his cash could purchase. Almost anything his heart desired came with a price tag, tidy and discreet: respectability, prestige, an honored place among his fellow men.

Why not?

Money, drugs and power. It was all the same.

He reached out for the wineglass and lifted it. The glass was halfway to his lips when it exploded, spraying wine across the table, startling a small cry from the servant girl. It took a moment for Escobar to notice that his middle finger had been cleanly severed just below the knuckle, pumping blood onto the table cloth. Confused, he was about to look for it, until he recognized the echo of a rifle shot.

"Ambrosio!" He bellowed out the name of his chief bodyguard, shoving his chair back with sufficient force to flip the table over on its side. "Ambrosio!"

The second shot caught Escobar an inch or two above the left knee as he vaulted from his chair. He felt the impact well before he heard the gunshot, crying out as his leg acquired a strange new angle, folding under him. He collapsed onto the flagstones of the patio. A scream drew Escobar's eyes to the servant girl, fleeing toward the house at full gallop, the ostrich feather still clutched in her small fist, bobbing with each step she took.

Ambrosio was there a moment later, standing over his employer with a stunned expression on his fleshy face. The sawed-off shotgun in his hands looked like a toy and seemed entirely useless in the circumstances. Shouting orders at the men who spilled out of the house behind him, deploying them as a human screen across the wide, sloping lawn, Ambrosio knelt beside his boss, dark blood soaking through his slacks.

"Boss!" he said. "What—?"

Only the first word of the question passed his lips, and then the lips themselves were gone, Ambrosio's face imploding as his head snapped back, the body following, surrendering to gravity. The distant tremor of the rifle shot was lost as other weapons opened fire across the lawn, spraying the tree line.

All too late.

The last shot from the unseen sniper found Calvino Escobar and flipped him over on his back, a rag doll devoid of conscious volition. His blood was brilliant in the sunlight, streaming down the flagstones on a slight incline to mingle with the grass.

REGAN KELLY WAS busy in the kitchen of her small bungalow when the radio drew her away. She stopped in the midst of slicing an onion, snuffled back sharp tears, and turned to give the news broadcast her full attention.

"Six men dead in Bogotá."

Why should that surprise her? What was so unique, or even noteworthy, about another killing in the capital?

It was a rare day, in fact, when no reports of multiple homicides were aired in Bogotá. Kelly suspected that a day without mass murder somewhere in the country would be cause for three-inch headlines in *The New York Times* and *USA Today*. Of late, left-wing guerrillas had been blamed for touching off a string of bombs throughout the city, theoretically intended to kill tourists and thereby subvert a portion of the state's economy. Then again, the blasts could just as easily have been set off by narcoterrorists, attempting to consolidate their turf.

Who knew? More to the point, how many people in Colombia—or in the world at large—still gave a damn?

"Calvino Escobar is dead...."

She recognized the name, stood rooted to the spot and listened to the rest of the report. The alleged cocaine exporter had been shot and killed while dining at his home, along with two men tentatively named as bodyguards of the deceased. Police refused to speculate on whether the Escobar murders

were somehow related to the afternoon slaughter of three
other men in a Bogotá penthouse apartment.

Kelly recognized none of the names in that case, barely
heard the female newscaster's heated speculation on whether
the crimes might be related, possibly the start of a new murder spree in Bogotá.

When had the old one ended? Kelly silently asked herself.
When would it ever end?

And then she thought about the stranger, Mike Belasko.

Rather, it came through to her that she was thinking about
him already, nearly as soon as she turned from her work at
the sink and started concentrating on the news report. His face
had come to mind, subliminally. The way he moved and
watched her as they spoke.

Did she believe he was responsible for the events reported
on the radio? Why should she leap to that conclusion? He had
come to Bogotá apparently unarmed— But guns were easy
to get. He'd asked her for names of individuals to contact in
the government, about the nether world of drugs, the paramilitary underground. How could he learn enough between
the time they separated and this moment to locate, much less
assassinate, a power in the drug trade like Calvino Escobar?

Unless...

She flashed back to the conversation in that very room, not
long ago, as Ciro Aguiar delivered his assessment of the
stranger.

"He's a soldier," Aguiar had proclaimed.

"Or an assassin," Gomez had amended.

Could a soldier or assassin come into a city, strange to
the surroundings, and begin to pick off targets in the space
of a few hours?

Possibly.

She only had Belasko's word, of course, that he was new
to Bogotá. For all she knew, he could have been there countless times before. For all she knew, the very name he used to
introduce himself might be a lie.

In which case, she was forced to ask herself—the onion in

her hand forgotten now, her tears long dry—why would Belasko waste time meeting her and talking to her in the first place? If he was some kind of killer and he had a death list in his pocket from the start, why bother setting up a rendezvous with members of the International Consultancy for Human Rights? The group was known to be nonviolent in all respects, opposed even to legal executions of the most egregious murderers. Why would a soldier or assassin bent on taking lives spend even thirty seconds in her company?

A flash of paranoia suddenly enveloped her. Kelly was dumbstruck, trembling in the length of time it took the thought to form and surface in her conscious mind.

Suppose it was a setup, some kind of conspiracy against the consultancy itself!

It was well-known among the members of the ICHR staff that they were hated by some leaders of the government, despised by most of the police and soldiers in the country. She and her colleagues were meddlers. They were outside agitators striving to disrupt the rule of law and order—as if any such thing had existed in Colombia since World War II.

Was it beyond the realm of possibility that someone in the government would hatch a plot to smear the ICHR by association with a murderer? Was the regime in Washington—or possibly some rogue subordinate at CIA—above cooperating in such tactics? Was there even any reason to believe that Belasko represented Washington at all, when he himself denied it? Or was his denial proof of the reverse.

Slow down!

Her mind was racing, circling back upon itself and going nowhere. Kelly put her knife and onion on the kitchen counter, rinsed and dried her hands, and sat at one end of the table while she still could trust her legs to get her there.

It wouldn't have to be the government, of course. In fact, the death of Escobar—who had, by all accounts, been lavish in his bribes to judges, legislators and policemen—sounded like an argument against official action, now that she had time to think about it.

Who else would profit from a scheme as convoluted as the one that Kelly visualized?

The drug cartels despised ICHR as much as any member of the government, because the consultancy opposed the cocaine trade in principle and spoke out forcefully against the virtual enslavement of peasants by the narcotraffickers. Some rival of Escobar might well have sought a way to solve two problems with a single stroke. In that scenario, again, American involvement could go either way. Members of the intelligence community had dealt with drug runners from 1940s Corsica to Vietnam, Nicaragua and Iran-Contra. On the flip side of that argument, Belasko might turn out to be an independent operator, someone representing syndicated crime.

Who else?

The paramilitary forces in Colombia, both left and right, were devious and deadly. They killed thousands every year, and while their style was normally direct—a highway ambush, for example, or the slaughter of a peaceful village while its people slept—there were no rules in the embittered civil war. Both sides had long since given up whatever principles they held at the beginning, to align themselves with rival drug cartels for cash and arms. They earned their keep by serving the cartels as private armies, killing who and when they were instructed to. The International Consultancy on Human Rights had criticized both factions vehemently for their crimes against humanity, and Kelly had no doubt that paramilitaries were responsible for the recent deaths of ICHR field observers in Colombia. It was entirely possible that one side or the other had devised a plot to smear the agency, perhaps while killing Escobar as a favor to one of their respective sponsors.

Confused and angry, Kelly realized that she had solved nothing, had in fact fallen short of even selecting a viable suspect. Her suspicion against Belasko was founded on nothing of substance, scarcely qualifying even as guesswork. Was he involved in the murders at all? And if so, where did he fit in any of the alternate scenarios her fevered imagination had churned out?

More to the pressing point, how could she satisfy her curiosity now that she had lost contact with the man and he was drifting somewhere through the streets and alleyways of Bogotá?

"You must be kidding me," she muttered, startled as she realized she had spoken the words aloud.

What was she thinking of? A manhunt through the capital, in search of someone who might be a killer operating under one or more false names? Where would she start?

Why should she start?

"It's not your job," she told herself. "It's not."

But was that true? Had she unleashed some new plague on the city by refusing to cooperate with the American visitor? Could she have delayed him somehow? Persuaded him to try a more pacific course, perhaps?

Could she locate him now? And if she did, what would she find? What could she do about it if he was some kind of killer, maybe operating with the sanction of her own elected government?

Where did she go from there?

"Nowhere," she said, and knew it wasn't good enough before the word had even cleared her lips.

She had to do something.

DARKNESS HAD SETTLED over Bogotá by the time Bolan parked his Passat downrange from the warehouse he had marked as his next target in the city. It was one of half a dozen standing fairly close together on a railroad siding, in the southwest quadrant of the city. Trains dropped freight and truckers picked it up, or vice versa. Bolan's briefing paper from the U.S. State Department noted that Colombia's chief exports were petroleum, coffee, coal, bananas and—of all things—fresh-cut flowers.

Not to mention the cocaine.

The warehouse he had targeted was labeled with a giant painted sign across the front that named it Alejandro Ltd. Bolan had no idea who Alejandro was or what his limitations were, but Saturnin Fermina had suggested that the warehouse normally contained at least one shipment of refined cocaine awaiting pickup for the long trip north. This fact was known to various police officials, whose myopia was compensated for by the inflation of their secret bank accounts. The titled owner of the warehouse and the source of the cocaine were unimportant at the moment.

Bolan meant to make a point and let the chips fall where they may.

There was a sentry on the warehouse loading dock, in front. He stood and chain-smoked cigarettes beneath a bank of lights that swarmed with insects, their flitting shadows casting shadows on the dock and warehouse walls like the effect sometimes achieved in cheesy nightclubs with a mirror ball. The sentry didn't seem to notice, paid the bugs no mind. He concentrated on his smokes, occasionally reaching down along his flank to stroke the barrel of an AK-47 that protruded from beneath the jacket draped across his shoulders.

Bolan didn't know if a visible guard meant a shipment was on hand or not. Crime being what it was in Bogotá, a warehouse operated by a drug cartel might well be watched around the clock. He also couldn't tell from where he sat if there were any other sentries presently on-site. There might be dozens in the warehouse, though he doubted it, with no activity apparent that would signal a delivery or pickup.

Either way, he meant to take it down.

He had switched off the rental's interior lights, no sudden glare to betray him as he opened the driver's door and stepped out into darkness. The individual warehouses were fitted with floodlights, some more brightly lit than others, but the street itself was one of those neglected byways found in most large cities, where nightfall hangs shadows that will only be dispersed by dawn.

Bolan was dressed all in black, from his long-sleeved turtleneck to his jeans and jogging shoes. His shoulder holster fit with the ensemble, and the OD webbing he slipped into as he stood beside the car did nothing to increase his visibility.

When he was buckled in, the Desert Eagle rode his hip, pouches distributed around his waist containing extra magazines.

He reached inside the car once more, retrieving the M-4 and a bandolier of 40 mm rounds for the M-203 grenade launcher. When the bandolier was slung across his chest, the rifle cradled in his arm, he softly closed the door and locked it, covering the sentry all the while and watching for any visible reaction.

Nothing.

Bolan crossed the street and started toward his target through the shadows, following the strip of hard-packed dirt that passed for sidewalk in this neighborhood. He watched for other lookouts on the way, at other warehouses, but any watchmen on the job were tucked away somewhere beyond his field of vision.

Thirty paces from the Alejandro warehouse, Bolan veered off course into the sprawl of dark waste ground between his target and its closest neighbor to the west. The chain-link fence that blocked his path wasn't electrified, and Bolan beat the razor wire on top by opening a flap below with wire cutters. He slipped through, closed the flap behind him so that it would pass a casual inspection from a distance and moved out to skirt the warehouse perimeter.

It was a standard layout, one side facing the street, the other butting up to railroad tracks. There were broad doors on both sides, all of them closed now, and smaller ones at the east-west ends of the warehouse. Bolan tried the smaller access doors and found both of them locked. Rather than blow one from its frame and go in blind, he circled back in the direction of the loading dock and the one sentry he had definitely verified.

The lookout was still smoking as Bolan rounded the last corner, just lighting a fresh cigarette from the butt of his last one. Shifting hands with the M-4, Bolan slipped the Beretta from its shoulder rig, thumbed the selective fire switch to semiautomatic and lined up his shot.

He had the sentry in profile, sights framed on the side of his head. A soft whistle from Bolan, barely audible across the space that separated them, and the rifleman swiveled to find the source of the sound, smoke billowing around his face from the cigarette between his lips.

Bolan fired once into the smoke cloud. The gunner did a little backward two-step, falling with his arms outflung as if he were preparing to be crucified. He struck the concrete with numbing force, expelling the cigarette from his mouth and a last puff of smoke from his lungs.

Bolan crossed the loading dock in a rush, moving to the door nearest the sentry's supine form. Finding it locked, he retreated to the smoky corpse and started checking pockets, spilling coins and currency, a comb and switchblade knife, before he found a ring of keys. The second one he tried opened the door, and Bolan slipped inside.

He followed voices and cigar smoke to his left, along a narrow corridor that led him to a kind of office. The glass above plywood partitions had been erected to create a room where none was ever meant to be. The warehouse proper yawned behind twelve-by-fifteen cubicle. Inside it, three men sat around a folding table, playing cards. As far as Bolan could determine, these three were the only ones inside the warehouse.

Shouldering the carbine, Bolan closed the gap between them, striding past the windows on his side before his presence had a chance to register on the card player facing that direction. He filled the doorway, covering the still-oblivious gamblers, noting one's shoulder holster as well as the row of Kalashnikov rifles lined up against the nearest plywood wall.

It was enough.

He raked them with a burst of 5.56 mm rounds, full-metal jackets on the slugs that sent them sprawling in a bloody mist, cards scattered, liquor glasses shattering. It took only a heartbeat, and the three gunners were sprawled in pools of blood that met and merged, filling hairline cracks in the concrete until the floor resembled a piece of grim abstract art.

Bolan waited a moment to see if the reports of gunfire would produce any stragglers from the depths of the warehouse. When no one appeared, he turned his attention to the merchandise on hand, deep rows of wooden crates and cardboard cartons labeled in Spanish. He had no way of confirming contents unless he opened each crate and carton in turn.

Forget it.

This was never meant to be a search. It was strictly seek-and-destroy.

He had the M-203 launcher loaded with a high-explosive round. Smoothly, he brought the carbine's stock to his shoulder, sighting down the barrel as his left hand found the launcher's trigger and released the 40 mm projectile.

It struck near the far end of the warehouse and exploded into smoky thunder, toppling a pyramid of wooden crates into smoldering ruin. Ears ringing from the detonation, Bolan fed the launcher an incendiary round and fired it down the middle of the big room, grimacing involuntarily as it blossomed into white-hot streamers. The chemical stench drove him back toward the door. He loaded one last incendiary round and pumped it after the first.

Scorched earth.

The thermite rounds would eat through steel, concrete, whatever they encountered as they burned with hellish intensity. Mere water wouldn't douse the fire, and little would remain of Alejandro's warehouse by the time the fire burned out. Cocaine or not, the place would be a write-off for its owners—and a message that the battle had been joined.

Outside, he took a deep breath of the clean night air and started back in the direction of his car. No sirens yet, but there was no one in the neighborhood to call in a report of gunfire and explosions. By the time they did, there would be little for the firefighters to do but shovel through the steaming wreckage, bringing out the dead.

There would be more work for the coroner before another day was done. The Executioner had barely gotten started, and there was no end in sight.

5

Yago Sebastiano paused for a moment to light a thin cheroot, drawing the rich smoke deep into his lungs, waiting for the nicotine rush that would suppress the first, faint stirrings of an ache behind his eyes. Snapping the ancient Ronson lighter shut, Sebastiano was relieved to see no visible tremor in his hands, no outward sign of nervousness that any other human being could detect.

Image was critical in politics and war alike, two fields wherein Sebastiano typically excelled. His strength lay in a natural ability to win the confidence of others and persuade them that they needed his approval to survive.

For many in Colombia these days, of course, that was a daily fact of life.

Sebastiano was the field commander of the largest right-wing paramilitary unit in Colombia, the People's Army of Democracy—more often simply called The Fist, after its symbol of a clenched fist raised to strike the leftist enemies of private property, free enterprise, Jesus Christ. Sebastiano was himself a jaded atheist whose faith in God had been discarded on some battlefield that he couldn't recall, but when it came to faking zealous dedication to the One True Church he could compete with any actor of the stage or silver screen.

Sebastiano's war was with the parasites who sought to undermine Colombian democracy, the socialists and labor organizers, intellectuals who spewed their ideas about the universal brotherhood of man, the petty criminals who made life in the cities dangerous and costly for all decent citizens. Conversely, while he recognized that the narcotics traffic was illegal and produced widespread corruption in society, Sebastiano felt no burning need to launch a war on drugs like that which had been churning futilely along in the United States for more than twenty years.

What was the point?

The narcotraffickers paid their own way in the world—and very handsomely, at that. Their trade supplied employment for whole villages whose people might otherwise go hungry. The drugs were mostly shipped to other countries while the cash poured in to Bogotá, Cali, and Medellín. It was the sort of trade balance that any staunch defender of free enterprise had to automatically admire. As for the bribery that flowed from drugs and other forms of consensual crime, it was a long-standing tradition where underpaid policemen and public officials were virtually expected to supplement their incomes with donations from the private sector.

No, the only bulk exporters who concerned Sebastiano were those who had forged alliances with leftist guerrillas like those of the Revolutionary Armed Forces of Colombia. Such men were traitors to their nation, to their families and to their history. If he had his way, they would be rooted out, erased from the face of the earth as if they had never existed.

But first, he had to deal with his boss.

"More wine, Yago?" Prospero Alarcon inquired.

"No, thank you."

They sat together in the smaller of Alarcon's two dining rooms, the massive house surrounding them and bearing down upon Sebastiano with the weight of wealth almost beyond imagining. The man seated across from him, while only two or three years older than Sebastiano, was a different breed entirely, born to money and the power it provided. Alarcon grew coffee and bananas on his vast plantations, owned a thriving emerald mine near Popayán and oil rigs at Tumaco. He didn't traffic in cocaine, but neither did he interfere with the elected livelihood of others who were wise

enough to leave him well alone. It had been whispered that
he owned as many politicians as the Medellín cartel, and
while Sebastiano couldn't prove it, neither did he doubt that
such might be the case.

"We have a problem?" the planter asked his guest, bringing the subject back to business.

"Possibly a small one." It would do no good to lie.

"I care nothing about Escobar," Alarcon said. "But Saturnin Fermina, this has me concerned."

They had been known to use Fermina's services from time
to time, when common enemies had slipped beyond Sebastiano's reach. While he wasn't the only international contractor working out of Bogotá, by any means, his loss would
still be keenly felt. Their program of elimination to the north
wasn't complete, and now Sebastiano feared they would be
forced to start from scratch with someone new. Discontinu-
ity was always troubling, more so when lives and large sums
of money hung in the balance.

"The incident is very recent," Sebastiano said, by way of
an excuse. "My people are investigating, talking to our friends
on the police force. There is no suggestion, yet, as to the men
responsible."

"This answer satisfies you, Yago?"

"No, boss." In fact, Sebastiano wasn't satisfied at all. But he
was skilled at masking his emotions under circumstances where
a grand display was pointless, even self-destructive. "We still
hope for some results before the week is out," he added.

"And do our friends in uniform believe the murders of
Fermina and Escobar may be somehow related?"

"They are of divided minds on this."

"Divided minds do not think clearly, Yago. They produce confusion which is detrimental to the orderly conduct of business."

"I understand."

"We must eliminate confusion, Yago, rather than compound it."

"Yes."

"You'll sort out this business, then, with all possible dispatch." It was an order, not a question or request. Dismissively, the planter added, "I will wait for your report."

Sebastiano rose with all the dignity that he could muster, bowing crisply from the waist as he prepared to take his leave.

"It shall be done," he said.

But on the long walk through the sprawling house, back to his car and driver waiting in the shaded courtyard, Sebastiano had to ask himself exactly *how* it would be done.

Admitting to himself that he, as yet, had no idea.

REGAN KELLY HATED meeting with the man most other people called The Monkey, but she found it was required from time to time, in order to obtain the sort of information that was otherwise unreachable. This time it would be worse than usual, she knew, because she couldn't simply ask The Monkey what he knew about the recent spate of unsolved homicides. To justify her interest, she had to share a measure of the truth with him, to win his trust, and that struck her as dangerous.

Still, she had made the date to meet him and she couldn't back out now.

The Monkey's given name was Jésus Galatria. While not a dwarf or midget, he was very nearly short enough to qualify, perhaps four-nine or -ten. Galatria waddled when he walked on short, bowed legs, his long arms dangling, leaving no doubt whatsoever as to how his nickname had been earned. As if his stature and physique weren't enough, the head perched neckless on his shoulders was completely bald and bullet-shaped, the features of his dark, perpetually scowling face distinctly simian.

He could have played the missing link without much makeup, Kelly thought, and whereas the uncharitable thought would normally have caused some guilty pangs, this day it echoed no remorse. Galatria had insisted that they meet in this disgusting tavern, where at least three-quarters of the patrons looked like ruffians and most of them kept staring at her, hard eyes crawling over her like restless hands.

She nursed a glass of wine—the house red, seemingly the

cheapest vintage readily available in bulk—and waited for Galatria to arrive. He was already late, ten minutes edging toward fifteen, and Kelly had decided she would leave at twenty, wasted trip or not.

Galatria arrived with two minutes to spare, resplendent in a lemon-yellow suit and matching wide-brimmed hat that made him look as if he had dressed up for a performance in a sideshow. What he took to be a strut was actually more a caricature of his normal waddling gate. A foot-long cigar protruding from his mouth completed the effect, setting various drinkers to gouging each other with elbows, pointing and snickering as Galatria made his way across the crowded room.

He was showing her off, Kelly thought, repulsed by the notion. He was acting as if they were on a date.

Galatria slid into the booth across from her, straining to pat her hand with one of his, blowing cigar smoke in her face. "Sorry I am late," he said around the smoldering speech impediment. "Got lots of business on a night like this, so much shit going down."

"You said you might have—"

"Information, yes," he interrupted her, at last removing the cigar to pick shreds of tobacco from his tongue. "You want to know about the murders, yes?"

"For God's sake keep your voice down!" Kelly whispered. She started to imagine half the people in the bar eavesdropping on their conversation, any number of them rushing off as soon as she departed to inform police, drug runners, paramilitaries—any one of which, she knew, could be involved with the assassins.

"There is no danger here," Galatria said, and flashed the first smile she had ever seen upon his face. A glimpse of his beige, crooked teeth, and she knew why he was stingy with his smiles.

"I'd like to be the judge of that, if you don't mind," she replied. "Now, can you fill me in discreetly, or is this a waste of time?"

"Discreetly, yes," he said, half rising from his seat as if to crawl across the table. Kelly nearly recoiled before she realized it was the only way Galatria could lean close enough to whisper. Suddenly embarrassed, she leaned forward, meeting him halfway. She was immediately thankful that her blouse was buttoned to the throat, with no display of cleavage.

Galatria took another pull on his cigar and fogged the air between them, making Kelly close her stinging eyes. At least it masked the short man's reeking body odor, which was normally severe enough to make her schedule their occasional meetings in open-air settings.

"It is like this," Galatria said. "Nobody knows who killed these men, but there is talk, you understand?"

"What kind of talk?" she pressed him.

"Street talk. Gossip." He brandished the cigar in front of her as if he were conducting a concerto. "All this talk I hear and I remember."

Reaching up to tap one twisted ear, Galatria grazed his hat brim with the tip of his cigar, smudging the hat and spilling ashes down across the shoulder of his yellow suit. Kelly bit off a squeal of spiteful laughter, concentrating on her stinging eyes and waiting for the impulse to subside.

"So," she prodded him, "are you going to tell me or what?"

Galatria rolled his eyes, twisting his head to scan the room. "This place," he said, "is not the best to speak of such things openly."

"You chose this place," Kelly reminded him, putting a hard edge in her voice.

"To meet you only," he replied, forcing a vague approximation of a grin. Two smiles from this one in a single sitting made her queasy. She experienced a sinking feeling that she had been had—or was about to be. "I think perhaps if we should go somewhere with greater privacy...."

"Is that what you think?" she retorted. "I suppose you're wanting something in exchange for this great information that you've gathered off the streets?"

Galatria shrugged, a move that made it look as if his skull were sinking into his thorax. "I don't reject the possibility of some negotiation for my services," he answered, feigning innocence.

"Oh, yeah? Well *I* reject it," she fired back. "Now, do you have the information that I asked you for or not?"

"Please, señorita! You misunderstand. I merely wish—"

"Blow out the candles, Monkey Boy," she snapped at him. "But that wish is never coming true." Rising to leave, disgusted with this creature and herself for trusting him, Kelly couldn't resist a parting shot. "And what's with that cigar? Could you be any more of a cliché?"

All things considered, Regan Kelly thought it was among her best dramatic exits, and her anger carried her all the way back to her car before she remembered that she was coming away empty-handed.

Leaving as she had without a backward glance, she didn't see Galatria staring after her, his face darkening as several larger men at nearby tables laughed at his predicament. It was a full two minutes later when he rose and went to find the public telephone.

FRACO TERCIERO LOVED his office. It was almost physical, the passion he experienced each morning when he entered and beheld the handpicked, handmade furnishings, the artwork on the walls, his view of downtown Bogotá through large tinted windows that constituted two walls of his spacious corner suite. The washroom included not only a toilet and sink, but his own private shower, with a hair dryer mounted on the wall.

Terciero had earned this relative luxury in his climb through party ranks to reach his present post as Assistant Minister of the Interior. Although he was subordinate to the appointed minister, in practice he made most of the decisions relative to problems that affected life for sundry elements of the Colombian population. He had his finger on the pulse of labor difficulties, unemployment, housing, education, agriculture and ecology. He shared information on a daily basis with the Assistant Minister of Justice and the Deputy Attaché for Military Affairs, thus keeping current likewise on the problems of law enforcement and the drug wars, terrorism and the army's campaign to suppress radical subversives.

Terciero sometimes regarded himself as all things to all men. He loved his office and, for the most part, he loved his job. What he did not love was the need to meet with killers on occasion and pretend that they were normal, decent human beings.

Still, it was part of his job, and Terciero plastered a smile on his face as he rose from behind his mahogany desk, circling the massive slab of hardwood to shake hands with Yago Sebastiano. The right-wing guerrilla leader wore a three-piece suit, which was a great improvement on his normal camouflage fatigues, and he had even shaved for the occasion, missing only one or two spots underneath his jaw. His hair was oiled and combed back from his face in what Terciero thought of as the Rudolf Valentino style—or maybe Dracula. One thing would never change, though. Even in his suit, Sebastiano stank of cheap cigars.

Terciero braced himself for the expected crunch of contact when their palms met, but Sebastiano didn't try mash his fingers this time, satisfied to pump his hand twice, like a jack handle, and let it go. Retiring to their separate chairs, the desk between them, both men sat. Terciero noted that the pistol underneath Sebastiano's jacket made an angular displacement of the fabric as he settled in his chair.

"Mr. Sebastiano—"

"Yago, please," the visitor corrected him.

"Of course, Yago. You mentioned on the telephone a matter of importance. As I have a busy calendar today, perhaps—"

"Directly to the business, then," Sebastiano finished for him. "That's good. You are aware, I take it, of the several incidents in Bogotá last night?"

There was no doubt which incidents Sebastiano meant. A spate of murders targeting some influential gangsters and their bodyguards, destruction of a warehouse owned by one of the cartels.

"These things are common knowledge, I believe," Terciero told his visitor.

"I bring you something that is not common knowledge, then."

"You have information on these crimes?" Terciero asked.

"Perhaps."

The assistant minister was instantly suspicious. "I appreciate your confidence," he said, "but surely if you have some information on a criminal investigation, you should take it to the Ministry of Justice?"

"It is most important at the moment," Sebastiano said, "that discretion be preserved."

"Of course, I understand," Terciero lied. "But still—"

"I was advised to seek you out by a mutual friend," Sebastiano said.

"I see." Another lie. "If it is not impertinent of me to ask the name—"

"Prospero Alarcon sends his regards," Sebastiano interrupted, flashing yet another jaundiced smile.

Fraco Terciero found himself momentarily at a loss for words, no comfortable state for a born politician. He had never met Alarcon, but knew the man by reputation. Who among Colombians did not? He was among the richest and most influential businessmen the nation had produced, including most of those who made their livings from cocaine. He was also a ruthless man who chose his friends with care and punished enemies unmercifully.

Depending on his mood, it was an honor or a hazard to be noticed by Alarcon. It seemed that Terciero had been singled out for praise, albeit secondhand. But why? What did he have that Alarcon desired? What would it cost him to cooperate—or to refuse?

The choice was made for pragmatism's sake before he spoke. "By all means, then, your information, please."

"You are familiar with the International Consultancy on Human Rights?" Sebastiano asked.

Terciero nodded. "Yes, of course. They meddle in affairs that don't concern them, asking questions best kept to themselves."

That put another smile on the guerrilla leader's face. "Indeed," he said. "Now, I have reason to believe a ranking member of the group is very interested, possibly involved, in last night's crimes."

"Involved?" Terciero wasn't quick enough to hide his open skepticism. "But the ICHR is a group of pacifists, old women when it comes to violence."

"Or so they want us to believe," Sebastiano said.

"Who is this person?"

"In a moment. We must first decide what should be done with one who meddles so."

Terciero felt the short hairs on his nape begin to bristle. If Sebastiano and The Fist planned to assassinate a member of the International Consultancy on Human Rights, he didn't want to know about it in advance. Why would Sebastiano even be here, sitting in his office, in that case?

"What is it that you wish for me to do?" Terciero asked.

"It is suggested that the matter may be of some interest to the state security police. Perhaps, if inquiries were made—"

"Of course." Terciero felt a stirring of relief. "But, once again, the most direct route to contact the agency you seek—"

"Is through the Ministry of Justice. Yes. I am aware of that."

"You wish that I should make that contact, then?"

"As an official of the state who has obtained this vital information for himself. No questions would be asked."

And nothing traced back to Prospero Alarcon.

Terciero managed not to sigh as he replied, "I'll need to know the name."

HILARIO BATISTA WAS a man who followed orders. He had learned the trait in childhood, from a hard-handed father, and it had been reinforced in military service. Now, with sixteen years in uniform as a member of the Colombian national police, it occurred to him that he had spent all of his thirty-eight years being told what to do by virtual strangers.

And it seemed completely natural.

Hilario Batista's half-dozen friends sometimes made fun of his given name—which translated as "Happy." When they told those tired old jokes he simply glowered at them, as he glowered all day long. If there was ever one whose name didn't appear to fit, Hilario Batista was the very man. It wasn't that he hated life, his job, or anything else in particular. He simply had a sour disposition that had followed him from childhood and would doubtless trail him to the grave.

Of course, some jobs brought out the worst in him.

The task at hand, for instance.

Batista cared nothing about the woman they had been sent to arrest. She was described as radical, a danger to the state, and that was good enough for him. The trouble lay in her identity. She was American and affiliated with the International Consultancy on Human Rights, which meant potential howls of outrage once the news of her arrest got out. If she should suffer any unexpected injuries in custody—as had been known to happen in Colombia from time to time—the affair could easily become an international incident.

And that was bad, Batista realized, because the men who gave him orders wouldn't wish to take the fall themselves. There would be fingers pointed, maybe documents destroyed or fabricated. And the crap, once it began to roll, would always flow downhill—straight to him.

Still, there was nothing he could do about it. That was life on the police force, in the army, in Colombia. There were a chosen few who gave the orders, others who were paid to follow them, and someone always had to take the blame when things went wrong.

At least they had been told to bring the woman in alive. That meant that if she later died in custody, it would be someone else's problem. Thinking well ahead, Batista knew that he should be conspicuous and concentrate on forging iron-clad alibis these next few days.

But first, he had to put the woman in a cell.

Three officers had been assigned to help him, which was overkill for one female affiliated with a totally nonviolent protest group. Batista understood about appearances, of course, and how they sometimes had to be maintained even at the risk of seeming ridiculous. He was part of the charade, and he would play his role to the utmost of his ability.

The woman occupied a small bungalow in one of Bogotá's working-class suburbs. The neighborhood was neither good nor bad in terms of crime, but merely average. Most of the criminals were thieves who stole from hunger, being either homeless, unemployed, or both. The normal crimes included burglary and shoplifting, some mugging, now and then a rape when things got out of hand. There had been murders, too— as everywhere in Bogotá—but they were typically domestic killings, with the occasional execution performed on strange turf for variety.

As to what the American had supposedly done, Batista neither knew nor cared.

They pulled into the alley behind her bungalow, a young corporal named Lazaro Ramirez driving the standard-issue unmarked sedan. It hardly mattered, since the Dodge Stratus sedans with government plates were obvious police vehicles and all four officers were dressed in full uniform, but it had been the only car available on short notice. For backup, Batista had two patrolmen—a rookie named César Costanzas and an old cop called Roano Ybara, whom Batista would be forced to watch in case he tried to feel the woman up en route to the police station.

"Wait here," Batista told Ramirez. "If she tries to run, we may need you to cut her off."

"I hope she runs," Ybara muttered from the back seat of the Dodge.

"Shut up and do your job, old man," Batista snapped at him. "You fuck this up and you'll be chasing purse snatchers in the parks again, I promise you."

Ybara muttered under his breath. Batista swiveled in his seat to face the older man, scowling, his right hand clenched around the riot baton that could scatter Ybara's teeth like mosaic tiles. There would be questions if he battered a subordinate, but with Ybara's record on the table and the other two officers backing him up, Batista was fairly certain he make a case for self-defense.

"What did you say, old man?" he challenged.

"I said nothing, sir." Ybara blinked once, forced a sickly smile, then looked away.

"Come on, then," Batista said. "Let's finish this."

BOLAN WAS FACING a problem now. He had come back to speak with Regan Kelly, unsure as to whether she would sit still for another conversation, but it seemed that someone else had plans for her as well. The three policemen in their khaki uniforms looked grim and businesslike as they pushed through the gate that served the courtyard of her bungalow, each officer with a baton clutched in his hand, a pistol holstered on his Sam Browne belt.

Police were problematic for the Executioner. From the beginning of his lonely war against the Mafia, he had maintained a pledge that he wouldn't use deadly force against duly recognized "soldiers of the same side" in the battle against crime. The fact that some police officers were themselves criminals—including some guilty of multiple murders—didn't absolve Bolan from that promise to himself. He had derailed a few police careers in his time and collaborated in sending some corrupt or murderous cops to prison where they belonged, and he tried to maintain his vow.

The problem still remained. These officers had come for Regan Kelly, and he knew that if they carried her away he would lose his last chance to speak with the ICHR's strong-willed spokesperson. Likewise, because he had no reason to believe that the woman had committed any crime, Bolan strongly suspected her arrest had to be political, and that her safety would be jeopardized in custody.

So, what to do?

He had three cops with side arms lining up at Kelly's door, a fourth cop waiting in the car out back. He could have taken them in seconds flat with the Beretta, left them scattered in the courtyard and the driver dead behind the unmarked Dodge's steering wheel, but that wasn't an option. He would have to circumvent their standing orders in some way that didn't lead to loss of life.

The point man for the team was knocking, waiting on the doorstep, with his backup flanking him. They hadn't noticed Bolan, crouching on the far side of the courtyard, hidden where the branches of a weeping willow grazed the flagstones. Bolan watched them as the officer in charge prepared to knock again, then drew his fist back awkwardly when Kelly answered, opening the door.

There was a sharp exchange in Spanish, growing heated in a hurry. The woman clearly didn't like what she was hearing, a combination of alarm and anger written on her face. She asked a question Bolan couldn't follow, and the officer in charge considered it for a moment, then nodded curtly. Kelly retreated from the threshold, starting to close the door, but the point man stiff-armed it open and followed her inside, one of the backup officers trailing him, while the other remained on the stoop.

Bolan counted the seconds without shifting to check his wristwatch. He was passing ninety-six when one of the cops reappeared in the doorway, followed by Kelly, with the leader of the squad bringing up the rear. He closed the door behind himself and locked it with a key he had apparently obtained from the woman. Pocketing the key, the leader of the khaki threesome took a pair of handcuffs from his belt and reached for her wrist.

Startled and frightened, she began to pull away. The older of the backup officers moved in behind her, wrapped his arms around her, one hand clamping onto a breast while his other pinned Kelly's left arm to her side.

Bolan palmed the smoke grenade without conscious thought, drawing the safety pin and pitching the grenade across the courtyard from his hiding place. The lead cop turned to see it coming as it bounced across the flagstones, frozen where he stood with handcuffs dangling from his fingertips. From the expression on his face, he recognized the canister as a grenade but didn't know what kind it was, the sudden panic in his eyes bespeaking mental images of sudden, rending death.

Instead of shrapnel, though, he got a sudden faceful of green smoke rising in a thick, enveloping cloud, blanketing the three policemen and their still-struggling prisoner. Bolan went in behind the smoke, dashing headlong toward his targets and navigating by instinct once he entered the swirling green fog bank.

The leader of the team had barely moved, except to drop his cuffs and fumble with the old-fashioned flap holster on his hip. Bolan snapped an elbow into his face and felt the nose crush, pulling the punch to avoid lethal contact. The cop staggered backward, arms whipping the smoke cloud as they flailed, and he dropped out of sight in the chemical mist.

Kelly was cursing her captors in a mixture of English and Spanish now, scratching at the rough hands that had somehow managed to cover both of her breasts. Bolan stepped in close and broke the grip by fastening his own hand on the grabby copper's ears, twisting sharply with a downward motion. A bit more force could have torn them from the skull, but he didn't plan to maim anyone if he could help it.

The patrolman dropped to one knee, squealing, and Bolan clipped him with the knife-edge of an open hand across the base of his skull. Before the rag doll toppled forward, the Executioner slipped the nightstick from the cop's belt and swung around to nail the third member of the team, jabbing the baton sharply into his solar plexus. The young man doubled over, retching, and Bolan left him to it, grabbing Kelly's arm in a grip that brooked no argument.

"Come on!" he snapped. "We're getting out of here."

"You," she blurted, focusing on Bolan's face with eyes gone teary from the smoke. "What are you... Why... Who are you?"

"We can talk about it somewhere else," he said. "Unless you'd rather sit in jail?"

"All right, let's go," she said, and followed Bolan as he led her jogging toward the far side of the courtyard, where they scaled the simple wooden fence easily.

"You owe me answers, damn it!" Kelly huffed at him, as they were sprinting toward his rental car.

"You show me yours," he said without a backward glance, "I'll show you mine."

6

There was a risk involved in taking Regan Kelly back to Bolan's rented flat, but he preferred that gamble to dropping her off at some point in the city, when police would probably be searching for her. She asked to use the shower and he pointed her in the direction of the bathroom, waiting in the combination living room and kitchen while he listened to the water run and thought about how much he could afford to tell her of his mission. She returned ten minutes later, damp hair sleek against her skull, most of the smoky odor gone except whatever lingered in her clothes.

"Okay," she said, as she joined him at the kitchen table. "Do you want to tell me what that scene was all about?"

"I'd call it self-explanatory," Bolan said. "Someone sent the police to haul you in."

"I followed that part of it," she replied. "You want to play games, let me spell it out: What were you doing at my house? Why did you interfere? Where did that smoke come from?"

He hit the questions out of order, starting with the last one first. "The smoke came from a standard-issue military smoke grenade," he said. "I came to see you with the thought that we should have another talk, but the police were there ahead of me. As far as stepping in, that was a judgment call. I couldn't think of any way you'd benefit from being locked up in a cell right now."

"So, you've made me a fugitive," she said.

"I didn't make you anything," Bolan reminded her. "You were behind me all the way."

"As if I had a choice. Now the police are after me."

He rapped the table sharply with his knuckles, leaning forward as he spoke. "They were already after you, remember? They weren't selling tickets to the next policeman's ball."

"But you assaulted them. And now they'll think I had something to do with it."

"If you want to fix that," Bolan told her, "we can find a pay phone, probably within a block or two. I'll drop you off. You call the cops and tell them you were kidnapped. Give them my description. You can have the license number of my car."

"Like they'd believe me," Kelly muttered, slumping backward in her chair.

"What you need to ask yourself," he said, "is why they came out to arrest you in the first place."

"It had already crossed my mind," she said, eyes narrowing to slits. "And I was thinking you might have an answer for me on that score."

He frowned. "And why would you think that?"

"My turn to ask the questions now," she said, ignoring Bolan's query. "Have you heard about the shootings in the city, overnight?"

"I haven't listened to the news."

"That's not an answer."

"No, it's not," he said, advancing one step closer to a leap of faith. "Before you ask that kind of question, first be sure you want to know the answer."

"Oh, I'm very sure."

"All right, then," he replied. "I am aware of certain incidents."

"Are you responsible?" she pressed.

"I wouldn't say that. But I was involved."

"You killed those people? Who are you?"

"I told you yesterday—"

"You told me squat!" she interrupted him, angry. "You claim to represent the U.S. government, and then you're killing people. Next, you turn up on my doorstep, gassing the police who want to haul me off to jail."

"Is that a 'thank-you'?" Bolan asked her, not quite smiling.

"Thank you?" Kelly's voice was sharp with incredulity. "You're saying I should thank you? I'm homeless now because of you. The cops are after me because of you."

That took him by surprise. "Why do you say that?" Bolan asked.

"Why else would they be after me?" she challenged him. "I meet with you, we go our separate ways, and you start shooting people. Hours later, I've got cops who want to slap the cuffs on, when they haven't given me a second glance in eighteen months. You think that's a coincidence?"

"Consider what you're saying, Regan. If they're drawing a connection, where did it come from?"

"What do you mean?" she asked him, losing just a bit of steam.

"I mean they didn't hear about our meet from me," Bolan replied. "There's nothing in your outfit's background to suggest that it—or you—would be involved in any violence, am I right? So, now you need to ask yourself, who spilled the beans?"

She frowned over that for a moment, plainly unhappy with the results of her consideration. "No," she said at last, shaking her head. "Ciro would never do that. As for Nestor, hell, he was run out of office as a prosecutor for refusing to play ball with grafting politicians and the drug cartels. No way. I'd stake my life on both of them."

"That's what you're doing," he reminded her, "unless you have a third alternative."

Something fell into place behind her eyes with an almost audible click. "Oh, God," she said. "There could be someone else."

"Tell me."

A sudden blush warmed up her cheeks. "I heard the news last night," she said, "about the shootings, and I started thinking. I was wondering if you...well, anyway, it looks like I was right. I wanted to find out more information, but I couldn't talk to the police, since they resent our criticism of their methods."

"So?" he prodded her.

"There's this...I don't know what to call him...man I know who always seems to know what's going on with criminals and politicians, things like that. I went to meet him last night, at a bar, but all he really wanted was to get me in the sack. He wouldn't tell me anything, so I walked out on him."

"And he has contacts with the state police?"

"Both sides, to hear him tell it. I don't know how much of what he says is true, but he's provided information in the past that checked out well enough."

"I'm guessing that he has a name."

"Oh, no," she said. "I won't do that. Besides, we don't know whether he had anything to do with this."

"Which is exactly why somebody needs to ask him."

"I won't be responsible for someone being killed."

"That's right, you won't," Bolan replied. "I'm here in Bogotá because somebody has been killing off Colombian exiles in the United States. It has to stop, and interdicting hit teams on the other end won't do the trick. To kill a snake, you cut off the head."

"And to kill a man?"

"I'm flexible," he told her bluntly.

"I won't be a part of this."

"You are a part of it. The cops are after you, and something tells me that it's not for unpaid parking fines. In custody, you're at their mercy. I haven't had a chance to check out all the rumors about right-wing death squads in Colombia—"

"They're true," she told him, softening. "Most of them, anyway."

"So going in a cage would mean that you're in jeopardy. You might not come back out again."

"What do you want from me, damn it?"

"I'll settle for that name."

She hesitated for another moment, then replied, "I can't decide this on my own. I need Ciro and Nestor."

"We don't have a lot of time."

"It won't take long, if I can use your telephone."

"No phone," he said. "Looks like we're going for another ride."

CIRO AGUIAR was waiting when she entered the café, alone in a booth at the back, near the rest rooms. Kelly caught him frowning at her as she waved off the hostess and made her way back through the long, narrow room that smelled of homemade salsa, pork and steaming rice.

He sniffed at Kelly as she slid into the booth across from him, and said, "You've started smoking now?"

"Don't ask," she said. "Where's Nestor?"

"He's not coming," Aguiar answered. Adding, "I think he's afraid."

"Of the police?"

"For starters, yes. Why not? He used to work with them and still has certain friends among them. He knows well enough what they can do, if they are motivated."

"Damn it!"

"Do we need him?"

"Maybe. I don't know." She paused a moment to collect her thoughts. How much should she tell him? How much did he need to know? What piece of information would be just one bit too much, and put his life in jeopardy whether he helped her or not?

"Regan?"

His soft voice brought her back. "All right," she said. "I told you the police were after me. I didn't tell you why."

"Tell me."

"This can't go any further, Ciro. Not for now, at least."

"You've known me now almost two years, Regan. You choose a strange time to insult me."

He was smiling as he spoke, and she ignored the gibe, the story spilling out of her, less well coordinated than she'd hoped, but Aguiar seemed to follow it. When she was finished, he spent a moment staring out the café's window, then he said, "The Monkey, eh? I never trusted that one."

"What? That's all you have to say?"

"You were expecting something else?"

"Now that you mention it." She leaned in closer, lowering her voice. "I thought you might have some comment about Belasko and the rest of it."

"That one," Aguiar replied, shaking his head. "I told you, he's a soldier."

"Nestor called him an assassin," Kelly said.

"Is there a difference?"

"I'd like to think so," she replied. "My father was a soldier, Air Force."

"It's all the same. Those who wear military uniforms are paid to fight, Regan. That means they're paid to kill. They don't choose their enemies, nor do they often act in self-defense, as the police are sometimes forced to do. They are dispatched by faceless men to seize and neutralize objectives in the name of policy. War always benefits the masters, never those who serve."

"You talk like that in Bogotá," she chided him, "and you'll have men with badges chasing you."

"In time," Aguiar replied, "I have no doubt of it."

"Before they come for both of us, then, tell me, what am I supposed to do, Ciro?"

"I can't make that decision for you, Regan. No one can."

"Terrific. So, I'm on my own?"

"I didn't say I wouldn't help you," he said. "I simply can't tell you what to do. Make your decision based on what your heart and mind tell you to do, and I will do whatever it may be within my power to assist you."

"You'll be in danger either way."

"We've been in danger from the start," Aguiar corrected her. "We've lost three friends already to the murderers."

"I'm not forgetting them. But there's no reason you should join them for my sake."

"I don't intend to die," he said, then cracked another smile. "At least not yet. Decide what you must do, either to help this soldier or to keep away from him, and then we make our plans."

"You're something else," she said and reached across the table, grasping his hand.

He smiled at her, replying, "Was there ever any doubt?"

YOU DIDN'T SEE the man who threw the smoke grenade?"

It was the third time that the question had been asked, in one form or another, and Hilario Batista thought that if he heard it one more time he might start raving incoherently. Of course, he knew that wouldn't happen in reality, because he was a noncommissioned officer in the security police and he had already received enough painkillers for his injuries that he didn't believe he could have staged a tantrum, even though frustration and anxiety were gnawing at his nerves.

"No, sir," he said again. "I didn't see the man who threw the smoke grenade."

"In which case," another voice asked, "how do you know it was a man?"

That was a new one, and Batista took a moment to consider it. "I don't know that a man threw the grenade, sir," he replied at length. "I only know a man attacked me moments after the grenade exploded."

"Moments?" a third voice demanded.

"Seconds, sir."

Batista had been cleared to leave the hospital after his broken nose was straightened somewhat, capped with tape, and sundry painkillers were forced into his hand. He had immediately swallowed three or four of them, hoping to quell the agony inside his throbbing head before he left for home.

Batista never made it, though.

The delegation had been waiting for him as he left the treatment area downstairs. He recognized the only one of them in uniform, a colonel of the national police named Pedro de Leon Lucero. His two companions wore dark, conservative suits. One of them had a thick mustache to compensate for his bald pate; the other wore horn-rimmed glasses, with the left lens made of what appeared to be black plastic, like a curious eye patch. Batista didn't need to hear that they were from the Ministry of Justice or some other agency that would pass judgment on his fate for failure to complete a simple task.

"You think it was the same man who threw the smoke grenade?" Colonel Lucero asked.

"I don't know, sir. I assumed it must be...but I have no proof."

"And this man broke your nose?" the man in the glasses asked.

"Sir, he struck me in the face."

"With what?" the cop with the mustache inquired.

"His arm, sir...or perhaps some other object. It's difficult to say. There was the smoke, things happened suddenly."

"And he disarmed your men, as well," Lucero said. He appeared to take the incident as a personal insult—or worse, as an insult to the force.

"I can't be sure of that, sir. I was knocked unconscious, as you know."

"By one blow to the face," the colonel said.

"One blow, yes, sir. At least, I think—"

"You saw the man before he knocked you down, I take it?" the man with the mustache asked.

"I saw someone," Batista said, "yes, sir. Of course, with all the smoke—"

"What did he look like?" This came from the man in glasses.

"He seemed to be a large man."

"Taller than yourself?" Lucero asked.

"Yes, sir. Also heavier. He moved quite rapidly, and with the smoke—"

"We've heard about the smoke," the man with the mustache said, interrupting him. "It's no excuse."

"No, sir." The spark that had been irritation turned to something more like panic, now. "I'm simply trying to explain that there was no real opportunity to see the man—"

"Before he knocked you out," the one with glasses completed the remark, fairly smirking.

Batista saw no point in answering the insult. If these men already had their minds made up that he was guilty of some negligent offense, his fate was sealed. Batista could no more dissuade them from their judgment than he could leap from his chair and fly around the room.

"This man," the colonel said. "Did he appear to know the woman?"

"They didn't speak in my presence, sir."

"That is to say, while you were conscious," Lucero clarified.

"Yes, sir. Perhaps if you asked César or Roano—"

"We shall speak to whom we choose," the cop with the mustache broke in. "Do not concern yourself with that."

"I take it, since you were unconscious," the other cop said, "that you didn't observe the woman as she fled the scene of the attack?"

"No, sir."

"Or which direction she and her companion ran?"

"I've said that I didn't see her escape, sir." The stupidity was overwhelming. These fools were investigators? Sleuths?

"And if you had seen," Lucero interjected, "you wouldn't withhold that information, eh, Hilario?"

This was bad! The accusation and his first name bundled up in one remark. The dull pain in his head began to throb again, as if it was acquiring new life of its own. Batista wondered whether it was possible to have a stroke from being asked too many questions after suffering a broken nose.

"Yes, sir. I mean, no sir! I have withheld no information from the court, sir."

"This is not a court."

"I feel as if I am on trial," Batista said, forgetting in the moment to add "sir."

"Not yet, Batista," Lucero said. Within the past half minute he apparently had managed to forget Batista's given name. "Not yet."

"Now tell us," the cop wearing glasses said, "whether you saw the man who threw the smoke grenade."

"I WANT NO PART of this," Nestor Gomez said, clutching his coffee mug in both hands, with such force that he feared it might shatter. "This is not the mission we are pledged to, Ciro."

"No one is asking you to fight, Nestor." There seemed to be no sneer in Aguiar's voice, though Gomez more than half expected one.

"It's all the same at law," the one-time prosecutor told his friend. "You make yourselves accessories—before the fact, if you provide this man with names. After the fact, if you conceal him from authorities in knowledge of his crimes. I can't do that. I won't, Ciro. It's why I first joined the consultancy, because the group is pledged to using only legal means, non-violence and—"

"They came for Regan, Nestor," Aguiar interrupted him. "The state police, at Regan's doorstep. This American kept her from a cage at the interrogation center. You, of all people, must know what happens there."

The comment stung, more so because it was true. Gomez had never taken part in a police interrogation while he was a prosecutor, but he had several times gone to court on matters where confessions made the case. And there were always rumors circulating in the halls of Justice—sometimes trailed by wicked laughter, other times by scowls of disapproval—that had let him know what happened in the case of certain suspects held by the security police. Those rumors and his grasp of the reality behind them were a major reason why he had abandoned his position with the government to join the International Consultancy on Human Rights.

"I understand, but—"

"Regan, Nestor!" Aguiar cut him off again. "Caged with those animals. And if they wanted her to disappear..."

"Enough!" Gomez snapped back.

As the interrogation methods of the state police were no great secret, so it rumored that certain prisoners were known to disappear entirely, turning up days or weeks later—if they turned up at all—as the victims of crude executions, presumably carried out by some right-wing pro-government death squad. The files would be empty if anyone went look-

ing for arrest records in such a case, the officers wise enough
to cover their tracks at least that far.

"Regan," Aguiar repeated, lowering his voice almost to a
whisper. "In the holding cells."

The mental image sickened Gomez, but he kept the tremor
from his voice as he replied, "What did they want from her?"

"They didn't say. What do they ever want?"

"There must be something, after all this time...."

"She asked about the killings."

"Killings?" The term was so generic, and there were so
many dead throughout Colombia that Gomez drew a blank.
"What killings?"

"Overnight," Aguiar replied. "The shootings here in Bogotá."

"What do you mean, she asked? Asked whom?"

Aguiar slumped back in his chair, the starch going out of his
spine. He shook his head, as if the words he had to say were un-
believable. "The Monkey, Nestor. Regan asked The Monkey."

"Good God."

Gomez closed his eyes and counted ten before he opened
them again. He had warned Kelly more than once about con-
sorting with Galatria, explaining to her that a petty criminal
who sold his friends to the police for money could never be
trusted at any level, but she had maintained the contact almost
as a perverse display of will. She insisted that the smirking
runt was a valuable source of inside information on both sides
of the crime war in Colombia, apparently placing her trust in
Galatria's illusory better nature.

"Why would he do this?" Gomez asked, thinking aloud.
"Who pays him?"

"Who always pays for information leading to a radical's
arrest, Nestor? As to the why of it, I think it is because Regan
rejected him. The Monkey may be small, but still he dreams."

"Bastard!" It took a conscious effort for Gomez to relax his
grip on the coffee mug. "But, Ciro, how could he know anything
of the American? Surely, Regan wouldn't tell that creature—"

"No, no," Aguiar said. "Galatria would have given up the
main prize if he could, to line his pockets. Regan asked for

any information on the shootings that hadn't been cleared for press release. He never answered, for this other business intervened and she embarrassed him. It was enough, perhaps, to raise some eyebrows and some questions with the state police."

"It would be, yes."

Most officials of the ruling regime disliked the ICHR at some level, for its outside meddling in matters of Colombian national sovereignty. Some mouthed platitudes of cooperation while dragging their feet and hiding behind red tape. Others were more openly defiant, calling upon the intruders—eighty-nine percent of them native Colombians at last count—to pack up and go home, leaving the government to solve its own problems without harassment and the daily glare of international publicity. Gomez believed that no group hated the consultancy so much as did the army and police, those men who operated on the cutting edge of the long war against subversives, radicals and other human scum.

There was no doubt in Gomez's mind that certain officers of the security police would seize upon an opportunity to smear the ICHR with purported links to violence in Bogotá. What better way to undermine the group and cast its education programs into disrepute? And if a ranking member of the group like Regan Kelly should perhaps confess her role in such illegal acts, the state would have no choice except to move decisively against its foes in the consultancy.

They would be searching for her now, and wouldn't rest until they had her in a cage. Failing in that objective, they would seek her known associates, including—

Good God!

"Where is Regan now?" he asked impulsively, then caught himself. "No, wait! Don't tell me."

The smile on Aguiar's face was sad. "I wouldn't let her tell me where she's going, just in case."

"They'll come for all of us," Gomez replied, stating the obvious.

"In time, perhaps. You may still have a chance."

"For what?" Gomez imagined running for his life, but had nowhere to go.

"You still have friends," Aguiar reminded him. "If they were asked the proper questions, they might tell you something. Names, perhaps."

"Of men to sacrifice?"

"We need to know who plots these deaths in the United States, Nestor. The same men plot our own destruction now."

"But what you're asking me—"

"And Regan, Nestor. Think of her."

Gomez could feel his shoulders slump. "It's not supposed to be a war, Ciro. We're noncombatants here."

"It was a war before we got involved," Aguiar replied. "And now we're in the line of fire. Regan, my friend. What do you say?"

Gomez stared down into his coffee mug, frowning. At last he said, "All right. I'll see what I can do."

JÉSUS GALATRIA NEVER, under any circumstances, thought of himself as The Monkey. He was aware of the derisive nickname, and while he sometimes scowled at his simian reflection in the mirror, there was little he could do about what others said or thought of him. Occasionally, he was blessed with opportunities to punish those who slighted or embarrassed him, by selling them to the police—or worse, to someone larger and more powerful, who wouldn't only meddle in an adversary's life, but actually bring it to an end.

This woman, for example, from the International Consultancy on Human Rights.

Galatria had lusted after Regan Kelly from the first time he had seen her, knowing even as he fantasized of sex and so much more that she would never soil herself with him. He had to have been demented, trying to negotiate an intimate encounter when they met the night before. He had been tipsy, certainly, which always managed to inflate his confidence. And when she had rejected him, as he subconsciously had known she would, something had snapped. The phone call to his contact at the headquarters of the security police seemed like a fever dream, but it was real enough.

And it couldn't be taken back.

So be it, then.

Whatever happened next to Kelly, he could tell himself that she had brought it on herself. Who needed an American with a fashion model's face and body meddling in Colombian affairs? Who was she to denounce and criticize a culture she would never truly understand—much less humiliate Galatria in front of men who already made fun of him at any given opportunity?

Perhaps the state police would teach her to behave herself, before they sent her back to the United States.

Or maybe they would never send her back at all.

It was the liquor, he insisted to himself, that had prevented him from thinking through his actions, following the chain reaction to its logical conclusion before he lit the fuse. In any case, it was too late for him to take it back, undo the damage.

And why should he care? There had been no thought for his feelings when the woman stormed out on him. Let her repent at leisure the insults she offered in haste. It was small enough recompense for a lifetime of humiliation, insults, snickering derision.

Still, Galatria would miss Kelly, whatever became of her in the next few days. That hair, those luscious...

He was suddenly distracted by a rapping on his door, so soft that he initially believed it was the sound of someone knocking at the flat across the hall, perhaps next door. Galatria waited, frowning, nearly jumping when the urgent sound repeated.

There could be no doubt this time.

Who could it be?

His address was no secret, but he had no friends worth mentioning and had invited no one home since he had moved into the place six years ago. Before that, there had been a string of other flats that no one visited. His neighbors never troubled him, and he in turn left them alone. Who could be knocking on his door now, in midmorning, when Galatria was barely out of bed?

He kept two pistols in the house and chose the nearest of them now. It was a Smith & Wesson Model 40, the Centennial hammerless revolver chambered in .38 Special with a 5-shot cylinder. Galatria kept it loaded with hollowpoints for maximum stopping power, but now found himself wondering if the bullets would penetrate his door.

Considering the cheap construction of the flat, he guessed that there would be no problem on that score.

The door was fitted with a peephole and a fish-eye lens apparently designed to make all human beings look like circus freaks. Galatria kept a plastic milk crate near the door, to help him reach the necessary altitude, though it was almost never used. Lifting the crate with his left hand, revolver steady in his right, he placed it silently before the door and stepped up to the peephole, closing one eye as he leaned into the lens.

And nearly dropped the Smith & Wesson.

It would have been a shock to find a woman standing at his door in any circumstance. To find that it was Regan Kelly, clearly not in custody, struck Galatria like a shot to the heart.

Despite the weird distortion of the fish-eye lens, Kelly's expression didn't strike him as unduly hostile. In fact, he couldn't honestly have said that she was even frowning. Was it possible that she had been released already? Or that the police had failed to pick her up at all?

In any case, why was she here?

Open the door, you idiot, and ask her! he thought.

Galatria was suddenly reminded that he wore a purple satin robe, with nothing underneath except a pair of boxer shorts. The shorts, as it so happened, were emblazoned with silk-screen depictions of Pamela Anderson in the nude, twining herself around his pelvis in sundry attitudes of passion.

Swallowing hard, Galatria stepped down from the milk crate and kicked it away, eyes tearing at the flash of sudden pain from his bare foot. Swiping at his face with a sleeve, he dropped the snubby .38 into a pocket of his robe, unlocked the dead bolt and opened the door.

"My dear," he said, "what a surprise!"

The tall man came from nowhere, stepping past Kelly, leveling a huge black pistol at Galatria's face.

"You ain't seen nothing yet."

7

Galatria had been hesitant to speak at first, despite his obvious fear and the Beretta's relentless pressure against his sweat-slick forehead. Bolan had resolved the issue by sending Kelly downstairs to wait in the car, thus eliminating any macho urge Galatria might feel to strike a pose before the woman of his dreams and simultaneously sparing her from the inevitable outcome of the interview.

Galatria had stalled for only moments after she was gone, before he spilled his guts. He copped to ratting out Kelly and named his contact with the state security police—whose name was only marginally valuable to Bolan while his rule against eliminating lawmen was in force.

The Monkey held more information, though. Almost enough, in fact, to justify his claim that he could find out anything and everything there was to know in Bogotá. He knew which politicians were bought and paid for by the drug cartels or other fat-cat businessmen, collaborating with such right-wing paramilitary outfits as The Fist. He had a fix on which members of high society were eyeball-deep in corruption, and which were merely bystanders, content to go with the flow. He offered names, addresses, résumés.

And none of it had saved him in the end.

Bolan had planned to kill him anyway, to insure that he wouldn't go running to his friends the moment Bolan left, but Galatria had seized the initiative, fumbling for a weapon Bolan had already noticed in the sagging right-hand pocket of his

satin robe. It was a done deal, then, and Bolan left him
stretched out on the carpet with a leaking hole between his
eyes.

Kelly had taken care not to inquire about the snitch's fate,
as Bolan drove her to a meet with Ciro Aguiar. They parted
after trading cell phone numbers, promising to keep in touch.

Three-quarters of an hour later, Bolan stood beside the
bulky air conditioner atop an office building and opened up the
metal case that held his newly purchased M-24 sniper rifle, un-
packing the components for the second time in as many days.

The basic weapon was a modified version of the classic Remington 700 bolt-action rifle, though its adjustable Kevlar-
graphite stock gave the piece a slightly different look from the
original. The barrel was heavier, also, and made of stainless steel.
The full kit for the M-24 included a bipod, separate ten-power
telescopic sights for day and night, and a field cleaning kit. The
rifle was chambered for 7.62 mm x 51 NATO rounds, packing
six into its box magazine. It boasted a muzzle velocity of 2,525
feet per second, with a maximum effective range of some 975
yards.

This afternoon, mounting the day sight on the rifle, Bolan
knew that he would need only a fraction of that killing range.

His target was less than a block away from where he stood,
due east from his position, on the far side of a busy intersection. He could see it with his naked eyes, but would require
the scope to pick out individuals and put the 140-grain projectiles where he wanted them to go.

The target was another office building, two stories taller
than the one atop which Bolan stood. The altitude would
make no difference, though, since his intended mark occupied
a ninth-floor suite, two floors below the Executioner's aerie.
The down-angle was sufficient to give his rounds extra velocity, without being so extreme that his view of the office interior would be compromised by perspective.

When the scope was mounted and the bipod attached,
Bolan made his way to the edge of the roof. Sighting on the
target, he counted down two floors from the rooftop, two

suites in from the northeast corner of the building's face. A slight tint on the plate glass of the windows muted reflection of sunlight without obstructing Bolan's view of the office within.

Its occupant was a large man with multiple chins and a receding hairline. The hair that he retained was gray, darkened with oil that slicked it down against his skull. He gnawed a fat cigar while talking on the telephone, gesticulating with his free hand as if someone on the other end could see him fan the air.

The target's name was Amadeo Ornelas, and he was first vice president of a megamillion-dollar agribusiness conglomerate controlled by Prospero Alarcon. Alarcon, in turn, had been named by Jésus Galatria in his final moments as one of the main corporate sponsors most active in supporting Colombia's right-wing paramilitary movements. Alarcon himself resided in the country on a fortified estate while Ornelas was available from nine to five, Monday through Friday, at his spacious desk.

The choice had been a simple one.

Bolan waited for his target to hang up the phone, then speed-dialed with his cellular phone and listened to it ringing on the big man's desk. Ornelas looked surprised in the scope's viewfinder, with the crosshairs centered on his florid face, as he saw the lighted button flashing for his private line. His hand was hovering an inch or so above the telephone receiver when it rang, and he scooped it up midway through the second ring.

"Yes?" Uncertainty in the big man's voice, not knowing who or what to expect.

"Señor Ornelas?" Bolan asked him, making doubly sure.

"Yes. Who is this?"

"I have a message for your boss," Bolan replied.

"Who is this?" A demanding tone, unaccustomed to practical jokes.

Which was no problem, since the Executioner was deadly serious.

"Prospero Alarcon," Bolan said. "I need you to tell him something for me."

"Ah. And what is that?"

"Tell him he's next."

Bolan set down the telephone and leaned into the Remington, edging its muzzle ever so slightly downward and to his right. A fraction of an inch from where he stood would mean a foot or more of difference on the receiving end. His finger curled around the rifle's trigger, taking up the slack gently, as if with a caress. The recoil, when it came, had been anticipated and was easily absorbed.

He saw the plate-glass window sprout a fist-sized hole downrange, the telephone on his target's desk exploded as if it had been packed with cherry bombs. Ornelas lurched backward in his swivel chair as Bolan worked the Remington's bolt, chambered another round and sent in the second bullet.

This one struck the marble base of an expensive pen-and-pencil set, spraying Ornelas with jagged slivers that stung his face, drawing blood. His reaction was so violent that the high-backed office chair bucked out from under him and dumped him to the floor behind his desk. That put him out of Bolan's view, but it made no difference. Racking the bolt with practiced ease, the Executioner slammed four more rounds through the shattered office window, wreaking havoc with the suite's decor.

He began to pack his kit a moment later. Ornelas could take that back to Alarcon and let him sweat a while.

"OF COURSE... Yes, I understand... Alone, yes...as you wish...the address is? I have it, yes. Thank you."

Nestor Gomez cradled the telephone receiver and scrubbed a hand over his face, wishing that he could wipe the tension from his mind with a simple gesture. It did nothing to help him, of course. His stomach remained tied in knots. The dull ache in his chest still lingered, a mixture of anger and anxiety.

Gomez was angry at his friends for using him, and at himself for being weak, allowing them to override his better judgment. At another level, he was furious that things had come to such a pass within his homeland that he had to be afraid of working to see justice done. Not long ago, he had drawn weekly paychecks to perform that very function—though, of course, the powers that be had always secretly intended him to fail. Now, a civilian with a few stray friends and contacts from the old days, Gomez wasn't sure how much he could accomplish, even with the goal of saving Regan Kelly's life.

And that was where the fear kicked in.

He was afraid for Kelly and, at some level, he was afraid *of* her. The feelings she called up from somewhere deep inside him troubled Gomez, not because they were unpleasant—quite the opposite, in fact—but for the fact that he felt weak in Kelly's presence, malleable, like a piece of unformed clay. He thought sometimes that she could overwhelm him with a glance, command him to transform his life upon her slightest whim.

It had to be love, he thought.

But soon, he knew, she would be gone.

The good ones never stayed for long, in his experience, and Kelly was already pushing it. With the security police pursuing her, she would be wise to leave Colombia at once, by any means available, and go back home to the United States. Gomez wouldn't see her again, but he could always dream.

As for the man they had picked up at the airport, he wasn't the sort to run away, nor would Colombia hold any terrors for him. Gomez suspected Mike Belasko had to have seen and done it all before, with variations, probably in half a dozen different Third World nations where the people all began to look alike. Soldier, assassin, it made no real difference what he was called in the end. He was a killer, and the killers tended to survive.

At least until they met a bigger, stronger predator.

Gomez didn't believe in violence, except in self-defense, but he had finally agreed to Aguiar's plan because it came from Kelly, and because denying her might leave her vulnerable to her enemies. Gut instinct told Gomez that he could never live with that, the thought of Kelly caged or worse because he sat back on his threadbare principles and watched the world go by.

So, he had made the call.

His friend was named Arturo Camarena, and he was a clerk with the security police. They had become acquainted in the days when Gomez was a gung-ho prosecutor, Camarena helping with the research on his cases, even doing legwork now and then, playing detective. Within a few short weeks they were fast friends, two bachelors on the town, with occupations and a certain basic loneliness in common. The day Gomez resigned, he had discussed it with Camarena first, and they had stayed in touch since then, although sporadically as time went by.

Camarena had been hesitant to help him. Indeed, he might have slammed down the phone had he known the truth of what Gomez was doing, his involvement with the recent spate of homicides. All friendships had their limits, and a man who tested that envelope risked everything.

Which was why Gomez chose to lie.

He had devised a story that was plausible, if one didn't examine it too closely or attempt to verify the facts. Gomez informed his friend that he had gone to work as a part-time consultant for a well-known private security firm. Kidnapping had become a cottage industry of sorts throughout Colombia, and with assassination being more or less routine, executive security was now a lucrative profession. The firm in question already had police contacts—Camarena would know that— but certain clients demanded an extra degree of discretion, information or cooperation obtained without going through channels with so many inquisitive eyes and ears.

Camarena had no problem understanding that, and he was happy to cooperate.

It had been the name Gomez dropped next that almost queered the deal.

Prospero Alarcon wasn't a man to trifle with. A friend and confidant to presidents and generals, a megamillionaire of international reputation and influence in modern-day Colombia, such men could snap their fingers and whole villages would be wiped off the map without a second thought. To crush one lowly clerk for the security police would be no chore at all.

It was for that reason that Camarena hesitated, finally persuaded by another lie, Gomez insisting that his interest in the great man was innocuous, a routine background check. Camarena should have known better; perhaps he did. In any case, he had agreed to meet with Gomez after hours in a park that lost most of its strollers when the sun went down.

Gomez would keep their date, but he would take a pistol with him when he went.

And long before that, he would make another call.

THE DRUG DEALER'S name was Julio Cristos. It was ironic, since the only thing Christlike about him was his hair, worn shoulder length and parted down the middle of his scalp. A closetful of thousand-dollar suits spoiled the effect, along with mirrored sunglasses that definitely weren't the savior's style. Instead of twelve apostles, Cristos traveled with a woman on each arm and half a dozen bodyguards whose upper-body muscularity was even more exaggerated by the weapons strapped beneath their jackets.

Cristos wasn't the top drug dealer in Colombia, but he may well have ranked among the top fifteen, and his rapprochement with the Medellín cartel allowed him to conduct his trade and life in relative security. The bodyguards weren't for show, of course, since this was still Colombia and life was cheap, but Cristos seemed to have no worries as he stepped from his Mercedes limousine, waited for his blonde bookends to catch up, then swept imperiously past the hotel doorman who had doffed his cap in a salute that went unnoticed.

Dirty money on the hoof.

Mack Bolan allowed the small parade to disappear inside the lobby, gave them time to board an elevator car before he crossed the street. The doorman didn't tip his hat this time, although he eyeballed Bolan long enough to log the unfamiliar face in memory.

No problem.

Doormen, bellhops and assorted other hotel service personnel were educated to remember guests and make them welcome, catering to whims and thereby earning tips. The doorman couldn't tell if Bolan was a guest, just yet, but he would be prepared next time he saw the face.

And since there was no name to go with it, it made no difference to the Executioner if a description later made its way to the police. If all went well, he would be only one of several hundred suspects, not on any register or videocassette, perhaps forgotten in the midst of the confusion he intended to create.

No one appeared to notice Bolan as he crossed the lobby. One of Cristos's men was staked out in a chair, off to the right, thumbing a magazine, and while he took in Bolan at a glance, he made no move to reach his weapon or the cellular phone resting on an end table beside his seat. Bolan passed by without acknowledging the goon's existence, but he had the other's measure. He was five foot ten, twenty-something, muscle-heavy for his height, and with extra weight added by the bulk of hardware beneath his right arm. Something compact but deadly. A mini-Uzi, perhaps, or an MP-5 K.

Bolan moved directly to the bank of elevators and rode the first available car up to nine. He had the floor—the room number, in fact—from Jésus Galatria, part of the information spillage that had failed to save The Monkey's life. A well-dressed woman shared the car with him as far as seven, then he had it to himself.

It stood to reason that the boss would want some privacy with the blondes he had brought back to his suite of rooms. Bolan wasn't surprised, therefore, to find his muscle lounging around the hallway in chairs, at the west end of the corridor. It was a curious arrangement to the unexpecting eye, but for the rent their master paid, Bolan imagined that the punks could sit most anywhere they wanted to.

One man downstairs, one with the car and four out in the hall made six. The dealer's full-time shadows were accounted for. This was no time or place for undue subtlety. The Executioner was looking for a simple in-and-out.

He flicked open his raincoat to produce the Spectre submachine gun on its makeshift shoulder sling. The weapon's thick four-column magazine loaded with 9 mm Parabellum rounds gave Bolan nearly twice the sustained firepower of any other SMG on the market, but he wasn't planning an extended battle here. Surprise and sheer audacity could mean as much as hardware in the short run, when the chips were down.

The shooters had divided their chairs, pulling two to each side of the hallway, the distance great enough that they were forced to raise their voices slightly when conversing. Add to that the young thugs' natural propensity for noise, and it was no great shock to Bolan that they missed the chiming of the elevator's bell as he stepped out into the corridor. It took another moment for someone to notice him, and by that time the Executioner was only thirty feet away, his weapon leveled from the hip.

The shooter who had spotted Bolan gave a startled cry and bolted to his feet, fumbling inside his linen jacket for a side arm of some kind. His three companions took a moment longer to react, but they were all professional about it, going for the weapons with a kind of grim determination even as they tried to rise and scatter.

Bolan wasn't having it. He raked them with a burst of autofire from left to right and back again, some of his bullets knocking divots in the plaster, others painting crimson streaks and splotches on the walls. He used up maybe one-third of the Spectre's magazine before his targets collapsed to the floor.

The Spectre had no sound suppressor, and Bolan had no time to lose. He took the locks out with a rising 5-round burst and kicked the door wide open without breaking stride. The blondes were screaming, somewhere to his left, and Bolan followed the sound in search of his target.

The bedroom was down a short hallway with art on both walls, ghastly paintings whose images ran toward abstract depictions of dismembered women. It was enough to make Bolan wonder what the hookers were screaming about, as he reached the open bedroom door and cleared its threshold in a crouching lunge.

The first shot from his adversary's pistol hit the door frame, gouging wood before it flew on down the hall and knocked one of the ugly paintings to the floor. The second might have done a little better, but Bolan had his target pegged by then, the Spectre stuttering a salutation that allowed for no reply.

Cristos, standing naked in the middle of a huge round bed, had two big guns for different kinds of action, but neither was enough to save him as the Parabellum manglers stitched their bloody tracks across his hairless chest. The impact pitched him backward, bounced him off the wall and dropped him facedown on the bed. The painting came down with him, smacking Cristos on the back of the skull, but he was past all feeling by that time.

The women cowered in a corner, afraid to lift their eyes to Bolan's face and thereby bring death down upon themselves. Without bothering to move them out, he left them there and backtracked through the suite, into the hall and past more corpses to the elevator. Riding down, he took the time to stow his SMG securely out of sight, leaving his coat open so he could reach both weapons in a hurry, just in case. The elevator stopped on four to board a pair of dowagers in bulky fur that would smell musty by the time they cleared three feet of rainy sidewalk from the hotel's entrance to a waiting cab. One of them sniffed at Bolan, to remind him of the cordite odor hanging on his clothes.

Downstairs, Bolan had barely cleared the elevator when he spotted the last bodyguard, hunched forward in his chair, the magazine forgotten as he spoke into his cellular phone. Glancing up as Bolan exited, his eyes locked with the Executioner's and the soldier knew that one of the blondes had recovered her wits enough to hit the panic button.

Timing. It would all come down to timing now.

There were perhaps a dozen people in the hotel lobby, counting various employees. If he had to take down the shooter in full view of an audience, this was the place to do it, rather than as part of some protracted running battle through the streets. He had a choice of weapons, thinking even as the bodyguard laid down the phone and started reaching for his hidden piece.

The Spectre or Beretta? Soft or loud?

The sound suppressor was no advantage, where those around him were about to view the action anyway. By contrast, sudden gunfire would incline most people to duck and cover, more concerned with personal survival than obtaining clear descriptions of the shooter for police.

The Spectre, then.

He caught the young Colombian half rising from his chair, with one hand buried underneath the roomy jacket that he wore. From ten feet out, the Spectre hammered him with half a dozen rounds that hurled him over backward, somersaulting right across the chair and out of sight.

Bolan kept walking, trailed by screams, until he reached the sidewalk. The doorman had his back turned, his nose in a corner, staring at the wall. He didn't turn or nod this time, intent on being deaf, dumb and blind until the gringo with the cold eyes had a chance to disappear.

"HE'S LATE," Orlando Chavez said, speaking around the stub of his cigar.

"Your watch is fast," Santos Zamora answered him. "It's always fast. You never set it right."

Chavez digested that, dismissing it. "Why are we killing this one, anyway?" he asked.

"What difference does it make?"

Chavez's shrug was almost eloquent. "No difference," he said. "I'm passing time. That's all."

"You talk too much," Zamora said. "We should be quiet now."

In fact, Chavez was whispering, and there was little chance of being overheard by anyone. The park had emptied out at sundown. There were no more baby-sitters pushing infants in strollers, children playing. The park belonged to predators at night, but there was none of them in evidence, either. No one at all to hear Chavez's whispered words.

The plain fact was that Chavez had a tendency to babble, as if silence were the enemy and he was duty bound to fill it up with noise. Zamora didn't fully understand this urge, preferring for the most part not to speak unless he had something of relevance to say. And even then he might keep still, if it wasn't an urgent matter, rather than risk drawing more attention to himself.

Assassins should be neither seen nor heard, in his opinion, and that rule applied particularly to an operation carried out in public, where they might be subject to discovery at any moment. If Chavez couldn't recognize that fact, he was a fool—and that meant he was dangerous.

Zamora, for his part, wasn't concerned about the reason why they had been sent to kill a perfect stranger in the park. A soldier of The Fist was taught to follow orders, trust his superiors to make the right decisions and advance the sacred cause for which they fought. If every member of an army second-guessed commands, nothing would ever be accomplished in the field. It was enough for Zamora to believe that greater minds than his had thought the matter through, weighed options and decided that the use of deadly force would yield superior results.

Which, when Zamora thought about it, had been true of nearly every situation in his life.

He had lost track of all the people he had killed, in combat or in executions, since he joined The Fist six years before. It was an endless uphill battle, trying to redeem his homeland from the criminals and traitors who were bent on making beautiful Colombia a kind of Communistic hell on Earth, taking a leaf from Castro's book to undermine justice, free enterprise and the religion of his forefathers.

Not that Zamora spent much time in church. His duties for The Fist gave him enough to do without attending mass, except on those occasions when his fellow warriors gathered for a special holiday or to bury one of their own. Even then, in the event of funerals, it was more likely to be a covert service, with some friendly priest transported to a grave site somewhere in the countryside.

As for the godless enemies they fought, there were no prayers or rituals to save their blighted souls.

Zamora and Chavez weren't alone on this assignment. They had brought along six other soldiers of The Fist to circle the perimeter and make sure that the target didn't slip away. It might be overkill, but preparation was the key to a successful strike. Zamora had a certain reputation to protect within the brotherhood, and he wouldn't allow a single nameless target to prevent his execution of an order.

Glancing at his watch, Zamora noted that their target was, in fact, three minutes late. Beside him, crouching in the darkness of a hedge, Chavez took note and said, "I told you."

"He'll be here," Zamora replied, wishing he felt as confident as he sounded.

No sooner had he spoken than a pair of headlights swung into the parking lot, three hundred meters from the point where he and Chavez waited. Though he couldn't see the man, Zamora heard a door slam, the faint suggestion of footsteps on asphalt. And then...

There he was!

Zamora lifted his small two-way radio and keyed the switch for a transmission. "We have target acquisition," he informed the silent night. "Be ready on my signal. No one fires before I do."

MACK BOLAN HAD checked in with Regan Kelly's people after he had cleared the neighborhood where Julio Cristos no longer lived. It had surprised him to find out that Nestor Gomez had agreed to help by touching base with contacts he maintained in the security police and prosecutor's office, but the kicker was that Gomez was supposed to meet one of those contacts at a public park, two hours after nightfall. Kelly was concerned about his safety, and while Bolan didn't overemphasize the matter, he believed that she was right.

And so he had decided he would shadow Gomez to the meet.

A tail wasn't required, since Bolan knew the lawyer's destination and the time that he was scheduled to arrive. It made things easier, no risk of spooking Gomez on the street and making him abort the mission, whereas Bolan could arrive ahead of schedule if he chose and check the park for hostiles.

As it happened, he had been delayed by one more raid before he disengaged to baby-sit the one-time prosecutor, and the hit had gone all frantic when a second carload of shooters had arrived unexpectedly to interrupt Bolan's torching of a drug stash on the north side of town. He had escaped with only minor injuries—more than his enemies could say, the few who still remained in any shape to speak at all—but it had cost him time, and it was after nightfall when he left his rental two blocks over from the park and started his approach on foot.

It didn't take him long to realize that Gomez had been marked for death.

The lawyer's so-called friend had either dropped a coin himself, or else he had been caught and squeezed until he gave up details of the meet. From Bolan's point of view it made no difference once way or the other. He had volunteered to back up the lawyer, and that was what he meant to do.

The first part of the job was counting heads. As Bolan worked his way around the edge of the intended killing ground, he made it six guns altogether, waiting for their target to appear. Before he made a move, the Executioner had satisfied himself that there were no more reinforcements lying back and waiting for a panic call. The rest of it was simple butcher's work.

Two of the shooters had staked out a spot together and would be the riskiest to drop, the other four spaced widely and alone at different points around the chosen field of fire.

Each man was armed with an assault rifle or submachine gun, but the Executioner didn't intend to duel with them if he could help it. He had silent work in mind, as far as possible, with nothing to disturb his adversaries as he worked his way around the killing field.

He started at four o'clock on the perimeter and worked his way around counterclockwise, using the stiletto and surprise to silence each shooter in turn. They gave it up with varying degrees of resistance, some thrashing fiercely before the blade went home, others stunned and helpless as he sprang upon their backs and cut their throats. No two were exactly the same, but none got off a shot before the Executioner was finished with his bloody work.

Bolan was rising from the fourth corpse when a walkie-talkie on the dead man's belt squawked out a warning from the leader of the team. He spoke in Spanish, announcing that their target had arrived. A glance downrange, in the direction of the parking lot, confirmed that Gomez was approaching cautiously on foot.

Bolan sheathed the stiletto and drew his Beretta before moving swiftly through the darkness, compromising stealth for speed. The last two shooters might cut loose at any moment, and it would be too late for their unsuspecting target once the bullets flew.

He had them spotted from a distance, knew exactly where they were, and started firing 3-round bursts from twenty yards, advancing at a sprint. One of the snipers gave a startled cry that turned into a gurgling cough. The other came up firing from the hip, an automatic weapon cutting up the night. Bolan ducked, squeezing off two more bursts as his adversary lurched, stumbled, fell.

By the time he turned to track Gomez, the lawyer was off and running for his life, back toward the distant parking lot. He didn't spare a backward glance, and Bolan quashed the thought of calling after him.

He had already saved the stranger's life.

It was enough for now, and he still had another rendezvous to keep.

8

"Nestor told us there was shooting," Regan Kelly said.

"Nestor was right," Belasko answered, the expression on his face revealing no hint of his thoughts or feelings on the matter.

"You were there?" she asked him, leaning forward slightly in her chair.

"I didn't get a chance to say hello," he said, as if that were an answer to her question.

"But you helped him," Aguiar put in. "We heard on television news about the...incident."

"That's not important now," Bolan said. "The thing you need to think about is how the shooters knew where Gomez was supposed to be. Who set him up? You've either got a leak, or he can't trust his friends. Of course, it could be some of both."

"Aside from Nestor and his contact," Kelly said, "no one outside this room knew anything about the meeting." She resisted a sudden urge to glance at Aguiar, refusing to question his loyalty.

"You talked about it on the telephone," Bolan pointed out.

"He called me from a public booth," Kelly replied. "The call came here. Nobody knows about this place."

"He knew," Bolan said.

"You think he put a hit out on himself?" She almost laughed aloud.

"I didn't say that. If he knew to call here, if there's a chance his call may have been monitored... You get my drift?"

"You're saying we should leave."

"I'm saying that you should have left by now," the tall American corrected her.

"I can't just—"

"Regan," Aguiar interrupted her, "he's right."

She turned to face her friend. "Where would I go?" she asked.

"There is a place...." Aguiar hesitated, glancing toward Bolan, then back to Kelly.

"For heaven's sake, Ciro!"

He blinked at her and said, "I thought...perhaps...my village?"

"In the mountains?" She was startled. "I thought you meant somewhere else in the city."

"It's not a bad idea," Bolan said. "Get out of town, out of the way. If they're still looking for you, let them chase their tails. And if they're not, it still can't hurt. Give them some time to be distracted and forget. Smart money says they may have other things to think about before too long."

Kelly could guess what that meant. Suddenly, she blurted out, "You should come with us!"

Now it was Bolan's turn to blink, surprised by the suggestion. "I have some unfinished business here," he said.

"It will still be unfinished next week."

"That's the problem," he told her. "It needs wrapping up."

"But the whole city's on alert. You can't—"

"Regan," Aguiar intruded once again, "if he's determined not to go, we can't—"

"Unless..." Bolan's tone was thoughtful now. He turned to Aguiar as he asked, "You mentioned going to the mountains?"

"Yes," Aguiar replied with visible reluctance. "I am from a mountain village. But to leave your work in Bogotá—"

"May be the change of pace I need," Bolan said. Adding, "Are there guerrillas in the area?"

"This is Colombia," Aguiar reminded him. "There are guerrillas everywhere."

That seemed to satisfy Bolan for the moment. "Right," he said. "Let's do it, then."

Kelly was startled by the feeling of relief that she experienced as Belasko spoke those words. She tried to keep it from her face, uncertain whether she had been successful from the way Aguiar was staring at her.

What was this about? she asked herself. They were about to leave the city, where the state security police were hunting her, and move into the mountains where guerrillas trained and skirmished on a daily basis. What was so unusual about a feeling of relief that they would be accompanied by a professional—the only man she knew, in fact, who would be capable of handling a combat situation?

Was there more to it than that? the small voice in her mind inquired.

"Don't be ridiculous!" she muttered, blushing furiously as she realized that she had spoken audibly.

"Regan? What did you say?" Aguiar asked.

"Nothing," she answered, avoiding his eyes. "Just talking to myself. More evidence I need to get away from here as soon as possible."

She caught Belasko watching her, as well, and wondered whether he had understood her mumbled words—and if so, what he made of them.

Forget about it, said the tiny voice. He was a soldier, not a psychic.

Still...

"We should call Nestor," Kelly said. She wasn't sure exactly where the thought had come from, much less how it wriggled into words, but there it was. "They've tried to kill him once. He needs to leave the city, too."

Belasko offered no reply, but she was startled by the frown on Aguiar's face, his hesitancy in agreeing with her. "Regan..." he began, with evident distaste for what he was about to say.

"You want to leave him here?" she challenged. "Ciro, I don't believe this. Not from you!"

"I didn't say that we should leave him," Aguiar replied. In his sudden desperation to mend fences, he glanced across the table toward Belasko, finding no help from that quarter.

"So, tell us, Ciro," Kelly said, "what do you mean?"

"If you know where to reach him," Bolan interrupted, "I'd suggest that you be careful."

"Careful!" Aguiar parroted with evident relief. "That's what I meant."

"Will you explain that for me?" Kelly asked.

"Same thing we talked about before," Bolan said. "If he's in a familiar place, there may be new ears on the telephone. If they don't have him tapped, there could be physical surveillance. If you arrange a meeting, he could show up with a tail. There are devices that a pro could slip into his car, his luggage, even in his clothing. He could lead a hunting party to the village and not even know it until someone slams the door behind him."

"You're not saying we should leave him here?"

"Use your best judgment," he replied, apparently deciding not to argue with her choice.

"We'll call him, then," she said, after a moment's guilty hesitation. "But we'll do it from the road. We can decide the rest of it later."

"Your choice," Bolan said, expressionless. "Right now, you really need to pack."

BOLAN HAD NO conception of how long the drive should take when they began. It troubled him to leave the city with his work unfinished, but he told himself he would return and see it through. And if he didn't make it back, then what the hell? It wouldn't matter, anyway. Brognola would find someone else to finish up, perhaps the men of Able Team or Phoenix Force from Stony Man Farm.

It would be settled one way or another. He was confident of that.

Their route of travel would be southward out of Bogotá, along the west face of the Cordillera Oriental. They stopped once in the suburbs, nearly out of town, Bolan and Aguiar remaining together in Aguiar's ten-year-old Jeep Cherokee while Kelly went to use the pay phone tucked away behind a filling station. She was back within five minutes, rattling some leftover coins in her fist and frowning over the memory of her brief conversation with Gomez.

"So?" the driver prodded her, before she had a chance to fairly settle in her seat up front.

"He isn't coming," she replied. "He doesn't want to leave the city."

Aguiar hesitated, firing up the engine, but he had to ask. "You didn't tell him...?"

"Ciro, God!" she snapped at him. "He had to know, all right. How could he make his mind up, otherwise? It's Nestor. He's our friend. Can you remember that?"

"I know this troubles you but..." Aguiar said. He didn't need to add any more. His face was grim with resignation as he drove, his shoulders slumped.

Bolan, seated in back beside his heavy duffel bags of military hardware, rode in silence as they left the capital behind and moved into the countryside. The mountains here were barely foothills of the Cordillera to their left, or east, but they would climb into the higher altitudes before much longer. Aguiar had explained that they would have to leave the Jeep a mile or so before they reached his village, but they'd have help with any luggage that they couldn't manage on their own. He had been looking at the Executioner's two duffels as he said it, Bolan reassuring Aguiar that he could manage on his own.

When they were roughly halfway there, about an hour on the road, the highway took them past a tract of land where it appeared that several dozen houses once had stood. Of the original community, four structures now remained and three of those were badly damaged by a sweeping fire that had destroyed the rest. The only house not burned was scarred by bullets, missing its front door, the windows empty rectangles devoid of glass. Beyond the burn zone, jungle had a good start on reclaiming one-time cultivated fields.

"What happened here?" Bolan asked, guessing that he might already know.

"This was the village of Piedras Blancas," Aguiar said, slowing the Jeep to give his back-seat passenger a better look.

"Its people cultivated maize and beans, some pigs and cattle. Many of them worked on the plantation of Prospero Alarcon. In season, they would harvest coffee beans."

"This wasn't any accidental fire," Bolan remarked, stating the obvious.

"One day a man came out from Bogotá," Aguiar continued, slowing further, staring out his window at the baked earth and the blackened ruins of this one-time agricultural community. "He claimed to be a Social Democrat, but some others said he was a Communist. Who knows if either story was the truth. This man—Rodrigo Obregon, he called himself—informed the people of Piedras Blancas that they were human beings of value, entitled to more for their labor than twenty pesos per day from the deep pockets of Alarcon."

Bolan tried to do the math but wasn't current on the daily rate of exchange between Colombian pesos and U.S. dollars. He knew that the average per capita income for Colombians with jobs fell in the neighborhood of six thousand dollars per year, and seasonal employment twenty pesos a day came in well below the pathetic national average. He saw where the story was going, but let Aguiar continue without interruption.

"The people of Piedras Blancas weren't fools," Aguiar said. "You may not know it, but the literacy rate in Colombia is eighty-seven percent. Nicaragua has only fifty-seven percent. El Salvador has only seventy-three percent."

"I get the point."

Aguiar forged on as if he hadn't heard. "My point is that these people weren't idiots. They read the pamphlets that Rodrigo Obregon distributed and understood the risks involved, but still they chose to strike against the men who kept them mired in poverty. What you see here is the result of too much courage, not of ignorance."

"So Alarcon did this?"

"No." The Jeep was gaining speed again, leaving the wasted village in its wake. "The man himself has no time for such trivia. He is too busy counting money day and night. He would, perhaps, remark to someone on his staff that there appeared to be a problem in Piedras Blancas, and the word would filter down. In time, that word would reach the People's Army of Democracy—The Fist—and then some action would be scheduled that the paramilitaries deemed appropriate."

Bolan kept silent, waiting for the end.

"The medical examiner's report suggests Rodrigo Obregon required at least three days to die. His executioners were patient men who took their time. It should have been enough, perhaps, but still the people of Piedras Blancas wouldn't yield. In fact, the death of Obregon appeared to strengthen their resolve. It was the harvest season, and an object lesson was required, before the poison of enlightenment had time to spread. One night, The Fist came down upon Piedras Blancas and the plague spot was removed. At least four hundred people occupied the village in those days. Before that night was over, forty-three of them were dead. You know what means this word, to decimate."

"I do," the Executioner replied. It meant the death of one in every ten.

"Those who survived the massacre were scattered to the winds. Widows, orphans, a few young women who were badly used and later bore the offspring of their tormentors. Who knows where all of them have gone? The village is no more, and it is only one of many that have suffered variations of the same experience."

"But not yours," Bolan said.

"No," Aguiar replied. "Not mine. Not yet."

"It's why we're here," Kelly said, "why the ICHR has to stay here and keep working in Colombia. The government takes interest of a sort if left-wing paramilitaries stage a raid—and they're as bad as anybody from The Fist or any of the other far-right groups, don't get me wrong—but when the death squads serve a man like Alarcon or one of the cartels that pays out millions every year in bribes, somehow the state police can never seem to find the evidence required for an indictment. It goes on and on."

"Have you made any progress stopping it?" he asked.

She swiveled in her seat and stared at him. "We're doing what we can," she said.

"That's two of us."

The drive went on in silence for another thirty minutes after they had left Piedras Blancas, winding up into the mountains, until Aguiar tapped the brake and told them both, "Here is the place where we must start to walk."

IT HAD BEEN TEMPTING, the idea that he could cut and run, but Nestor Gomez had refused. His reasons were diverse, but all of them could ultimately be reduced to one. And that was shame.

He was ashamed of being frightened every time that Aguiar or Kelly asked him to perform some task on behalf of the ICHR. He was ashamed of hiding how he truly felt from those who were supposed to be his closest friends. He was ashamed of being foolish when he trusted his old friend Camarena. And he was ashamed of running in the park last night instead of standing where he was and fighting like a man.

Of course, in that case, Gomez knew he would be dead.

But even death was better than betraying the two friends he knew that he could still trust in the world. One of them was as close to Gomez as a brother, and the other was the woman whom he loved, though she would never hear him speak the words.

He would remain in Bogotá because he was a city boy at heart and feared that he would prove himself an even greater coward in the mountains than he had last night. Because in the city, at least he had some clue to who his adversaries were and how they might attempt to snare him.

And because he had at least a fighting chance to be avenged against the "friend" who had betrayed him.

The pistol in his briefcase was a Browning Model 1910, manufactured in the early 1960s. Chambered for .380 ACP, the semiautomatic carried six rounds in its magazine and one in the chamber, its hammer concealed to prevent snags on clothing in emergencies. Gomez had owned the pistol for three years and he had fired it only once, on a private target range, but he could still recall the sense of power it had given him.

Oddly, he picked up no vibrations from the weapon now. It was a deadweight in his briefcase, nothing more.

But when he needed it, this afternoon, Gomez assumed that it would serve him well.

He hadn't called ahead this time to warn Camarena that he would be coming. Gomez may have been a fool to trust his former friend one time, but he wouldn't repeat the same mistake. He understood that no one else could have betrayed him to the men who nearly killed him in the park.

The second object in his briefcase, nearly the same size and weight as the Browning, was an audio cassette recorder. Gomez didn't plan to kill Camarena if he could avoid it, but he did plan to obtain the filing clerk's confession to participating in a murder plot, including names of those whom he had called after arranging to meet Gomez in the park. The evidence wouldn't stand up in court—coerced confessions never did, unless they were obtained by the police, supported by the perjury of officers—but he could take his information to the ICHR, to the media, wherever it would do the most harm to his enemies. The same men who had ruined his career now sought to have him killed, but Gomez wouldn't go without a fight.

There would be no more running, no more cowardice.

He wished Aguiar and Kelly well—particularly Kelly—though it was unclear to him what they hoped to accomplish in the mountains. Granted, it was possible for them to hide, if they were smart and kept a low profile among the peasants, but they couldn't carry on the fight, the ICHR's information war, from some backward collection of shanties where indoor plumbing was a dream and electricity a rumor.

Gomez had killed the afternoon awaiting the hour when he knew Camarena habitually left work, stopping for a drink or two on his way home. It would be folly to attempt abducting him from the saloon, likewise a confrontation on the public street. The only way to do it, Gomez knew, was to confront the traitor at his home and force him to admit his crime. That done, Gomez would be content to leave Camarena there, leave him to flee, warn his superiors, perhaps to kill himself. What did it matter to the end result? As long as Gomez had the tape and could convey it to some trusted contact for dissemination to the world, it was enough.

The next hard question, then. Who could he trust?

First get the tape, Gomez chastised himself, as he approached Camarena's home on foot. He had expected nothing in the way of special guards and saw none present. Why should Camarena be in any fear, when Gomez was expected to be running for his life, perhaps already gone from Bogotá?

The doorbell sounded flat, off-key. Gomez was ready with the Browning automatic when Camarena answered, backing him inside without a word, the cold expression on his face enough to silence any planned pretense of innocence.

Gomez was ready with the gun and with his accusations, but he wasn't ready for the truncheon that came slashing down across his wrist as soon as he had crossed the threshold into Camarena's flat. Nothing could have prepared him for the officers who sprang upon him, one from either side, and crushed him to the floor.

Condemned to play the fool again, Gomez could only pray that they would kill him swiftly.

But his prayers wouldn't be heard this night.

IT WAS ILLUSION, Ciro Aguiar decided, but the hike from where he had to leave the Jeep until the point where he first glimpsed his village seemed to grow a little longer every time he made the trek. A few more years, at this rate, and the mile he knew it was might stretch to feel like two, or even three.

But that assumed he had a few more years, and any effort to predict the future in Colombia—much less to claim a stake in it—was folly. After the attempt on Gomez's life in the park, which member of the ICHR might be next? For that matter, what guarantee did he have that next time he passed through this forest to his home, he wouldn't find a field of cold, dead ashes where his family and friends once lived? Each visit thus became potentially the last, more bittersweet for that, and Aguiar never took for granted that his loved ones were secure against the savages who seemed to run his homeland—and the world at large—as if it were their private game preserve.

Two hundred meters out, their guide in front of them, with Kelly and Belasko bringing up the rear, Aguiar could smell meat cooking, guessed that it was either pork or goat.

"Supper," he called across his shoulder to the others, smiling at the thought.

This time, at least, the village still remained.

An old man with a world war-vintage rifle guarded the village's western perimeter. As to which world war the rifle might belong to, or the date when it had last been fired in anger, that was anybody's guess. The old man was a second cousin of Aguiar's father. Sometimes it seemed to Aguiar that every member of the village was related in some way and should be banned from intermarrying on general principals. In truth, though, as the village aged and younger ones like Aguiar sought their fortunes elsewhere, there would soon be no more marriage, no more children, and the village would begin to die a slower, more protracted death than would be offered by The Fist.

"This way," he told the others, leading them along the main street of the village toward the home his mother and his youngest sister occupied. His father had been bitten by a fer-de-lance three years ago while hunting in the forest. He was dead within the hour, one of those the village lost with no one from the outside world to blame. Aguiar's two brothers and an older sister had moved on to lives and families of their own in Bogotá and Medellín, but Aguiar seldom heard from them. They seemed to know he felt the ties of blood and soil more strongly than they did, and couldn't stand to see the mute recrimination they imagined in his eyes.

"You haven't told us what it's called," Kelly reminded him.

"What's that?"

"This," she said. "The village."

Aguiar frowned. "It has no name," he said. "That way, it feels like less to lose if it is swept away."

THE NAMELESS VILLAGE had an easy rhythm to its life. There was no challenge, falling into it, and Bolan was a bit surprised at the easy acceptance Aguiar's people accorded to himself and Kelly. In the absence of a native son, he thought, it would have been a different matter, though. The old man with the antique rifle hadn't been the only posted watcher on their trek to reach this place, and Bolan guessed that some who tried to pass that way without permission from the tenants of the land might not return alive.

Bolan had briefly dwelt in native villages before, in Southeast Asia and in other parts of the so-called Third World, and while he admired the simple routines of life among "primitive" people, he was ever conscious of his own disruptive role as an outsider, set apart not only by his language and the color of his skin, but also by technology, knowledge, the avaricious need to seize and own that drove his kind. He recognized himself as an intruder and followed Aguiar's lead as far as interaction with the people who had first claim on this piece of Mother Earth. He hoped the outside world wouldn't intrude too swiftly or too harshly on this simple place, and that his war wouldn't accelerate the process.

Propriety dictated that Kelly should stay with Aguiar's mother and sister, while Aguiar himself bunked with a childhood friend and Bolan was accepted by a couple in their mid-sixties who seemed constantly amused to have a gringo in their home. They didn't ask about the clanking contents of his duffel bags, although he guessed they had to have known that he wasn't some kind of wandering mechanic laden down with tools. The past half-century had taught Colombians to live with violence and the men who used it as a daily implement for good or ill, and questioning a heavily armed stranger would rank low on any long-term survivor's list of things to do.

His gear stowed safely as it ever could be in this place, Bolan observed the evening routine and pitched in where he could, drawing water from a nearby mountain stream, collecting wood to keep the cooking fires alive. There were few children in the village, but the ones he saw didn't appear to feel the lack of cable television, video arcades, or hundred-dollar sneakers. Bolan wasn't ready to declare this life the best available—he knew a fair bit on the subjects of disease, hard work and poverty that went along with it—but living in the moment, he was hard-pressed to determine how a spoiled brat from the Hamptons or Beverly Hills would grow up any more humane or decent than the children he saw here. Quite the reverse, in fact, if his experience was any guide.

A scuffling footstep and the scent of perfume told him Kelly was behind him. "This is what we're fighting for," she said, as Bolan turned. "Of course, you wouldn't call it fighting."

"There are different ways to fight."

"And some are more equal than others?"

"It depends on the situation," Bolan said. "If the carrot doesn't work, sometimes you have to use the stick."

"And you're the stick."

"Maybe a twig."

She smiled at that but caught herself before it turned into a full-blown laugh. "I'm not sure that I want to meet the really tough guys, then," she told him, sobering.

"Some of them aren't so bad. If you passed them on the street, you'd never know the difference."

"That's what scares me."

"Don't let it worry you. The real tough guys aren't all that common, anyway. The ones you have to watch for are the bullies and the scavengers."

"Just face up to them, right?"

"It works sometimes."

"Or you can always kill them."

"Right. There's always that."

There was a bleakness in her eyes as Aguiar found them, calling them to share the evening meal.

9

After a time, the pain almost began to seem routine. Nestor Gomez convinced himself that he had plumbed the blackest depths of suffering and sampled all the horror lurking there. The probes and skewers. Alligator clamps attached to hand-crank generators. Heat and cold. Blunt trauma. He was almost persuaded that he could endure anything.

Almost.

Unfortunately for his resolution, the interrogators knew their business better than he did. They understood when he was fading, losing touch with the indignities they inflicted on his mind and body. They could sense the distance growing and were wise enough to offer him a respite from the torture, letting Gomez slump against his bonds and doze, if he could manage to lose consciousness. They granted him the opportunity to rest, regain a measure of himself. To feel again.

Before they started over, from the top.

Gomez had no clear notion of how long it took the team to break him. He thought it had been hours, at least, but his ordeal could just as easily have stretched for days on end. In which case, Gomez told himself, perhaps it was too late for the interrogators to make good use of the information they had pried from his unwilling mind and lips.

Perhaps Kelly and Aguiar were no longer in the village.

Maybe they had traveled on to parts unknown.

Gomez hoped so, for at the end—when the all-devouring pain became too much and he could barely speak because his throat was raw from screaming—he told them everything. Kelly. Aguiar. The village, though, at least in that case, he couldn't direct the hunters to their target with precision, since he had only a vague sense of the settlement's location.

What had interested his interrogators most, however, was the news of the American, Mike Belasko. The first mention of his presence in the city had excited them, prompting a rash of questions Gomez couldn't answer. The inquisitors had shocked and beaten him into unconsciousness, then let him rest and brought him back for more, until they realized that he had told them everything he knew about the stranger in their midst. The questions he hadn't been able to resolve clearly disturbed his captors. After yet another hour of pain and pressure, they had brought an officer to see him, stately in his tailored uniform, with medals on his chest. The officer asked questions while the torturers applied more pain. Gomez was on the brink of making something up to please them when the officer gave up and went away.

Gomez had been alone for what seemed hours now, or was it days? He ruled out the latter at last because no one had brought him food or water, and he knew he would be dead if they had left him gasping in his chair for days on end.

Hours, then. How many? Time enough to find the village and prepare a strike force for the raid? Had there been time for them to track down Belasko? Did they even possess a clue to his identity, beyond the fact that he was almost certainly American? That aspect had intrigued them most of all, and Gomez understood the problem. The regime that ruled Colombia had been propped up by U.S. foreign aid for decades, the assistance going far beyond cash payments to include military equipment and counterinsurgency training for Colombian soldiers and policemen, special lessons in "debriefing" for selected officers at the CIA's notorious Academy of the Americas, and undercover aid in carrying elections when the odds weren't supportive of a landslide for the candidate endorsed by Washington.

Gomez wondered briefly if his own interrogators had studied at the CIA training facility, learning different ways to make him scream, his flesh convulse. If so, they had to have been among the brightest students in their class, or maybe they came by it naturally, having found a way to mix business with pleasure.

The main thing was that Gomez had some time alone, a few short moments to himself, and he had to use them to coordinate his frayed and tangled wits. He had to rank priorities and act accordingly—assuming that he found some way to act at all.

First thing, he needed to discover if the enemy had found Aguiar's village and overtaken Kelly. Gomez had no great concern for the American, but if Kelly had been caged or killed, then anything he tried to do would be in vain. The guilt would crush him, and the best thing he could hope for would be speedy death.

It was unlikely that his captors would provide a prisoner with updates on the progress of their hunt for his best friends. There was a chance, however, that they might return to gloat if they had been successful—or to ply him with more questions if they didn't find what they were looking for. In either case, Gomez would have at least a vague idea of what was going on. The solitary silence was his enemy. Within it he fell prey to his imagination, sketching scenes that might be worse than anything the enemy could think of on his own.

Next thing, if Kelly and Aguiar were alive and still at large, if Gomez's jailers hadn't found the village yet, it was his duty to alert them, let them know that he had broken down and placed their lives in jeopardy. Forgiveness was irrelevant. They needed time and a head start. If he could somehow give them that, Gomez would gladly sacrifice himself to see them safely on their way. It was no more than fair.

Last thing, the sheer, grim hopelessness of his position in the torture cell. He occupied a straight-backed wooden chair, bound tightly to it with a yellow rope that felt like nylon or some other man-made fiber where it rubbed against his skin. Gomez was naked, to allow his tormentors no end of possibilities, and he was badly weakened by the battering, by the electric shocks, by loss of blood. If they returned to loosen his bonds right now, he wasn't certain he could stand unaided, much less fight or run away.

One thing at a time.

He was working on the rope that bound his wrists behind him, flexing and twisting against it, thankful for the lubrication of his blood, when he heard footsteps closing from behind him, and a noise like squeaky wheels.

A moment later, his two old friends in khaki stood before him, the taller of them leaning on a handcart with the generator, insulated cables capped with shiny alligator clamps.

"Mr. Gomez," the other one addressed him, smiling like a hungry shark, "we have a few more questions."

FRACO TERCIERO WAS uneasy as he waited for the meeting to begin. He had rushed home from work to change his suit, but Terciero still felt shabby standing in the library of the exclusive country club. The members here were seriously rich, if not beyond Terciero's wildest dreams, at least light-years beyond his realistic hopes of ever catching up.

And he was waiting for the richest of them all, summoned as if by royalty, to appear upon demand. There had been no thought of ignoring the command. Terciero might be venal and corrupt, perhaps a trifle slow at times, but he wasn't insane.

"Fraco, it's good of you to come on such short notice."

Terciero spun, surprised, thankful his glass of rum was almost empty so it didn't spill. Prospero Alarcon had entered silently, closing the space between Terciero and the doorway like a wraith. He stood six feet away and gestured to some nearby chairs in lieu of shaking hands.

They sat, and Terciero said, "It was my pleasure, Mr. Alarcon." A lie, preserving the illusion both men recognized.

"Prospero, please," Alarcon said.

Now, that was new. Calling the big man by his given name was something only other big men normally were privileged to do. Terciero recognized the gesture for precisely what it was: bait in a trap.

"Thank you," he replied, avoiding the perilous name and quaffing the last of his rum for courage. "How may I serve you, sir?"

"We have a minor problem, Fraco." Making it a thing they shared before he ever spelled it out, so that Terciero would be doubly bound—by his financial obligations and the frail illusion of fraternity—to put himself at risk in the pursuit of Alarcon's objective.

"Anything that I can do, of course." The mantra that would someday be his epitaph.

"You are familiar with the International Consultancy on Human Rights," Alarcon said.

"Yes, sir." Terciero flashed back to his recent meeting with Yago Sebastiano, wondering what had gone wrong in such a short time that he found himself summoned by Sebastiano's master to discuss the self-same thing.

"I have discovered, quite by accident of course, that certain members of this so-called public service group are acting in collaboration with left-wing guerrillas to subvert out lawful government."

Terciero might have smiled at the absurdity of that, if he hadn't been trembling with the fear of what would follow. "Yes, I see," was all that he could manage in response.

"In fact," Alarcon went on, "it seems they have imported an assassin from America. He is the man responsible for the most recent chain of homicides in Bogotá."

"If you're aware of his identity..." Terciero let the statement trail away, uncertain where he meant to go with it and suddenly appalled that he had been about to offer help in what could only be an execution.

"Sadly, no. Not yet," the big man said, apparently ignoring Terciero's hesitation. "But it's known that two employees of the ICHR are presently in conference with a group of Marxist sympathizers in the Cordillera, not so far from Bogotá."

"This is confirmed?" Terciero asked. He didn't want to

know the names or details, but his instinct told him that it might be unavoidable.

"Confirmed? Oh, yes. The source is unimpeachable, another member of the traitor's nest. There is no doubt."

"In that case, sir, the army or the state police—"

"One of the terrorists is an American," the big man interrupted him. "An American woman, in fact. You may recall the furor that erupted, some years back, about the nuns in Guatemala?"

Teaching sisters of the Holy Church who had been raped and murdered by militiamen. What politician in Latin America would ever forget it? The embarrassment had come close to toppling a government. Worse, it had jeopardized foreign aid to the military and security police.

"It was...unfortunate," Terciero said.

"Indeed." Alarcon was nodding as he spoke. "A wise man, Fraco, learns not only from his own mistakes, but also from the errors of his fellow men. You understand?"

To lie, or not to lie? In this case, Terciero felt that he had more to lose by feigning comprehension than by openly confessing ignorance.

"Sir, I am not precisely—"

"We must not repeat the error of our brothers to the north, Fraco. The military and police must not involve themselves to any serious extent in what may prove to be...how shall I say it?...an inflammatory circumstance."

"In that case, sir, I'm not sure that—"

As if by habit, Alarcon broke in to cut him off. "The matter will be handled privately, Fraco. There are among us citizens who rise from time to time, spontaneously, to defeat their homeland's enemies."

The Fist, Terciero thought. All right, then. But if Alarcon was using his militia for the job, why had he summoned him here? Was there more risk in asking or in waiting to be told?

He waited.

"There is one small problem, though," Alarcon said, dropping the other shoe. "I hope you may be able to assist me in resolving it."

"Of course, sir. If I can." Sealing his fate. Again.

"It is a simple transportation matter, Fraco." Alarcon was smiling now, convinced that he had won. "If there were three, perhaps four helicopters not in use this evening, perhaps tomorrow morning early, their loan would be appreciated. Naturally, expenses for their fuel and pilots would be paid in full...and in advance."

The envelope seemed to appear from nowhere in the big man's hand. Its bulk impressed Terciero, but he didn't reach for it immediately.

"Sir, the Ministry of Military Affairs—"

"Is very busy, I am sure. Perhaps you may be able to assist me with this one, small thing?"

Terciero felt a lump form in his throat and swallowed it. He thought he heard his bones creak as he shifted forward in his chair to reach the envelope.

"Of course," he told the big man. "You can count on me."

"IT MUST BE HARD to live this way," Regan Kelly said.

"All depends on what you're used to," Bolan answered.

They sat together on the great bole of a giant tree that had been felled by wind or flooding, possibly some other force of nature, in the not-so-distant past. The forest hadn't finished with its reclamation work on this one yet. It still served as a fairly decent bench.

"Is that your way of calling me a city girl?"

"I'm curious," he changed the subject. "Do you take offense at everything that's said to you, or is it only me."

That silenced Kelly for a moment. When she spoke again, there was a measure of contrition in her voice. "I'm sorry, Mike. I have a problem with what my family likes to call 'constructive criticism.' Maybe it's in the genes, I don't know."

"So, you pick a career where someone's virtually guaranteed to be criticizing you at all times?"

She couldn't help but smile at that, although with obvious reluctance. "It's something I felt I had to do," she said, pausing a moment before she continued. "You are—or were—a military man?"

"I did some time in uniform."

"You'd recognize my father's type, then. He was a gung-ho Marine, a lifer. Do you remember General Patton's son, I think it was, when he was over there? One year he sent a Christmas card around to all his friends that had a photograph inside of villagers killed by artillery. The card read, 'Peace on Earth, Goodwill Toward Men.'"

"It rings a bell."

"My father framed that card and hung it on the wall above his desk at home."

"And now you try to counteract the military mind-set," Bolan said. It didn't take a graduate degree in Freudian analysis to see where this was going.

"Not the military mind," Kelly corrected him. "The brutal mind. There is a difference—or there should be, anyway. And if there isn't, then we need a drastic change."

"You're waiting for an argument?" he asked her, softening his tone.

"Am I about to get one?"

"Not from me."

"But what you do—"

"Has nothing whatever to do with the military," he told her, fudging a little, but still hewing close to the truth. "I told you going in, I'm not on Uncle Sam's payroll."

That was true enough. Despite his link to Stony Man Farm and Hal Brognola's covert management of many field expenses, he had never drawn a salary from any branch of government since he'd deserted from the Army to avenge the slaughter of his family.

"But you kill people."

"Regan, I respond to predators in situations where the law has either broken down or cannot be applied. I speak the only language my opponents understand. It's neither just nor civilized that they escape accountability for lifetimes spent degrading, murdering and terrorizing innocents."

"So you're a vigilante, then?"

"I'm not concerned with labels," he replied. "Only results."

She turned away from him, lowered her voice. "I'm sorry, Mike. You saved my life, and Nestor's. I feel hypocritical, attacking you, but still...I can't help how I feel."

"And if you didn't feel that way, we wouldn't be here," Bolan said. "You'd have a nice, safe job back in the States. Maybe a family."

"Oh, please. I'm so not the maternal type."

Of course not, Bolan thought. You're just adopting every victim of oppression in the country. And he said, "It will be getting dark soon. We should probably head back."

"Right now?" The sound of disappointment in her voice surprised him. "Do we have to?"

"In the forest after dark you never know what may be creeping up behind you."

She stepped in close and raised her face to make eye contact.

"But I have you to protect me, don't I?" Kelly asked him. "Even if it's only for tonight?"

"IT IS ARRANGED," Prospero Alarcon declared. "The helicopters are available. You have a fourteen-hour window, as they say. Two hours' notice is required to make them ready for the air."

He watched Yago Sebastiano check his watch, as if the mission had been scheduled for some time within the next few minutes. Satisfied by what he saw, Sebastiano said, "I think it best if we go in at dawn."

"Such matters are within your field of expertise," Alarcon said. "I'm not concerned with details. Simply do the job."

"Of course, boss."

Sebastiano didn't take offense—or, if he did, wouldn't allow his face to register the fact. In either case it was the same. A soldier did as he was told by his superiors, the men who paid the bills and pulled the strings.

"You must watch out for this American," he reminded Sebastiano. "He is obviously dangerous, and we have no idea whom he may represent."

"I can't believe the Company would send a man against us," Sebastiano said. "They love Colombia. So many opportunities, so many games to play."

"So many players, Yago. Don't forget that Langley is a rat's nest, and not all rats savor the same kind of cheese."

"You mean a rogue? Some element within the CIA that works against the orders of the White House?"

"Who knows what the White House wants or what its many statements mean from day to day," Alarcon said. "I trust men I can see and touch."

Men he could buy, that was. Men he could terrorize. If all else failed, sometimes it was enough to touch their families. But even then, Alarcon trusted such men only within the limits of his reach. He had a long arm, granted, but his reach wasn't infinite. He wanted to believe the CIA wasn't involved, that the mysterious American was some kind of mercenary operating on his own, without official sanction, but the only way to end the threat was by eliminating him.

If Sebastiano's people were skillful or lucky enough to capture the Yankee alive, perhaps they could learn something from his dying breaths. At least, that way, the troops would have some entertainment for their trouble. Either way, though, the intruder known as Belasko had to die.

"There is a chance," Sebastiano said, "that he won't be found among the others in the village."

"In which case," Alarcon replied, "you will complete your business in the mountains and return to Bogotá. It's well known that the state security police are overworked. I've no doubt that they would appreciate your help in settling a minor problem such as this one."

"As you say."

It was the kind of answer that Alarcon preferred.

As you say.

So be it.

Thy will be done.

In fact, it was the only sort of answer that a man in his position could accept. His wisdom and his leadership couldn't be questioned—not without significant reprisals, at the very least—if he intended to remain on top. A weak man could afford to vacillate, and no one was surprised. A strong man who didn't retain his grip on the controls was swiftly beaten down and torn apart by rivals, rapidly forgotten as a new lord of the manor took his place.

But that wasn't about to happen to Alarcon. Not from two worthless Americans, and one of them a woman. He would kill both of them for daring to infringe upon his territory, and if others died in the process, so be it.

It was all a part of doing business, and Prospero Alarcon was still the consummate achiever in his field.

YAGO SEBASTIANO stood before his men, six ranks of ten, all of them ramrod straight and rigid at attention in their jungle camouflage fatigues. They were supposed to keep their eyes straight forward, but he sensed that every one of them was watching him, imbuing him with their collective strength.

"Three helicopters have been placed at our disposal," he announced, his voice ringing in the warehouse where they had assembled. "I'm told that each has space for eighteen passengers. This means, regretfully, that six of you will have to stay behind this time."

No murmur of displeasure from the ranks. The soldiers of The Fist were too well disciplined for anything resembling an emotional display.

"Each one of you received a number on arrival." As he spoke, Sebastiano raised his right hand, showing off a slip of pastel blue paper. "In just a moment, I will draw six numbers from the lot and those who hold them are exempted from the mission. There shall be no shame attached to this. It is simply a logistic matter. Those excused are guaranteed first call on the next mission."

Again, there was no hint of a response. He had expected none.

"Our target, first thing in the morning, is a village in the Cordillera Oriental, known to breed and harbor forces of the FARC." Referring to Colombia's premier leftist guerrilla

army—the Revolutionary Armed Forces of Colombia—
would, Sebastiano reckoned, heighten the anticipation and
alertness of his troops. "It is our task to guarantee that no more
terrorists are born or sheltered there. It is our duty to the nation and the God we serve!"

It looked as if a couple of his soldiers in the front rank were
about to cheer, but they contained themselves. One of them
bit his lip, bright tears of patriotic fervor shining in his eyes.
It was incredible, he thought, how easily these peasant youths
could be manipulated by clichés and slogans. Sebastiano
wondered how long it would take for this one to wake up, or
whether he would sacrifice his life before he understood what
he was really fighting for.

Most of the men who served The Fist still clung to some
ideals and principles of how society should operate and how
the system ought to be maintained. Those things were basic,
fundamental, and provided them with will to keep on fighting through the years. At the same time, most of them—all
the veterans, certainly—had learned by now that their long
struggle wasn't geared toward crafting a Utopia.

The Fist had been created for one reason and one reason
only. It was meant to hold the line against subversives, parasites and the disrupters of society. Some of their enemies
were Communists, while others knew no more of politics
than any suckling babe. It mattered less to Sebastiano and his
soldiers what another man believed than what he said and did.
In time, all parasitic criminals would have to go, except, of
course, for those extremely wealthy ones who generated jobs
and paid their own way in normal company. It was the way
of things, God's plan, perhaps, that mankind suffered certain
vices, and that some men would be chosen to accommodate
those appetites. If there had been no outlet for those needs,
no sin, how would the Holy Church survive?

Sebastiano's mind snapped back without missing a beat in
his pep talk. "It is your task," he told the troops, "your duty
and your honor to destroy this nest of traitors as if it had never
been. So cursed is this plague spot that it has no name. No

name! As if the Lord himself had marked it from the day it was created for the judgment that is coming."

Sebastiano heard himself slipping over the top, but this kind of thing was expected in a patriotic movement pledged to the defense of God and country. He could hardly tell his men that leaders of the Holy Church were paid to close their eyes and turn away at certain times, the same as politicians and policemen were. What was the point? Were they not wise enough to understand the workings of the world themselves? Had it not always been this way, from the beginnings of recorded history?

"In just a moment," he continued, wrapping up his speech, "we will draw lots for those who stay behind. The rest of you will then prepare your weapons and equipment. At four o'clock tomorrow morning, buses will transport you to the helicopters. By this time tomorrow night, you will be heroes celebrating victory."

Sebastiano jabbed his fist into the air and cried, "Hail victory!" The shout and rigid-armed salute came back to him, reverberating through the warehouse as his soldiers answered him three times.

They were prepared to kill or die on his command.

Sebastiano smiled, completely satisfied.

10

A dream woke Bolan in the darkest hour of the night, before pale dawn could break across the upper strata of the forest canopy. He sat bolt-upright on his sleeping pallet, reaching for the pistol at his side, his mind and body instantly alert.

What was it?

Details of the dream were lost to him, despite the ingrained instant-waking reflex that sometimes allowed him to retrieve scenarios and fragments from the other side. He felt the small hairs bristling on his nape and knew that it wasn't a dream of Regan Kelly and the hour they had passed together on the outskirts of the nameless village.

This was something else.

He rose in darkness, silent, drawing on his shoulder rig. His loaded duffel bags lay ready at the left side of his makeshift bed, but Bolan left them there. He had to pin down his feeling, find out if there was anything behind it first, before he broke the big guns out.

For now, he reckoned the Beretta 93-R was enough.

His hosts were sleeping as he passed their room, a muffled snorting as the old man grumbled in his own dream, shifting restlessly. Bolan continued on and stepped into the night.

It would be dawn soon. He could tell from the shifting sounds of birdsong in the forest, nightcallers giving over dominion to those who greeted the day. Nocturnal hunters would be winding down their endless search for prey, returning to the lairs where they would pass the daylight hours, either sleeping off a meal or listening to sounds from an empty stomach. In another half an hour, maybe less, the sky would lighten slowly and the village would begin to stir.

One tenant of the village was already stirring.

Bolan heard him coming first, then saw the man emerge from shadow on his left, between two houses. He was carrying a rifle in his hands, not slung across his shoulder as was usual. A few steps closer, and Bolan recognized the man as a friend of Aguiar's, introduced to him simply as Lorenzo.

Bolan waited for the sentry to notice him, no sudden movement to startle or trigger a shot in the dark. Lorenzo picked him out, approaching with the muzzle of his weapon pointed toward the stars. He closed the gap between them with determined strides.

"You feel it too, señor?" he asked.

"I wasn't sure," Bolan replied.

"You feel it." Not a question, this time.

"Did you hear something?"

"Sí. There was a sound, but far off, northward. It reminds me of—"

The sudden, ringing silence was as obvious to trained ears as a gunshot in the middle of a cocktail party. In the time it would have taken for the Executioner to snap his fingers, every bird, monkey, tree frog and insect in the neighborhood had lost its voice, as if someone had pulled the plug on a recorded track of forest sounds. The sound of Bolan's thudding pulse echoed inside his skull.

"Somebody coming."

"Yes."

"From that direction." Bolan nodded toward the north.

"I think so, too."

"That sound you heard..."

"Like motors," Lorenzo said. "First, it comes this way, then stops, then goes away."

Drop ships.

"How quietly can you get everybody up and out?"

"We practice this," Lorenzo said. "The sleepy children, I don't know."

"Just do the best you can."

Inside the house, he roused his hosts and urged them to get dressed without a light, to find Lorenzo or another sentry and evacuate as quietly as possible. Returning to his borrowed room, he knelt beside the duffel bags, unzipped one and removed the M-4 carbine with its grenade launcher attachment, setting the weapon beside him as he fished inside the bag for bandoliers and combat webbing. Seconds later he was ready, shouldering the bags—one of them noticeably lighter now— before he made his way outside.

The villagers were leaving, slipping from their homes in family clusters. Whispered warnings stilled the cries and questions of the older children; strong hands gently covered the mouths of those too young to understand.

Lorenzo and a few more of the younger men, all armed, had set them moving southward, away from the approaching enemy who still had made no sound that reached as far as Bolan's ears. He would feel foolish if it proved to be a false alarm, but with Lorenzo's testimony fresh in mind that didn't seem to be the case.

Drop ships could put a strike force down within an easy march of almost any target on the globe. They didn't have to land. The soldiers could rappel from treetop level if they had to, plummeting through darkness like a swarm of spiders coming down to feed. If they were trained and disciplined, they could advance upon a target almost silently or at least quietly enough to keep from rousing those they meant to kill.

Facing due north, the Executioner moved out to find himself a vantage point from which he could await the coming of his enemies.

RUFIO SANTIAGO, a lieutenant in the People's Army of Democracy, had been elated when he was selected to command the strike force that would wipe another nest of traitors off the map. He was determined not to fail and thus betray the commander's trust in him. When he was finished with the nameless village now no more than several hundred meters distant, nothing recognizable would remain.

Santiago stayed back near the middle of his marching column, twenty-five or thirty men in front of him, including scouts, the other twenty-odd behind. They had lost one man while rappelling from the army helicopters, his ankle cleanly snapped despite the high-topped combat boots he wore, but that still left Santiago with fifty-two guns besides his own.

He told himself that it would be enough.

Most of the village would be sleeping at this hour, early risers still groggy from their dreams and busy brewing coffee or preparing breakfast. Any sentries posted in the darkness would be starting to relax—another night almost gone, without incident—and they would die in the first fusillade. From that point onward, it would be a swift and seamless massacre.

Santiago had no qualms about killing Communist rebels, whether they were able-bodied men, old people, women or children. Such tactics drew criticism from the self-righteous Americans, of course, but who on Earth had less right to complain? The young lieutenant knew his history. It was a president of the United States who once declared that the only good Indian was a dead Indian. American military commanders had justified the slaughter of native women and children for decades by declaring that "nits make lice."

This morning's mission was important, even critical, to the redemption of his homeland from the enemies who threatened Santiago's way of life. He would succeed or give his life—and that of every soldier under his command—in the attempt.

He checked his wristwatch, pressing a button on the side to illuminate its face. They were on schedule, even early. At this rate—

The first explosion seemed to steal Santiago's breath away, though he was well outside the killing radius and only felt the shock wave as a kind of dirty, cordite-smelling breeze that brushed across his face. It came from farther up the column, near the point, and from the ragged sound of voices crying out in pain he knew that he had lost the precious margin of surprise.

Was it a booby trap of some kind? Possibly a land mine?

Someone started firing up ahead. Santiago recognized the sound of Kalashnikov assault rifles like the ones his point men carried, stuttering in the darkness split by muzzle-flashes now. He vaguely recognized a popping sound—grenade launcher—and then a second blast ripped through the trees, immediately followed by more screams.

Panic hit Santiago like a rabbit punch to the solar plexus, but he swallowed the bile in his throat and began shouting orders to his men. The time for stealth had obviously passed, and they were losing their advantage. He needed to regain control of the situation, and swiftly, before his startled soldiers lost their nerve.

"Advance!" he shouted, to be heard above the gunfire rattling across the front line of the column. "Forward and find cover! Mark your targets! Fire at will!"

Santiago rushed forward with his men, clutching the Uzi submachine gun that he carried to his chest, careful to keep his finger well outside the trigger guard. He needed every man he still had left and didn't wish to open fire on one of them by accident, in the confusion of the moment. Stumbling on the tangled branches of a fallen tree that lay across the path, he took advantage of the great log's cover, huddling low while bullets snapped and whistled overhead.

"Forward!" he shouted to his men once more, from hiding. "Push on to the village! We must not be stopped!"

THE FIRST EXPLOSION startled Regan Kelly, froze her in her tracks. The frightened villagers continued moving past her in the darkness as gunfire erupted from the far side of the village. She imagined Belasko and a handful of the others fighting for their lives, barely conscious of her own change in direction even as she started back along the trail.

Hands clutched at her, tried to restrain her, but she threw them off and soon the villagers quit trying. It wasn't their job to save this crazed American from herself. Her presence in the village had most likely brought this doom upon them, and they owed her nothing. Most of them, although they might not speak the words aloud, were satisfied to see her go.

She moved toward the sounds of battle, picking up speed as she went. The crowd of village refugees was thinning out, most of them well behind her now and off into the forest. They might lose their homes, but it would take a large, determined force to track them down in the mountains, an investment of time and manpower Kelly doubted the enemy was prepared to make.

Who was the enemy?

As far as Kelly knew, Aguiar's people hadn't made any particular enemies among the left- or right-wing guerrillas who operated in this area. They were simple, hard-working people whose daily routine should have held no interest for the army, state police or pro-government death squads. Unless...

My fault, she thought, and cursed herself. Could it be a coincidence that gunmen were raiding the village less than eighteen hours after she and Belasko had arrived? It seemed impossible.

Another loud explosion startled Kelly, made her stumble over something on the narrow trail before one outflung hand found purchase on a gnarled tree trunk. The sounds of fighting had intensified and they were closer now, but she couldn't decide if that was due to her advancement or some progress of the raiders toward the village.

Kelly understood that someone—Belasko, sentries from the village, both together?—had somehow intercepted the attackers in the woods before they reached their target. It had given the villagers time to escape, but how long could the defenders hold that line? Were they already weakening, retreating, running for their lives?

More to the point, what could she do to help? Why was she even going back, unarmed and absolutely unprepared, into a zone where men were being killed?

Kelly couldn't have answered that one if her life depended

on it—and it might, within the next few moments. Even so, she pressed ahead.

And found that the defenders had already been pushed back into the village proper. They were fighting from the cover of the houses, some of them apparently inside, while others moved more freely through the shadows cast by dawn's encroaching light. For just a heartbeat, Kelly picked out Belasko, one of those who flitted here and there among the houses, pausing long enough to fire in the direction of the tree line where his enemies were firing back. He raked the forest with a burst of automatic fire, then triggered something that produced a popping sound, followed swiftly by a thunderous explosion among the trees.

So this is what he does, she thought, and watched him duck back out of sight between two wooden homes.

Some of the attackers were firing tracer rounds from their weapons, lethal fireflies arcing through the gray murk of the forest clearing where the village stood. Where tracers burrowed into aged wood, they set the wood on fire, half a dozen of the small homes burning within moments of the first hostile exchange. Kelly could smell the smoke mingling with the acrid reek of gunpowder, fouling the primeval forest.

Aguiar found her out of nowhere, looming in front of her, a bolt-action rifle clutched in his hands. "You must leave here," he said, raising his voice to be heard over the gunfire.

"Go now, Regan!"

"Ciro," she responded, "I can't go and—"

"Go!" he bellowed at her, punctuating the command with a menacing step forward, raising the rifle as if he might strike her. His face was contorted into a mask of rage she barely recognized.

"Ciro—"

"Go now!"

She ducked his clumsy swing, sobbing, and fled into the forest, following the other refugees along a narrow game trail through the trees.

BOLAN SLIPPED ANOTHER HE round into the M-203 launcher's breech and snapped it shut, cocking the 40 mm weapon automatically. He glanced around the corner of the house that sheltered him, then ducked back as another swarm of AK-47 rounds and tracers flew past.

The sky was swiftly lightening, and while the tracers would be losing their intimidating power in the daylight, they could still set fire to any target made of flammable material. Perhaps a quarter of the wooden homes were already on fire, most of them at the north end of the village where the battle had been joined.

From the sudden smoky smell and crackling near at hand, Bolan determined that the house whose bulk provided cover for him had, likewise, begun to burn. He didn't know whose house it was, how badly they would miss it, but the only consolation he could offer to these total strangers was that most of them had gotten out alive. The armed men who remained behind to join him in the battle might not prove to be so fortunate.

At least one of them was dead already. Bolan didn't know the young man's name and couldn't recognize him when he burst from a burning house, screaming, his clothing and hair all in flames. Bolan had snapped the M-4 to his shoulder, ready to end it in the only way he could, but a Kalashnikov burst from the tree line got there ahead of him, slamming the rag-doll figure down into a crackling, smoky heap.

One down, and that left five of the half-dozen who had stayed behind to help him fight. Their arsenal consisted of vintage bolt-action rifles, one pump-action .22-caliber repeater, and an antique double-barreled shotgun. The woodsmen were presumably accomplished hunters, but he couldn't tell in the confusion whether they had managed to disable any of the steadily advancing enemy.

He risked another glance around the corner, just in time to see three figures clad in jungle camouflage advancing from the tree line in a rush, firing from the hip as they came. The lack of any recognizable insignia on their camous had con-

firmed the unofficial nature of the raid. Now Bolan shouldered the carbine and lined up his shot, left index finger
curled around the M-203's trigger, taking up the slack. There
was a hollow-sounding pop, with no recoil to speak of, as the
HE round went spiraling downrange.

And detonated in the midst of Bolan's running targets.

A cloud of smoke and flying sod erupted at ground zero,
hurling bodies this way and that, tumbling through somersaults
that would have impressed a gold-medal gymnast. The land-
ings left much to be desired, though, limp forms crashing to
the deck as gravity asserted its command and drew them back.

It was a tricky proposition, fighting men with high explosives. The concussion and resultant shrapnel could be deadly,
but in many cases the direction of the blast, diverted by some
solid object into open space, spared targets who would certainly have been disabled by a more specific antipersonnel device. The HE rounds could shatter houses, but the folks inside
might walk away with only superficial injuries. In open-air en-
gagements, it was just as likely to knock down soldiers and
kick dirt in their startled faces as to kill them where they stood.

Bolan tracked the tumbling figures, following their
progress with the M-4's sights. Two of them seemed to be unconscious, maybe dead, but number three was more resilient,
lurching back to all fours, struggling awkwardly to gain his
feet. The gunner was almost there when the Executioner
slammed a quick burst into his chest and put him down for
good.

More soldiers were rushing from the tree line now, and
Bolan met them with a storm of automatic fire, strafing their
ranks, watching the runners stumble, stagger, fall. Some of
them broke stride, lapsing into jerky little dances as the 5.56
mm rounds tore into them, while others simple toppled forward in their tracks and never moved again.

Five...six...seven...

The M-4's bolt locked open on an empty chamber, Bolan
ducking back under cover to switch magazines. He heard the
hostiles coming. Boots slamming hard-packed earth, orders

and curses shouted in Spanish, the stutter of full-auto weapons. He could stand and die where he was or find a new strategic position and fight on from there.

It was no contest.

The Executioner broke from cover, sprinting toward the nearest shadowed sanctuary, with a swarm of bullets snapping at his heels.

CIRO AGUIAR SAW Belasko ducking, weaving, returning fire as he ran. The invaders of his village had a target now, a focus for their wrath, and they were charging after him, even as one of them fell to Belasko's raking fire, then another and another.

He couldn't kill them all alone.

Without hesitation, Aguiar raised the Mauser Model 98-K rifle to his shoulder, tracking the invaders with its open sights. They were a hopeless blur in front of him until one of them stopped suddenly, bent over his weapon, grappling with it, trying to clear a jam.

Aguiar released his pent-up breath as he squeezed the rifle's trigger, felt the steel-shod butt plate slam against his shoulder as the 7.92 mm bullet hurtled toward impact with its target. The camouflage-clad stranger shuddered as a piece of his skull was dislodged, spilling crimson and gray in the dust, the lifeless body toppling over backward as if in slow motion.

Aguiar was stunned. It was the first time he had fired a rifle since his fourteenth year, the one and only time that he had ever fired upon a man. He felt a sudden rush of power, nausea coming close behind it, and he swallowed hard to keep the scalding bile out of his mouth.

There was no time for weakness now. His village was about to be destroyed, including the home he had grown up in and other homes belonging to his relatives and lifelong friends. A foreigner and total stranger had done more to stop the enemy so far than anyone who had grown up within the confines of the village.

It was time to even the score.

Aguiar worked the smooth bolt on his borrowed Mauser,

ejecting hot brass and chambering the second of the rifle's five rounds. Spare cartridges were heavy in his pockets, dragging down his jeans and clinking when he walked. He hoped he lived long enough to fire them all.

Two other members of the raiding party had seen their comrade fall, turning to face the general direction where the fatal shot had come from. One of them spotted Aguiar, standing in the shadow of a house that had so far been spared from tracer fire, and called his friend's attention to the target.

Aguiar saw them, nearly froze as the twin Kalashnikovs pivoted to bring him under fire, but some new sense of reckless courage had invested him. He harbored no illusion of his own invincibility, but death seemed less important now than fighting back—and fighting back with something more than words.

He sighted quickly down the Mauser's twenty-four-inch barrel, squeezing off another shot almost before his sights had found and framed a second target. Once again he saw the splash of blood, his target lurching out of frame and going down. He didn't know if this one was a kill, but there was no time to consider it as the survivor opened up with his Kalashnikov.

Aguiar threw himself backward, into the space between two simple houses, where the bullets couldn't find him. He racked the bolt, round three in the chamber, clutching the rifle hard enough to blanche his knuckles. He was trying to decide what he should do, which way to go, when he heard footsteps rushing toward him down the main street of the village. How many of them after him? He couldn't tell. There was no time to run, nowhere to hide.

He turned to face the street, lifting the Mauser, butt tight against his shoulder. When the first man came around the corner, Aguiar shot him in the chest, dead center, the explosive impact punching his enemy backward and clear of the alley with a startled whoosh of air emptied lungs.

The bolt again, round four, and Aguiar instinctively dropped to one knee as others came running. Two of them cleared the corner together, both firing automatic rifles, bullets fanning the air where his chest would have been a moment earlier.

He shot the soldier on his left, fired through the other's blinding muzzle-flash to strike him in the thorax. Dying on his feet, the gunner slouched and fell against his comrade, both of them off-balance as Aguiar attacked in blind fury, no time to reload, swinging the Mauser as a bludgeon and cracking the second shooter's skull. Blood sprayed across his face and hands, across the wall immediately to his right.

Aguiar reached down to grab one of the automatic weapons lying at his feet, surprised at the brutal weight of it. Its strap had wound around the pistol grip somehow, but he cleared it in a moment, found the trigger as he spun to face the others who had found him now.

Three, four, five. Aguiar gave up counting as they rushed him, holding down the trigger of his captured weapon.

A sharp metallic snap announced the hammer falling on an empty chamber. Aguiar could only stare at the six guns arrayed before him, the grim faces poised behind them, and he felt the giddy laughter welling up from somewhere deep inside him.

He was laughing when the firing squad let go, killing him where he stood.

BOLAN HAD SHAVED the odds, perhaps cut them by half, but it wasn't enough. At least half of the houses in the village were on fire, and hand grenades were going off in others as the hunters tried to find him, flush him out. He had lost track of the remaining village sentries, but he still heard isolated rifle shots or shotgun blasts from time to time, suggesting that a few of them were still alive.

Bolan decided that he had to turn the game around before it was too late.

He found a place between two houses at the southwest corner of the village, dropped his duffel bags and unzipped them, rummaging inside. It took only seconds to prepare the Spectre submachine gun and drape its strap over his left shoulder, so that the weapon slapped against his hip. Spare magazines were tucked inside his web belt, though he didn't know if he'd have the time or opportunity to switch. He filled his hands with frag grenades and clipped them to the rings on his suspenders, others on his belt.

It would be chaos when it started, and he had no way of knowing whether he would be alive ten seconds later. While he lasted, though, he had to spread as much confusion in the hostile ranks as possible, inflict as many casualties as he could in the minimum amount of time. It was impossible to get a fix on the remaining enemies, but he would have to do the best with what he had.

Beginning now.

He checked the street, saw a contingent of perhaps a dozen shooters bearing down on his position. He could make his move or wait and maybe never have the chance to move at all.

He moved.

Stepping clear of the space between houses, Bolan lobbed an HE round from his 40 mm into the midst of the approaching rifle squad. Before it even had a chance to detonate, his left hand found the Spectre's pistol grip and raised the compact SMG, his right hand leveling the M-4 carbine with its stock wedged tight against his ribs.

He started firing, short bursts from each weapon, as the HE canister went off among his adversaries, somersaulting bodies, flinging some to earth while others flew into the air. His 5.56 mm tumbling projectiles, interspersed with hot 9 mm Parabellum rounds, ripped through the men still on their feet and sent them spinning into crumpled heaps.

More soldiers coming in a rush, telegraphing their approach with shouted warnings and commands. Bolan took full advantage of the momentary lull to feed his weapons two fresh magazines, before drifting across the street to find a slightly better vantage point. Another moment and the enemy was there, the sight of scattered, broken comrades slowing the advance just long enough for Bolan to attack.

He fell upon them in a blaze of gunfire, his two weapons firing independently and chopping through the ranks. Some of his would-be killers broke and ran, but bullets reached out from behind and brought them down. Others stood fast and Bolan felt the hot wind of their automatic fire crackle around him, ignoring the fact that a lucky round might pierce his skull or chest at any moment.

Instead, he hit them. And when the stragglers rushed to find out what was happening, he dropped his empty weapons in the dust at his feet, drawing the Desert Eagle from his hip and the Beretta 93-R from its armpit sling. He met the dazed survivors of the raiding party with whispering death and thundering ruin, scattering their corpses with the rest.

It took a moment for the empty killing ground to register on Bolan's mind before he realized he was alone, no enemies remaining to be slain. He slowly turned and found three of the village sentries watching from a distance, rifles drooping in their hands, with dazed expressions on their faces.

He had seen that look before.

"This may not be the last of them," he said, mouth dry. "We should go now, while there's time."

But he could only wonder if it might already be too late.

11

Adriano Aznar was puzzled. It didn't happen often, and he hated the occasions when it did. It was unseemly for the district commander of the Revolutionary Armed Forces of Colombia to be caught unaware and uninformed of any transpiring in his area. More to the point, it could be dangerous.

Particularly when it involved a neo-fascist paramilitary outfit like The Fist, against which he had waged incessant war for years on end.

"What was the village called again?" Aznar inquired.

"It seems to have no name," replied his chief of staff, Carlos Tavares.

"And will need none now, I take it."

Tavares shrugged. "The field reports are incomplete," he said. "From what we've heard, it seems most of the people managed to escape, although the village was nearly obliterated."

"Most unusual," Aznar remarked, "for any operation by The Fist."

"Yes, sir."

The real unusual aspect of the raid, however, didn't lie with how many intended targets of the fascist death squad had escaped. The marvel of it was that someone had fought back, and so successfully that many members of the raiding party—possibly the whole contingent—had been killed.

"This no-name village," Aznar said, "am I familiar with it?"

"No, sir." Tavares made a steeple of his fingers as he spoke.

"It was a small place, no resources of real interest to our movement. Older people, for the most part. All the young ones go away to Bogotá or Medellín. Those who remain work mostly for Prospero Alarcon."

"Alarcon." Aznar pronounced the hated name as if it were a curse. "He kills his own stoop labor, now?"

"It wouldn't be the first time."

"But if they weren't political, then why? Was there some labor issue?"

Tavares shook his head. "Nothing that I'm aware of, sir. We're looking into it, for information purposes."

Which meant, of course, for propaganda use against the government and its fascistic goons. The FARC's minister of information was assigned to handle matters on that front, grinding out pamphlets by the carload every time another incident occurred, but Aznar's interest was distinct and separate from any propaganda goals or tactics.

He was worried that The Fist and its supporters in the government might be preparing for a new offensive in his district, one more in their endless series of attempts to decimate the FARC and eliminate dissent by means of force. It wouldn't be the first time they had tried to purge Colombia of honest voices speaking freely.

Aznar's thoughts were interrupted by the ringing telephone on his desk, situated midway between himself and Tavares. The rebel leader scowled, regarding the instrument as if it were some loathsome object, perhaps a heap of offal dropped onto his desktop.

Aznar waited for the fourth ring, a routine that ruled out any of the several hang-up/call-back signals he had worked out with his officers as an alert to sundry forms of danger. Satisfied that this had to be a simple call, however grim the news he may receive, Aznar brought the receiver to his ears.

"What?" he demanded without preamble.

"Adriano Aznar?"

It was a deep male voice, clearly more accustomed to English than Spanish.

Aznar frowned at Tavares across the desk, replying, "Who did you say?"

"You heard me," the caller said. "Can you put him on or not?"

"Tell me. If it's important, I can give him the message."

Momentary silence, Aznar wondering if he had scared the caller off, but before he could cradle the receiver, the nameless stranger spoke again. "All right. There was a village hit this morning in the mountains south of Bogotá. Word is, the raid was carried out by soldiers from the People's Army of Democracy. You know those guys?"

"I don't have time for questions," Aznar said. "Is that your message?"

"Part of it," the caller told him.

"Say the rest, then, and be done."

"Word is," the caller said, "these soldiers hit the village thinking they might find Aznar and catch him napping. As it turns out, though, they had bad luck. A lot of them got wasted. Now they blame Aznar for that. They say it's payback time."

"How you know so much about these things?" Aznar inquired, still frowning.

"Maybe I was there to see it happen."

"So," the rebel leader growled, "you are with The Fist, and still you tell me this?"

"Who said I'm with The Fist?"

"You just said—"

Aznar realized that he was talking to an empty line, the dial tone humming in his ear. He held the receiver at arm's length, glaring at it for a moment, then dropped it back into its cradle.

"Who was it?" Tavares asked him.

"I don't know," Aznar replied. "A gringo, maybe."

"What?" Tavares appeared confused. "What gringo? That's your private number, yes?"

Aznar ignored the question, since Tavares knew the answer. Instead, he addressed himself to the subject of the call. "He says The Fist attacked this village we were speaking of."

"We know that, Adriano."

"He also says The Fist thought I would be there. They were trying to catch me sleeping, so he says."

"That's foolish," Tavares said. "Who would expect to find you in a village that you never saw and maybe never heard of? There's no sense in that."

"Who says The Fist always makes sense?" Aznar replied. "There's more."

"What else?"

"The gringo says they blame us for their losses in the raid and want revenge. 'Payback,' he calls it."

"How does this gringo know so much?"

Aznar could only shrug at that. "Says he was there to watch the killing."

"I think he's lying."

"Why?"

"Who knows? Could be he's with The Fist and wants to frighten you. Or the security police hope you will lose your nerve, perhaps. Maybe surrender if you think your life's in danger."

"And a gringo works for the security police?" Aznar was skeptical.

"Why not? We know they get money and weapons from the CIA. Why not a phone call from the embassy?"

"And if he tells the truth?" Aznar inquired. "What, then?"

It was his chief aide's turn to shrug. "What of it, Adriano? The Fist has tried to kill you many times. You're still alive."

"Because I never take unnecessary chances, Carlos. That is why I am still alive."

"What would you have me do?" Tavares asked.

"Reach out for the lieutenants," Aznar said, "and have them meet me in an hour. We have plans to make."

YAGO SEBASTIANO left one of his men to get the telephone, grimacing as the shrill sound rasped across his nerves. He poured himself another double shot of whiskey, downed it, already reaching for the bottle by the time the liquor scorched his throat.

Sebastiano thought of all the soldiers he had lost and asked himself again how such a thing was possible. He had dispatched his finest warriors, more than fifty of them, to complete a relatively simple job. Wipe out a smallish peasant village and destroy two nosy members of a pacifist society who would be found there.

Nothing could be simpler, but the whole thing had gone horribly, inexplicably wrong somehow.

He had no living witness to the massacre, which made it all the worse. The helicopter pilots had stayed well back from the action, though they heard some of it, saw the firelight and the tracers from a distance. It was only later, when Sebastiano's men didn't return to keep their rendezvous for the extraction as agreed, that one pilot had overflown the village, making out a scene of carnage that had sent him racing back to Bogotá.

All dead, the pilot had reported back. He could be wrong about that part, of course. The darkness, smoke, confusion, his own fear—all these and other factors may have blurred his vision. Still, one thing was clear: Yago Sebastiano's men had walked into a trap, and none of them had lived to tell the tale.

"Sir," the voice behind him cut into his thoughts. "The telephone."

"I heard it."

"It's for you," the soldier told him.

"Who?"

A cautious shrug. "He will not give his name."

The frown carved furrows in Sebastiano's weathered face. "You told a stranger I was here, you idiot?"

"No, sir!" His subordinate was frightened now, and rightly so. "I told him I would try to find you."

Sebastiano felt like pistol-whipping this one for his sheer stupidity. The first rule of the telephone was to acknowledge nothing, offer no incriminating statements or admissions. This one—Bonafacio, his name was—would most certainly, and at the very least, be barred from answering the telephone in future.

"Go back and tell this person with no name that I couldn't

be found. In fact, there is no reason to believe that I was ever here or ever will be. If he cares to leave a message, take it. Otherwise, hang up the goddamned phone!"

"Yes, sir!"

Bonafacio rushed off to do as he was told, his voice a low-pitched mutter on the far side of the room. When he returned to stand before Sebastiano several moments later, the man stood well back, out of arm's reach.

"Sir?"

"Get on with it," Sebastiano ordered.

"This one speaks English. I think he was American."

"And his message was...?" Impatience strained Sebastiano's voice.

"He says he knows who killed our soldiers in the village."

"Ah." The news was out by now, of course, with speculation on the radio and television that the dead men from the village were associated with The Fist. Still, for a call to come directly from a stranger not associated with the media was most unusual, if not unique.

"Who did he blame for this?" Sebastiano asked, his tone a trifle softer now.

"FARC," the smaller man replied at once. "He tells me Adriano Aznar brags of murdering our men."

"And you believe him, Bonafacio?"

Sebastiano's subordinate was startled, as much by his boss's amiable tone as by the fact that his opinion should be asked on such a matter. Blinking at the question, he first shrugged, then said, "He may speak the truth."

Sebastiano nodded, almost smiling at the answer that had been the only safe and prudent thing to say. "I see," he said, and watched the other flinch as he unfolded from his chair.

There were too many unknown variables, for him to make a judgment. Sebastiano almost wished that he had spoken to the stranger himself, attempted to deduce if he was being truthful, but he judged it would have been a wasted effort. If he couldn't see a liar's eyes, how could he ever truly know his heart.

There was no reason to believe the village they had raided

was an FARC enclave. That had simply been a story he concocted to inspire his troops for battle. Still, if it were true, that would explain the way in which his men had come to grief. They had gone in expecting no significant resistance, but if they had walked into a hornet's nest of Communist guerrillas...

Yes, it fit.

Sebastiano wasn't ready to pronounce the statement true, but he was wise enough to recognize a danger to himself and to the movement which he led. Such losses couldn't be sustained for long, and they could never be allowed to pass without swift retribution.

"I want my officers," he said at last. "Reach out for them, wherever they may be. I want them here within the hour."

"YOU THINK THESE calls will do the trick?" Regan Kelly asked.

Bolan frowned and said, "Chances are I'll have to help them a bit."

She looked away from him. "Oh, God. I know what that means."

"You're no part of it," he told her bluntly. "There's no reason you should be involved at all. In fact, I ought to make some calls and see if we can get you out of here this afternoon."

"What makes you think I'm going anywhere?" she challenged him.

"I understand about your friend...."

"Oh, really?" She was angry now. "You do? Why don't you tell me all about him, then? For starters, you could tell me why he had to die."

"He didn't have to die," Bolan replied. "He could have run away. The fact that he decided not to, that he chose to stand and fight, says something about his character."

"Fat lot of good it did him, right? I mean, he's dead, no matter how you try to dress it up."

"That's right," the Executioner agreed. "He's dead."

"And if he'd run away, the chances are that he'd still be alive."

"I'd have to know his definition of the term. Some men— some people—need a certain minimum of self-respect to make it worth the effort, Regan."

"Self-respect? Is that what this comes down to?"

"What do you want to hear?" he asked. "That it's a God-and-country thing? That altruism's all that counts? How many people do you really think adopt a cause because it serves the planet or mankind instead of some more personal concern?"

"We're back to me again," she said. "I should have seen that coming. Look, I don't know what you *think* you know about me, just because we...we..."

"I thought we were discussing Ciro and his choice," Bolan said, interrupting her.

"Were we? I heard you saying that you think I chose to work with the consultancy because it fit some purpose of my own."

"I thought we were agreed on that," he said, "but that's beside the point. Not everything that happens in Colombia is your responsibility. It may be hard to grasp, but some events may have nothing at all to do with you."

"That's cute. And what about this morning in the village? Do you think that was some kind of wild coincidence? How do you think that came about?"

"I think somebody tipped off the shooters that we were there," he told her honestly.

"So, there you are. My fault. Those people dead because of me."

"Not necessarily."

"Look, you just said—"

"I said I thought somebody tipped off the shooters that *we* were in the village, not just you. In case it slipped your mind, they have more cause to take me out for what's been happening in Bogotá the past two days than you for anything you've done the past year and a half."

"I think there was an insult in there, somewhere," Kelly muttered.

"Not at all," Bolan corrected her. "I'm simply going with the odds."

"But the police came after me," she said. "Remember that?"

"Right. To squeeze you for whatever information you might have about the shootings in the city. We confirmed that from the guy who sold you out, remember?"

Kelly clearly didn't want to think about Galatria or his fate. "So, what you're saying is—"

"That none of this is your fault," Bolan finished for her. "The police were after you because of something I did. Ciro volunteered his village as a hideout after the ambush on Nestor—who, you may recall, now has a disconnect recording on his telephone."

"They got him, too," she said. Her voice was sorrowful.

"And if that's true, I guarantee he gave you up. Smart money says that's where they got their pointer to the village."

"Nestor wouldn't turn on us that way," she said, but ugly truth had robbed her voice of truculence.

"I didn't say it was his choice," Bolan replied. "Each human being has a breaking point. There are academies devoted to resistance of interrogation. It's the only thing they teach. You graduate from one of those, you think you're made of steel—until the first time you get hit with a specific drug or some new pain technique the teachers didn't think of. And you break. Nobody goes the distance and survives. They break you one way or another, even if you don't give up a certain name, address or fact. You give them things they never even asked for, give your mother up to make it stop."

"Voice of experience?" she asked him, trembling on the edge of tears.

"Not quite," he said. "I've started down the chute a time or two, but luck can also factor in. Each time, I found a way to talk them out of it."

"You killed them, right?" Still holding back the tears, but only just.

"It's not an option Nestor would've had. Don't think too harshly of him."

"You believe he's dead?"

He saw no reason that would justify a lie. "It's probable," he answered. "Keeping him alive would be a major liability."

"I've just lost my two best friends on Earth."

The tears came then, and Kelly took a lurching little step into the circle of his arms. Bolan expected nothing of the heat from the past night's brief encounter and he felt none. This was grieving, and the pain would simply have to run its course.

Long moments later, Kelly stepped away from him, wiping her eyes. "What happens now?"

"I stir the pot," he said. "Turn up the heat and see what bubbles to the top."

PROSPERO ALARCON was restless, pacing in the spacious study of his vast suburban home. Broad windows faced a garden filled with luscious flowers, some of which the master of the house had never learned to name. This day, it might as well have been a rock garden or slag heap, for the pleasure it provided Alarcon.

His mind was churning with the news of what had happened to the raid initiated on his orders and the implication of that outcome for himself. He didn't care about the men who had been killed on either side, because it wasn't in his nature to have true regard for anyone except himself. That shortcoming had made Alarcon a lifelong bachelor, childless—except, perhaps, for two or three stray bastards he would never claim—and on the whole he liked his life the way it was.

Except when things went wrong.

Granted, that didn't happen often to a man as wealthy as Alarcon, a man with friends or friends of friends in places high and low. Ninety-nine times out of a hundred, he could solve a problem simply by producing cash and paying it to go away.

This morning's grim fiasco in the Cordillera was a problem that stubbornly refused to yield—or worse, threatened to turn and bite him in the ass.

He had been on the telephone most of the morning, speaking urgently to men whom he had trusted to resolve such matters in the past. Yago Sebastiano had been one of them, but his reports of late were even more disturbing than the news of his initial losses. Now, it seemed, there was some possibility that FARC paramilitaries may have been responsible for the bloodbath. And while that should have come as no surprise, all things considered, still it gave Alarcon new cause for worry.

In the early days of this most recent strife that tore Colombia apart, he had refused to speak—much less negotiate—with those whom he despised as Communists and traitors to their homeland. Later, when it had become apparent that the war might last for decades, Alarcon discovered that the FARC and assorted other leftist cliques no longer cared to speak with him. They held him in contempt, not only for his wealth, but for his cavalier approach to crushing human beings when it suited him to do so. There was irony behind that show of principle, since every private army in the country, left or right, was led and staffed by murderers. For that insult, he knew, they wouldn't rest until they saw him dead or, at the very least, compelled to live in exile from his home, with nothing but huge bags of cash for company.

The threat from killers on the left was nothing new, but this time something told Alarcon that he might be at greater risk than usual. He thought—feared would have been too strong a word—that this time there might be a more concerted effort to collect the standing bounty of two million pesos that the FARC long ago had placed upon his head.

He paused, midway through one more circuit of the study, and reached out to straighten an original Picasso on the northeast wall. He lurched back, startled, when the pane of glass fronting the masterpiece shattered and the painting crashed at his feet.

It took a moment for Alarcon to realize exactly what had happened. Spinning toward the garden windows, he beheld the bullet hole, and he was diving for the cover of a massive teakwood desk before he heard the distant echo of the rifle shot.

A second bullet came through just behind the first, seeming to chase Alarcon as he leaped for the safety of his desk. It clipped his In tray, flinging correspondence toward the ceiling, and flew on to drill the high back of his cowhide-covered swivel chair. The chair spun happily without him, stuffing spilling from the bullet's exit hole in back.

The third, fourth, fifth shots ran together in Alarcon's ears and in his mind, one bullet drilling through the heavy teakwood six or seven inches from his face, another sweeping the telephone onto the floor beside him. He was reaching for it, thinking he might call for help, since all his bodyguards had seemingly deserted him, when he discovered that the handset had been snapped in two.

Alarcon began to scream.

12

Fraco Terciero knew there was trouble when he found himself summoned to a meeting with Prospero Alarcon and Yago Sebastiano. The two of them together were more than doubly dangerous, the risk of being in their presence when one or both were angry multiplied exponentially. Alarcon had but to speak a word or raise an eyebrow, and Sebastiano would be ready to kill on his patron's behalf.

And Terciero knew, both men had ample reason to be furious.

He had deliberately avoided learning any major details of the Cordillera raid that had gone so completely, disastrously wrong for Sebastiano's men. It had turned out to be a massacre, he knew that much, but not the usual sort where all of the victims were peasants lined up for machine guns or killed on the run. This time some had stood and fought, taking the raiders down and leaving them to feed the forest scavengers.

Instead of Alarcon's estate, Terciero had been ordered to report to an exclusive high-rise apartment building in the heart of Bogotá. He had passed by the building many times, occasionally wondering about the filthy rich who lived inside, never supposing that he would be summoned there for a royal audience.

Uniformed doormen surrounded him in the lobby, checking his ID and calling upstairs to confirm his appointment. They didn't pat him down, but Terciero found four men with submachine guns waiting when he stepped out of the elevator car. A flash of panic subsided as he realized Alarcon wouldn't have brought him here to be killed, spilling blood and God knew what else on the expensive beige carpet.

Two of the gunmen stood aside and covered Terciero while their comrades searched him thoroughly. They didn't make him strip, but by the time they finished poking, prodding, probing him, undressing would have been superfluous. His cheeks were flushed with anger and humiliation, but he offered no protest as the smirking gunmen stood aside, one of them nodding for Terciero to follow him.

The apartment was smaller than Terciero had expected, but lavishly appointed, reeking of blood money. He assumed there were servants on call, but none was visible as the gunman ushered him into a parlor without windows, steering him toward a tall bronze-colored door that stood ajar between bookcases. The sentry left without a word, and Terciero made his way across deep-pile carpet, embarrassed to catch himself walking on tiptoe. At the door, loath to touch it, he knocked on the stout frame instead.

"Come in, Fraco."

Alarcon didn't sound friendly, his grim face confirming the impression of his tone. Terciero judged that he was no longer permitted to address the man by his given name.

"Señores." He addressed the two of them together, Alarcon reclining in a bulky chair constructed out of some dark wood, upholstered in rich leather, while Sebastiano stood beside an artificial fireplace, smoking a cheroot.

"You've heard about our problem, I assume?" Alarcon asked. He held a brandy snifter in his right hand. Could it be the hand was trembling just enough to make the dark liqueur move slightly in the glass, rippling?

"The...um...the village, yes," Terciero said. How did one casually describe a slaughter that had taken more than fifty lives?

"The village was a disappointment, certainly," Yago Sebastiano said, unconsciously providing a reply to Terciero's silent question. "But Mr. Alarcon refers to the recent attempt on his life."

Terciero was stunned, speechless. Glancing about the study where they had assembled, he found himself in another room without windows, beginning to understand.

"Not here, surely?" he asked.

"At my estate," Alarcon said, as if deciding he could manage for himself. "There was a rifleman."

"Perhaps the same one who attacked Calvino Escobar and Amadeo Ornelas," Sebastiano stated.

Alarcon dismissed the comment with a flick of his free hand. "We don't know that," he said. "There is no end of gunmen in Colombia. The problem, now, is that we think the FARC may have been responsible for both the village incident and the attack upon myself."

Terciero felt like saying that the village "incident" had been their own damned fault, but it would have been tantamount to suicide. Instead, he swallowed hard and said, "FARC? Then you must certainly contact the state security police."

"I am responsible for Mr. Alarcon's security," Sebastiano said, shifting posture slightly as he spoke, to puff out his chest.

"However," Alarcon cut in, "we may require assistance from the military and police if it appears that Yago's men are overmatched."

Sebastiano scowled at that, his complexion darkening. His eyes dared Terciero to agree that such a thing was even possible.

Sidestepping the apparent trap, Terciero said, "As I suggested earlier, a man of your influence and connections certainly must have contacts within the ministries of Justice and Defense. My normal duties for the Ministry of the Interior—"

"Include accommodating those who make it possible for you to keep that job," Alarcon remarked, cutting him off. "Tell me, Fraco, do you suppose that you attained your present post through merit and intelligence? Can you be that naive?"

It was Terciero's turn to flush with anger, but he bit his tongue. It was impossible to win an argument with someone

on the level of Alarcon. As for Sebastiano, he might call one
of the gunmen from outer corridor, have Terciero taken out
and shot, dumped in the gutter like a sack of trash.

"What is it that you wish of me?" he said at last.

"Merely cooperation, Fraco," Alarcon replied. "You've always been so helpful in the past."

"If it's within my power, certainly."

"I wouldn't ask for something it wasn't within your power
to provide. You shall continue as my personal liaison with the
other ministers, remembering that my name must be mentioned sparingly—and never without pressing need."

"Of course, sir."

"For now, I only need to know that there are forces on alert,
prepared to move if necessary on a moment's notice."

Terciero reckoned that should be no problem. The security police and military in Colombia had been on a near-con-
stant red alert for close to twenty years. He was relieved that
he hadn't been asked to do something more difficult.

At least, not yet.

"It shall be done, sir."

"Then you may leave us, Fraco. You'll be contacted at
once if we need something more."

Dismissed, he turned and left the lush apartment, past the
gunmen clustered near the elevator, feeling them observe him
with a combination of amusement and contempt. Downstairs,
it was all Terciero could do not to sprint through the lobby
and into the street, running like a madman to his waiting car.

He wondered if he could afford to flee the city, flee Colombia, and find himself another life before it was too late.

REGAN KELLY SAT alone in the small apartment where Mike
Belasko had left her, working up nerve to cross the room and
switch on the radio. She was afraid to let the world in, as if
it might somehow attempt to grab her, drag her back outside,
into the city where her life was next to worthless.

So much death already, and her instincts told her that the
worst was yet to come.

She thought of Ciro Aguiar and Nestor Gomez—one dead in the village where he was raised as a child, the other almost certainly murdered in Bogotá. They had been her only true friends in the city—in the whole damned, bloody country when it came to that—and in her heart she knew that each of them had loved her in his way. She was oppressed with guilt now, both for her part in events that led the two men to their deaths and for the fact that she hadn't been able to reciprocate the feelings she had sensed from both of them.

It hurt that Belasko, after such a short acquaintance, could see through her, reading her private thoughts, the feelings— anger, guilt, and all the rest of it—that she had always thought were hers alone. It was unfair, a total stranger somehow empowered to see inside her mind and heart, expose her to herself without half trying.

Where was he now, this man of blood and mystery? Out stalking someone, she supposed, and feeling not the least bit guilty as he framed another target in his sights. Life seemed so simple, viewed through Belasko's eyes: the guilty had to be punished, and it didn't matter how that end was finally achieved. He was like something from the old American Wild West, or even further back, a kind of transplanted Medieval knight, his cruelty balanced by a sense of chivalry.

"You're being stupid now," she told herself, speaking aloud into the empty room. Disgusted, she compelled herself to get up from the sway-backed sofa and switch on the radio, turning the dial until she found a station with the news in progress. After several moments with no fresh reports of slaughter, Kelly didn't know if she should feel relieved or disappointed.

If Belasko somehow failed at whatever it was he meant to do, did that mean she had failed as well? That her two friends had died in vain? Was everything that she had tried to do in Bogotá these eighteen months a total waste of time? Was it reduced to some bizarre and egocentric self-indulgence, serving no one but herself?

She told herself that she had traveled to Colombia in hopes that she could make a difference for the war-torn country and its people who were suffering...but what if she had only sought to make a difference for herself? Could it be true that she believed a change of scene would also change her life? Had Aguiar and Gomez died because she was a selfish dilettante with delusions of altruism? And if true, did that make her a murderer of sorts?

A part of Kelly now wished she had gone with the police, that Belasko hadn't arrived to help her when the officers had come for her at home. Would anything be different now, if she had gone off to the cells and the inevitable questioning that would have broken her? Would Aguiar and Gomez be alive, or would she have condemned them with her own words, thereby marking them for death?

She felt the burning in her eyes and sinuses that presaged tears, refusing stubbornly to let the feeling carry her away. She could do nothing about what had happened in the past, and there appeared to be no way for her to help Belasko with his struggle, either. If she tried, she was convinced that she would wind up being killed or captured, either one of which might be the ultimate distraction that resulted in Belasko being killed.

Or did he even care that much about her to begin with?

Had he simply stashed her in this place so that she wouldn't be in his way, run off on some wild tangent of her own and spoil his plans?

And in the end, what difference did it make?

Kelly didn't delude herself into believing she would ever see the man again, assuming either one of them survived the present crisis. He was from a world she barely knew existed, rootless, brutal when he had to be. The moment they had shared in the village meant no more than any rash, impulsive action taken under pressure, when tomorrow's promise seemed about to be withdrawn.

They weren't lovers.

Kelly wasn't sure if they were even friends.

Depressed by that as much as anything that she had witnessed in the past days, she made a concentrated effort now to focus on the news from the radio.

With any luck, she might hear something that would tell her if Belasko was succeeding in his quest—or whether he was even still alive.

"ALARCON HAS DESERTED his estate," Aznar explained. "He hides in Bogotá, a place he keeps downtown. Who knows when he'll go home again?"

Vidal Mendoza paused, sipping a glass of tepid beer, considering the problem. "I assume his hideaway is well protected, Adriano?"

"It is three blocks from the main headquarters of the state security police," Aznar replied. "A busy intersection in the city's heart. He has armed guards inside. Not many, granted, but the very placement of the flat makes it a trap. To send men there..." Aznar put on a frown and shook his head. "It would save time and effort if I had them shot before they left the barracks."

"You know best, of course," Mendoza said, although he didn't sound convinced. "There must be some way to persuade this pig that he should go home to his sty."

Vidal Mendoza was Cuban, the equivalent of a lieutenant colonel of the DGI—Castro's Dirección General de Inteligencia—that was responsible for "exporting revolution" throughout Latin America and around the world. He had served briefly in Angola, some years earlier, before he was recalled to concentrate on building up leftist guerrilla movements in Honduras, Guatemala and Colombia. The latter nation was his great success, verging on total chaos, though Mendoza naturally couldn't take credit for the natural bloodthirsty leanings of the natives.

Still, it never hurt to try.

"I have discussed this with my people," Aznar told him. "We believe that if we threaten him at the apartment house, he'll simply reinforce his bodyguard and summon the police to watch more closely."

"But of course," Mendoza said, nodding. "I thought, perhaps, if someone threatened the residence itself..."

He left the notion dangling between them like bait for a sluggish, not particularly clever fish. Aznar examined it, considering the possibilities.

"He might still call the army," Aznar answered, "or The Fist. It's understood that Alarcon has purchased many friends in the establishment. As for the People's Army of Democracy, it's said he helped create it as a private force of strikebreakers and killers, also as a death squad to support his friends in government."

"You have troops at your disposal," Mendoza said pointedly. "It surely can't be that you're afraid of confrontation with these running dogs of the American fascist regime."

He saw Aznar bristle, gratified by the impact of his words. "It is not a matter of fear, Mendoza," the guerrilla leader answered stiffly. "Fidel himself has taught us to conserve troops and resources, has he not?"

"The Comrade President also demonstrates by his example that we must be bold, not timid. You remember his attack on the Moncada Barracks, I assume?"

"I am aware of the event," Aznar replied. "Regrettably, Comrade, I wasn't born in 1959."

Mendoza sighed, already weary of the game. "You were not born in 1848 or 1917 but still you learn from Marx and Lenin, yes?"

"Of course, Comrade."

"Prospero Alarcon values his house and property, I would assume?"

"Indeed. It's said he loves his horses most of all. The pig maintains a stable filled with sleek, fat Thoroughbreds while hundred of his workers nearly starve."

"Let this love be your weapon, then. It is a weakness in the strongest men."

"Attack the stables?" Aznar seemed confused.

"Threaten what he loves most," Mendoza clarified, his patience tested almost to the breaking point. "He will defend it, Adriano. This I promise you."

"Defend it with the army and The Fist," Aznar muttered.

"In which case, you find him unprotected somewhere else.

Use this—" Mendoza raised a hand, the index finger tapping lightly at his skull, then dropped the hand to pat the pistol hidden underneath his coat "—before you reach for this."

"Perhaps," Aznar suggested, "you might have some interest in observing the attempt. I'm sure my officers would benefit from your experience and criticism."

The trap was set. Mendoza was within his rights to turn down the rebel leader, chastise him for his impudence. The role of an adviser was, quite simply, to advise. He wasn't meant to gallivant about the countryside on exercises where his liberty, perhaps his very life, would be at risk. The downside of refusing, though, was that he would immediately lose respect from Aznar and whichever other members of the FARC Aznar chose to share the story with.

And that, Mendoza had no doubt, would be the whole damned team.

"I would be pleased to supervise the action," he replied, turning the game around on Aznar, claiming for himself at least a theoretical position of command. "It always benefits a field adviser to observe the troops."

If Adriano Aznar felt the barb, he gave no sign of it. His dark face broke into a smile. "Good," he said. "I'll give the orders and reach out for you when it is time to move. You'll be available? The usual phone number?"

"Certainly." Mendoza forced a smile. "I wouldn't miss it for the world."

MOBILITY WAS PARAMOUNT. The Executioner had learned that fact while he was still a green recruit in basic training, had it reinforced through combat service in the Special Forces and the private wars that followed his departure from the mainstream military. Movement in battle—what the Executioner sometimes called combat stretch—was often critical, whether for feints, advances or retreats. The soldier most at risk for being overrun and slaughtered was the one whose position was static, immobilized by geography or circumstance.

Bolan's problem in Bogotá was peculiar. He no longer had eyes inside the enemy camp, no one to brief him on the movements of his targets, so he had to mount surveillance by himself, alone. That instantly ruled out observing different factions, forcing him to choose a single mark and play it out that way, whatever happened down the road. He had also lost track of Prospero Alarcon following his deliberate near-miss at the man's estate, and reacquiring the target could be problematic—unless he chose the right figure to shadow from that moment on.

The final choice came down to Yago Sebastiano, for dual reasons. First, Bolan had his home and office addresses on file in his mental Rolodex, which gave him concrete starting points. Second, and more importantly, Sebastiano, as commander of The Fist, was most likely to deal with Alarcon directly, maintaining at least some degree of personal contact. It would go against the big man's grain to haggle through subordinates when he could reach out for the man in charge. And if the local skinny was correct, in assuming that Prospero Alarcon had funded The Fist to begin with, he would most likely pull his ranking puppet's strings directly, rather than delegating the pleasure.

Two phone calls had convinced Bolan that his quarry would be found at the office where he normally spent two days every week, pretending to administer a patriotic political action committee. In each case, calling the intended target's home and office, he had been informed that Sebastiano wasn't present, but the man who picked up at Sebastiano's home had said it quickly, without thinking, while the office flack had gone offline for several seconds, as if asking for advice. Bolan had thanked him when he finally returned and cradled the receiver, satisfied.

Parking his rental on a side street with an angular view of the office, Bolan had settled down to wait, a Spanish-language newspaper open in his hands to provide an illusion of belonging to the neighborhood. With his dark hair, olive complexion and suntan, he thought he could pass if no one stopped to talk—and since most residents of violent Bogotá were as reticent of contact with strangers as the average New Yorker, Bolan thought he was safe. There were no signs or meters to suggest restricted parking on the street that he had chosen, nothing in the way of sentries visible around the storefront office where Sebastiano put in time. As long as The Fist didn't have some kind of roving neighborhood patrol in place, Bolan thought he would be fine.

And if they did, he was prepared, with the Beretta slung beneath his arm, the Spectre submachine gun on the seat beside him, hidden underneath a second newspaper.

He had been watching the office for three-quarters of an hour when two men emerged wearing leisure-style suits that had gone out of style in the States years before. Their jackets were cut loosely to hide concealed weapons, but not loose enough for the hardware these soldiers were packing, bulking out their slender torsos. They surveyed the street in both directions, missing Bolan as he slouched behind the rental car's steering wheel, then one of them retreated briefly, sounding the all-clear inside.

A moment later he returned, with two more gunners in tow. These also sported leisure suits, which Bolan was beginning to suspect might be The Fist's official uniform for urban operations. The four guards were on station, ringing the office entryway, when a black two-year-old Continental pulled up to the curb and waited, engine idling.

Only when the car was in place did Yago Sebastiano show himself. He wore a suit of more traditional cut, but its khakilike fabric still gave him the look of a soldier in dress uniform. Behind Sebastiano, as he stepped into the waiting car, two more shooters emerged from the office, all six piling into the car with their leader and the wheelman.

They were rolling out in seconds flat, Bolan giving the Lincoln a lead before he pulled out behind it, taking up position for the track. He didn't know where they were going, but Bolan meant to follow them—straight to Prospero Alarcon.

13

"Are the horses all right?" Prospero Alarcon demanded as he stepped out of the car.

"Yes, sir!" Two voices reporting as one, his security chief and ranch foreman responding in unison.

They glanced at each other, these nervous two, and it was the foreman who continued. "The device was found by Manuelito. He is—"

"I know who he is!" Alarcon snapped. "You think I don't know my own stable boys? Get on with it."

"He found the...object and called me. I immediately called Miguel."

It was the other's turn. "It was a small incendiary bomb, sir," Miguel Cervantes said. "Not large, but it would have razed the stables. It has been disarmed."

"Tell me how such a thing can happen here," the master of the house demanded. "Are you not paid adequately to keep bombers from this place? What's next? My bedroom? Shall I find plastique inside the toilet bowl?"

"No, sir," Cervantes said. "We've checked the house most thoroughly, and—"

"Goddamn it!" Alarcon exploded. "How can someone creep in here unseen? It's daylight! Are my so-called body-guards all blind and deaf? Or are they merely stupid, soon to be among the unemployed?"

"Sir," the foreman said, eyes downcast, with a tremor in his voice, "we now believe it was another of the stable boys.

He's missing, and...we think...at least it may be possible he planted the device."

"A stable boy." Alarcon's tone was flat, his features etched in stone. "Give me his name."

"Isidro Mondregon."

"Find him. And find his family. I want them all. If he's responsible for this, the parents must know something. One of them will talk before the night is over."

"I have men out looking for them now," Cervantes said.

"I want the names of those who treat me with such disrespect, Miguel. I want them punished. Do this quickly and correctly, if you wish to see another paycheck with my signature."

"It shall be done as you say."

"And you," he said, rounding on the foreman, fairly snarling. "If this one—" a thumb cocked toward Cervantes— "can't keep the stables safe, it falls to you. Understand?"

"Yes, sir."

"Five hundred pesos extra to the boy who found the bomb."

"Yes, sir!"

Alarcon turned and left them standing there to fight about whose fault the problem was. He had been seething since the phone call had announced discovery of the incendiary in the stable, with its timer counting backward to the flashpoint that would have destroyed his precious Thoroughbreds and several hundred thousand dollars' worth of property.

In spite of his demands, the big man was convinced that he could name the rebels who had left this package on his doorstep. Adriano Aznar had the nerve, and he was also fool enough to think that he could do such things without incurring any major consequence. Alarcon was still unclear on what had happened in the village where Sebastiano's men were killed, but somehow it all seemed to revolve around the FARC and the International Consultancy on Human Rights.

Moving swiftly toward the house, surrounded by his retinue of bodyguards, Alarcon wondered if the ICHR had somehow decided to cast itself with the leftist guerrilla fighters in Colombia. It seemed unlikely, given past denunciations of both sides by consultancy spokesmen, but stranger things had happened in Colombian politics. The strangest part, in Alarcon's opinion, would be the ICHR's decision to side with those who were destined to lose.

And if Aznar sent men to kill Alarcon at his home, the schedule of the FARC's loss would only be advanced. Sebastiano and his men were already en route to reinforce the plantation, men and guns enough arriving to deal with any significant threat short of air strikes or nuclear warfare.

Alarcon now regretted fleeing his home in the wake of the afternoon sniper attack. It set a bad example for his servants and would make him seem less than courageous to any business competitors who might learn of the incident. Still, nothing could be done about that now. He had returned, and he would stay until the issue was resolved. In the improbable event that battle was joined here, in his backyard, Alarcon had every confidence that he would triumph.

And that would be the lesson his competitors and enemies remembered to their dying day.

It would be Alarcon's sincere pleasure to watch them scream and beg before they died.

"WE LEAVE THE ROAD soon," Adriano Aznar told his Cuban traveling companion, smiling at the vague look of discomfort on the other's face.

"Of course," Vidal Mendoza said. "To take them by surprise."

Aznar had never been especially impressed by the adviser from Havana, though he never failed to thank Mendoza for the bags of cash be brought or for the arms and ammunition he supplied. It seemed to Aznar that the little Cuban thought himself some kind of modern Che Guevara—but without Guevara's wit, courage or fighting skill. He was a talker, not a fighter, in Aznar's opinion.

"Comrade Fidel no doubt led many marches through the jungle after nightfall," Aznar said.

"Of course." Mendoza took the needle with only the slightest hint of irritation. It was rather disappointing.

Aznar lapsed into silence until they had reached the point where they would leave their vehicles and proceed overland on foot, penetrating the private domain of Prospero Alarcon. A spy on Alarcon's staff had reported his return to the estate, thus validating Mendoza's prediction that a threat to the horses would bring him home.

What a fool this one was, Aznar thought. Risking his life for the sake of dumb animals, when thousands were worked to death or slaughtered on his plantations every year. Where was the logic, the rationale?

Aznar had brought seventy-five of his very best men, crammed into four-wheel-drive sport vehicles and army-surplus trucks. The small convoy had drawn some curious stares in transit, but they had encountered no opposition thus far, and the authorities had missed their one best chance to intervene. The next enemy Aznar and his people faced would be The Fist, whose troops had also been reported as arriving at the big man's home.

It was to be a battle, then. So much the better.

Aznar's men had come prepared. Each soldier had an automatic weapon with an ample supply of spare magazines. Many had side arms for backup, and most had grenades. One man in every dozen wore a Russian RPG-18 light antitank weapon strapped across his back, loaded with a 64 mm shaped charge capable of knocking out an armored personnel carrier—or shattering the walls of a mansion.

Forming the soldiers into loose ranks, Aznar double-checked the compass heading with his rifle team commanders and the column set off through the forest in lowering darkness. It would soon be full night and they would have to proceed without flashlights, avoiding any giveaway that would betray them to their enemies.

"We have two kilometers to go, perhaps a little more," Aznar informed his Cuban paymaster, "before we cross into the land owned by Alarcon. From there, it is another six or seven kilometers more to the house. Three hours, more or less, if we don't encounter great obstacles along the way."

Like armed patrols, he thought, but kept the comment to himself.

"They are expecting us?" Mendoza asked.

"They are expecting trouble, in accordance with our plan," Aznar replied. He longed to say, "your plan," but again he bit his tongue, remembering the guns and money.

"So, a bold initiative," Mendoza said, with less enthusiasm than Aznar would have expected from a hero of the People's Revolution. "Tonight, your enemies will learn to walk in fear."

"Our enemies."

"Of course."

"We should be quiet now," Aznar advised. "I'm sure you understand."

The guerrillas made steady, cautious time, alert to any dangers present in the forest after nightfall. Enemy patrols weren't the only hazard that they faced; the land itself could be an enemy to those of reckless disposition. Cultivation of coffee and other crops in the region had driven away most large predators, but Colombia still harbored more than a dozen venomous snakes, and two of them—the bushmaster and Barba Amarilla—were aggressive biters, the latter responsible for more snakebite deaths than any other serpent in the Western Hemisphere. There were banana spiders that could kill a man if help wasn't available, and scorpions whose sting, while rarely fatal, could result in days of wretched pain and nausea.

Wildlife aside, the forest was an unforgiving place for careless travelers. Flash floods could change the landscape overnight, producing deep gorges where a man might fall and snap his leg or spine. Some trees were undermined, nearly uprooted by erosion, insects and disease, awaiting human contact or an errant breeze to bring them down with crushing force. Burrows and roots could twist an ankle, sidelining a soldier or slowing the troops to his lame, halting pace. On hillsides, there was always danger that the earth itself would move, loose soil and boulders plummeting to bury hapless men.

All things considered, then, it came as a relief to Aznar when his file of soldiers, thus far undiminished, found itself at last within a half kilometer of Alarcon's great manor house. The lights were clearly visible beyond a cultivated field of beans and maize.

"From here," Aznar advised Mendoza in a stage whisper, "the danger will be great."

He half expected that the Cuban would elect to stay behind and watch the battle from a distance, but Mendoza managed to surprise him.

"Let us meet the danger, then," Mendoza said, and flashed the first smile he had ever shown Aznar.

It was a sight the guerrilla leader could have lived without.

MACK BOLAN knew the forest.

Not this one specifically, although the present visit to Colombia wasn't his first. Rather he knew the forest as a concept, a milieu where life-and-death dramas were played out in daylight or darkness, winner take all. He had come of age in the steamy rain forest of Southeast Asia, sampling others from Canada to South America and Africa in the course of his wars. Each was unique, of course, in terms of its inhabitants, climatic quirks and so forth—but the rules were constant, immutable laws of nature.

Respect the land, its denizens, your enemies.

Rely upon preparation and yourself.

Survive at any cost.

Bolan had come prepared to face Alarcon, his bodyguards and soldiers of The Fist, plus anybody else who happened to appear. He hoped they might have company, but if no other hostiles showed, Sebastiano had already stationed close to seventy armed men around the grounds of the estate on full alert.

Bolan was dressed in blacksuit and black webbing, face and hands darkened with combat cosmetics, although there was no moonlight to betray him. Better safe than sorry in the killing game. He carried the M-4/M-203 combo, with the Desert Eagle autoloader on his hip, Beretta 93-R slung beneath his left arm and the Spectre SMG riding a quick-release strap on his back. Spare magazines, hand grenades and rounds for the 40 mm launcher completed the ensemble, adding almost fifty pounds to Bolan's normal weight.

At least, he thought, he didn't have to wear a full field pack with canteens and survival gear. He would be in and out of Alarcon's estate in relatively decent time...or he would never leave at all.

Bolan had scouted the perimeter, marking the guards, remaining just beyond the range of their senses. No dogs were in play, a fact that improved his chances for survival, and the floodlights that illuminated Alarcon's mansion hadn't been installed to light the surrounding fields or forest. The guards carried flashlights but used them sparingly, conserving the batteries unless they heard some unexpected sound or hit a rough patch of terrain.

They were about to hit a rough patch soon, from which no flashlight would permit them to escape.

Bolan was finishing his second circuit of the property, his targets memorized, when he picked up on the approach of an assault force from the south. He knew the troops approaching weren't friendlies, since they took great care to keep their progress quiet.

FARC? Perhaps the payoff from his call to Aznar's headquarters? It hardly mattered, in terms of individual identities. Any distraction was a benefit to Bolan now. He would take what he could get, and give it back tenfold.

The soldier's smile was grim as he began advancing on his target's home.

YAGO SEBASTIANO was sipping coffee on the veranda, wishing it had whiskey in it, when the bats began to circle overhead. The sonar they employed to guide themselves in flight couldn't be registered by human ears, but they made other chirping sounds in their pursuit of insects that were drawn to the floodlights surrounding Alarcon's vast home. Their voices set Sebastiano's teeth on edge and made him wonder if there might be vampires winging through the night, mingling with those who fed on bugs, waiting to swoop and steal a taste of blood.

He wondered if there would be blood enough to go around this night.

His soldiers were as ready as they'd ever be. Beyond a certain point of preparation it was all waiting, killing time, boredom and disappointment. The readiness was obviously wasted. It was then that troops sometimes lapsed into negligence, fatigue and ennui joining forces to debilitate, sometimes to kill. If there was no contact by midnight, Sebastiano knew that he would have to circulate among the troops and keep their spirits up.

In fact, he wondered if—

The first reports of gunfire sounded far away, around the northeast corner of the house. He heard a single crack of rifle fire, immediately followed by an automatic burst, and then another, longer one.

Goddamn it!

It was probably a false alarm, one shot triggered by accident igniting the perimeter, and if so, Sebastiano had to deal with it swiftly, before panic spread, setting off firefights between groups of his own men. At the same time, any display of firepower would minimize the chance of enemies trespassing within range of his guns, thus prolonging the virtual siege.

Setting his mug down on a nearby wrought-iron table, Sebastiano took off jogging toward the nearest corner of the house. His right hand clutched the Uzi submachine gun slung across his shoulder, to prevent it slapping painfully against his hip. The gunfire was continuing, spreading as he had feared, but he was still not ready to admit it constituted any true cause for alarm.

The explosion shocked his mind blank, stunning him. He broke stride, almost stumbled, then recovered his balance and poured on the speed. The blast had been produced by some explosive far more powerful than any normal hand grenade, but what? And how?

Sebastiano suddenly felt terribly conspicuous in his street clothes. He had relieved himself of tie and jacket when he went out to enjoy his coffee and review the troops on sentry duty, but his white shirt, khaki slacks and street shoes reminded him with every step that he wasn't dressed for battle. Indeed, he wore no side arm and carried only one spare magazine for the Uzi, carelessly thrust into a hip pocket of his slacks as an afterthought when he left the house.

All wrong. A danger to himself and others.

Still, there was no time for him to turn back now and grab more ammunition, much less change into fatigues and boots. He had to find out what was happening.

The second blast seemed closer, but Sebastiano couldn't tell if this was due to his own progress or if someone was advancing on him with the weapon that produced those thunderclaps. He was aware of fine dust drifting down around him from beneath the eaves of the three-story mansion, sifted loose by the explosion, gritty in his eyes and on his lips.

He reached the corner of the house and paused there, with the ragged sounds of battle ringing in his ears. Sebastiano slipped the Uzi off his shoulder, making sure the safety had been disengaged and that it had a live round in the chamber. Dropping to one knee, unmindful of the dirt and grass stains that his slacks would suffer, he leaned out to risk a peek around the corner, ready to duck back if he was threatened or came under fire.

Across the broad north lawn that sloped away toward darkness and the forest, he saw eight or nine of his commandos fanned out in a ragged skirmish line. Two more lay prostate on the grass, one firing toward the distant trees, the other limp and still. Downrange, the darkness of the forest was alive with muzzle-flashes and he heard the rattling hiss of bullets swarming toward the manor house.

No accident, goddamn it! No mistake!

They were under attack by a force of some strength, and

that fact alone narrowed the range of suspects. Who but Adriano Aznar and the FARC would attempt such an assault upon Prospero Alarcon?

No one.

He was about to join his soldiers when he saw a brighter flash, down near the tree line, and a rocket streaked across the north lawn, hurtling toward the house. Sebastiano just had time to turn and sprawl facedown, arms clasped above his head, before the rocket detonated twenty feet away and showered him with smoking pieces of debris.

VIDAL MENDOZA LOVED the smell of gunpowder. He found it physically arousing, better than perfume behind a woman's ear. He liked to practice on a firing range, and while excitement never spoiled his aim, he often left the sessions giddy and light-headed.

He was in a kind of private heaven now.

When he was young and new to Castro's DGI, Mendoza had been stationed in El Salvador, and then in Nicaragua. Though his mission was to counsel and report, he'd found himself pursuing any opportunity to fight, go on guerrilla raids, participate in ambushes or executions. He had earned a reputation for himself, and it had raised some eyebrows in Havana. He had been recalled after an incident involving several prisoners, and there had been a period of strict reeducation wherein he had learned to put the Party and its needs before his own.

He was reformed.

But this was fun.

Mendoza caught one of the fascist paramilitaries in his AK-47's sights and fired a short burst, watching as the target staggered, lurched and went down. It was his second kill so far, and he was confident it wouldn't be the last. These peasants might have guns and uniforms, but he wasn't impressed so far with their ability as soldiers.

Moving toward the house where floodlights blazed, Mendoza swept the field for targets and found that the first line of defenders had apparently retreated—those who weren't killed. Another armor-piercing rocket streaked across the broad expanse of lawn and slammed into the house with stunning force, striking the northwest corner of the topmost floor, spewing debris into the yard below. It looked to him as if the house were burning now, a flickering of red-orange light in blasted rooms.

The fire excited him. Racing across the lawn, with Aznar's soldiers fanning out on either side of him, Mendoza was reminded of the reason he had pledged his life to the advancement of the People's Revolution in the first place. Politics ingrained from early childhood was a minor part of it. Mostly, he craved the action, any chance at all to lash out violently against selected targets. He had managed to conceal that from his counselors in the reeducation program—well enough, at least to win a second chance with Castro's covert diplomatic corps. Now, here he was, back in the thick of it, and he was happy, verging on ecstatic.

Alarcon's defenders were returning fire and scoring hits. Already, Mendoza had seen half a dozen of the FARC soldiers killed or wounded, but they pressed on regardless, shouting battle cries that had been drilled into them with countless rehearsals, to remind them why they were risking their lives to kill strangers.

Mendoza needed no slogans to drive him. The thrill of combat was motive enough.

He glanced around briefly, in search of Aznar, and found the rebel leader lagging a few yards behind, to Mendoza's left flank. It amused the Cuban to think that he had startled—even frightened—Aznar by his transformation in battle. If they both lived through the night, Aznar would never look at him the same way again.

And if they didn't make it...well, at least it was an interesting and exciting way to die.

Nearly two hundred meters yet, before they reached the house and other buildings—a long detached garage, some kind of barn, outbuildings for storage, the stables to the west—the defense still showed no sign of crumbling. The first line had retreated, it was true, but now they held their ground as if invested with a new combative spirit, more determined not to yield.

An explosion tore through the advancing FARC ranks, thirty meters or so to Mendoza's right. He flinched involuntarily but never broke stride, advancing steadily, albeit with his shoulders hunched against the anticipated sting of shrapnel or bullets.

They had some kind of heavy artillery, perhaps grenade launchers, but it would do them no good.

The end was coming for Alarcon.

Mendoza hoped that he would have the privilege of taking out the fascist pig himself.

BOLAN FIRED another HE round in the direction of the charging troops and turned away without waiting to view its effects. He had seen enough examples of HE's impact on flesh and bone that no further displays were required. The targets who survived the blast would be shaken at best, maimed at worst. Either way, they were out of the fight for a while.

Bolan turned his attention to Alarcon's defenders. He hadn't seen Sebastiano since the shooting started, but he had no doubt the field commander of The Fist would be among his soldiers somewhere, rallying the troops, exhorting them to give their all.

And Bolan meant to see them do exactly that.

His game was simple and as old as time: when heavily outnumbered, use your adversary's *other* enemies against him to your own advantage; let them kill off one another while lending any personal assistance possible. The more who die on either side, the better. Ideally, if it all worked out, the two opposing sides would neutralize each other and be done with it.

A group of reinforcements, eight or ten in all, had just arrived from somewhere as he moved in closer to the rambling manor house. One of them flicked a glance his way and saw the black-clad, camou-painted apparition bearing down upon them like Death. The soldier squeaked a warning to his comrades, turning in midstride and squeezing off a burst from what appeared to be an MP-5 K submachine gun.

Bolan was impressed.

The move was smooth, professional and nearly did the trick.

Almost too late, he threw himself aside and tumbled through a rather awkward shoulder roll, while bullets swarmed through empty air behind him, drilling space that he had occupied a heartbeat earlier. He came up firing with the M-4, punching round after round through the agile gunner's chest to drop him in a squirming heap, before he could recover and adjust his aim.

The others knew they were in trouble now, but they were still confused as to its source. They had expected to confront invaders from the northern quadrant of the property, not someone charging from their western flank. Bolan took full advantage of the momentary lag in shifting gears, strafing the squad from left to right and back again before they could recover from the shock of losing their companion and react accordingly.

The storm of 5.56 mm tumbling projectiles ripped into his human targets, flinging them about in all directions, drilling futile hands and arms thrown up to shield themselves. A few of the defenders managed to return fire, but their hasty efforts placed the Executioner in no real jeopardy. In seconds they were down and Bolan moved among them, swiftly dealing out a point-blank coup de grâce to three who still showed signs of trembling life.

Beyond his line of sight another rocket detonated, number four by Bolan's count. This one hadn't impacted on the house, as far as he could tell, and from the secondary blasts that followed he surmised it had been fired at one of the cars parked in front of the mansion.

Were Alarcon's people attempting to flee? Or were the raiders simply canceling the options?

Bolan shrugged off the question and turned away from the main battlefront, circling around the damaged house to the south. It pleased him when the floodlights died along that side, whether from damage to the wiring or a blown-out fuse, he neither knew nor cared. The Executioner would take whatever edge he could get in a situation like this one, with the odds so long against him, and use it to his own best advantage.

As far as Bolan could tell, approaching the south side of the house with its veranda facing cultivated fields and trees beyond, no raiders had approached from that direction, but a number of defenders had been detailed there to cover the approach, the multicar garage and other outbuildings. He counted seven men and judged that there were probably at least a few more whom he couldn't see.

But time was short and he couldn't wait for the others to reveal themselves, if they were there at all. Bolan was looking for a way inside the house before it burned to its foundation. These troops stood between him and the best route.

He took a breath, prepared himself.

And fell upon them like the wrath of God.

14

Prospero Alarcon didn't enjoy admitting he was frightened, much less verging on a state of panic. He had spent the best part of his life developing the image of a man immune to fear, a personality commensurate with his wealth and prestige. It wouldn't do for him to crumble now, before his bodyguards and servants, yet he found the mounting dread inside himself increasingly hard to control.

His lavish home was damaged, possibly beyond repair, and it was burning now. He smelled the smoke, although it wasn't visible as yet, and Alarcon had detailed men to fight the flames with fire extinguishers, though they were needed to repel invaders from outside. It seemed that he was damned whichever course of action he elected now that the assault was under way.

It served no purpose to debate what steps he might have taken to prevent things coming to this pass. He had trusted Sebastiano to place sentries where they were needed—if not to head them off entirely, at the very least to give some warning of their advance before they came too close. Now, the rebels were nearly on his doorstep, and Alarcon had no faith that he could keep them away with the troops he had on hand.

Someone would suffer for this failure if he lived, but at the moment even that remained in doubt. There was a chance the FARC raiders—it could be no other group, in Alarcon's opinion—would attempt to capture him for ransom if they could, but the chaotic battle raging just outside his door didn't bode well for recognizing individuals or taking prisoners. Besides which, Alarcon had no intention of submitting to the Communists who meant to steal what he had worked for all these years.

His best hope was escape, but there were problems with that plan, as well. Evacuation of the property with no more than a handful of his bodyguards would mean abandoning his Thoroughbreds, and Alarcon had no doubt as to how the red guerrillas would vent their anger when they found that he had slipped their clutches. They had tried to kill the horses once already, and it pained Alarcon to think of what would happen to those fine, proud animals if he abandoned them.

It almost broke his heart.

Almost.

If he was forced to choose between his own life and the animals, of course, they were only animals, albeit damnably expensive ones. But if he could protect them, even to the mere extent of freeing them into the nearby forest while he fled, there was a chance he could come back, retrieve at least some of them later when the raiders had withdrawn and he had military troops on hand, instead of Sebastiano's amateurs.

Yago.

If both of them survived the night, Alarcon intended to replace Sebastiano as commander of The Fist. He hadn't made up his mind yet, what should become of his most disappointing aide, but at the very least Sebastiano had to be stripped of power and influence, cast back into the gutter Alarcon had plucked him from so long ago, to let him lead the People's Army of Democracy.

And if the damage to his grand estate was as extensive as Alarcon suspected, if his precious Thoroughbreds were lost, Sebastiano would be called upon to pay in blood.

Alarcon thought he just might do that job himself, instead of delegating it to a subordinate. If nothing else, it might assist in the rebuilding of his image after word began to spread that he was driven from his home.

Escaping was the trick—after delivering the horses, if he could.

It came to Alarcon that simple plans were normally the best. The main assault against his home had been directed from the north, and Alarcon had heard no gunfire from the rear or south. It seemed to him that a selected team of soldiers should be able to sneak out the back and reach the stables unobserved—the more so, now that many of the outer floodlights had gone dark—and free the horses before retreating to the seven-car garage and bailing out.

The plan, he thought, seemed like simplicity itself.

But who would lead the foray into darkness?

Clearly, Alarcon had to go along to calm the horses if he could—and to be ready when the cars were loaded with those chosen to evacuate the property. As for the rest, he grudgingly admitted that Sebastiano should command the party. There was no one else whom Alarcon could trust to rally soldiers now or match the ever-dwindling faith he had in Sebastiano to command and make it stick.

His course decided, Alarcon reached out to collar the first soldier who came running past him, stopped the young man short, demanding to know where Sebastiano was. The soldier shrugged at first, then saw something behind Alarcon's eyes that made him try a little harder.

"Outside with the others," he suggested. "Fighting with the rest!"

Alarcon nearly ordered him to go find his commander, but he knew the order would most likely be ignored. As soon as he was out of sight, the young man's fear would be replaced by more immediate concerns, including how to save himself.

"If you want something done correctly," he said, muttering beneath his breath, "do it yourself."

And he set off to find the leader of the People's Army of Democracy.

ALTHOUGH SURPRISED, the sentries on the south side of the house fought back with more skill and tenacity than Bolan had expected. After killing two of them with his initial fire, he'd hope the other five—and any backup they had lurking in the shadows of the outbuildings—might scatter in a rush to save themselves.

Instead, they stood and fought.

It was a brave attempt, but they were badly overmatched. There is a point where massed firepower smothered skill, experience and courage, but the Executioner had never found that to be true with odds of only five to one. His enemies were also shaky at the moment, some of them perhaps unblooded in a showdown where their adversaries had a chance of shooting back. Coupled with the advantage of surprise, Bolan believed he had an edge that ought to see him through.

The nearest of his five opponents fired an AK-47 burst, fanning the air a foot above his target's head, then kept firing as he toppled backward with a ragged line of holes stitched left-to-right across his chest. He went down kicking, short legs flailing air, then drumming turf before his last wild spurt of energy ran out.

Sweeping on, Bolan caught two more huddled together, near the southwest end of the long garage. One of them was standing, shouldering his automatic rifle, while the other knelt in front of him and slightly to his right, clutching a submachine gun tight against his ribs. Bolan dusted them together, the burst that sheared off most of one man's face ripping across the other's midsection, slamming both of them back against the pale yellow wall that was suddenly daubed and streaked incarnadine.

Two left, and Bolan had to roll out of the way as they cut loose on him in unison. The two survivors both had SMGs and they knew how to use them, even if their aim was hampered by excitement and the shock of seeing their associates cut down. There was no chance of dropping them together like the last two, since they were positioned thirty feet or more apart, angling for interlocking fields of fire, their bullets chewing up the turf.

Incoming rounds spit dirt and grass in Bolan's face, stinging his eyes, but he could still see well enough to sight on muzzle-flashes, and he still possessed enough control to fire back even as he rolled to avoid the hostile fire. A rising burst from Bolan's M-4 cut the nearest shooter's legs from under him and pitched him over on his side, huffing as impact drove the air from his lungs and nearly made him drop his weapon.

Twisting awkwardly to bring his other adversary under fire, Bolan squeezed the carbine's trigger before he had full target acquisition, the flash and racket of his own weapon helping to spoil his enemy's aim at the critical instant. He heard and felt the SMG rounds whipping past him, almost kissing-close, and held his weapon steady by sheer force of will as he replied in kind.

The gunman staggered, taking hits between the waist and throat, losing his SMG when he was halfway through a clumsy, crimson-spouting pirouette. He went down in a heap, and Bolan gained his feet in time to find the last man he had wounded struggling upright in a seated posture, one arm braced behind him, while the other laid his submachine gun horizontally across an upraised knee.

Bolan didn't wait for the dying man to find his mark. A quick burst from twenty feet chopped through his skull an inch below the hairline, ending it. Surprised, mouth dropping open as he died, the shooter flopped backward, spilling his wasted hopes and dreams into the grass.

Bolan was on his feet and ready to defend himself when it became apparent that the field was his. There were no other sentries in the neighborhood. He had destroyed them all.

That left Prospero Alarcon and anyone who tried to shield him from the Executioner.

ADRIANO AZNAR WATCHED Mendoza running like a soccer player through the hail of automatic weapons' fire that crisscrossed Alarcon's great sprawl of lawn. The broad expanse of well-tended grass had turned into an open-air abattoir, dotted with corpses from both sides of the conflict still raging, the failure of floodlights surrounding Alarcon's mansion a mixed blessing. While it made the work of the defense more difficult and sheltered Aznar's troops, it also hid obstacles in the raiders' path—such as the corpse Aznar tripped over, nearly falling, as he tried to keep up with Mendoza.

The Cuban had been radically, almost supernaturally transformed since the beginning of their march through darkness to Alarcon's plantation. Mendoza was a man possessed, once battle had been joined. It was a side of him Aznar had never seen before—and which he would have been content to miss.

It wasn't that the Cuban's sudden spasm of ferocity repulsed Aznar. Such exhibitions were a necessary thing in combat when the cause and personal survival were at stake. Rather, the FARC leader was concerned because he misjudged his adviser so badly, mistaking him for a poseur who aspired to seeing action as a revolutionary, but who never found the nerve to test himself in action. Now, it seemed, he had been wrong across the board.

Mendoza was some kind of wild man, rushing forward in the skirmish line instead of hanging back to watch the action from a safer distance. Aznar wondered how this fit his role as an adviser and decided that it would be safer not to ask. Something was wrong with this one, well beyond the scope of simple zeal or agitation in the face of danger. It occurred to Aznar that he should begin considering some tactful way to have Mendoza recalled to Havana, replaced by someone more stable.

But first, Aznar thought, they would have to survive this night.

The defenders were falling back, slowly but surely, yet they were exacting a price for the yardage gained toward the house. Aznar could only guess how many soldiers he had lost so far, killed or wounded since the shooting started, but he had a feeling that the final body count would be substantial. On the good-news side, his raiders weren't meant to capture and hold the estate, merely to raze it and slaughter the fascists inside. No garrison troops were required. Any losses he sustained would be acceptable, as long as the mission was accomplished.

And, of course, as long as Aznar himself escaped with his life.

That was foremost in his thoughts as Aznar advanced toward the burning mansion, trailing yards behind the Cuban and his other forward troops. Aznar spoke often to his men of dying for the cause, but he had never seen himself as a martyr, lay-ing down his life for the People's Revolution like some sacrificial goat. Death was part of a soldier's bargain, and he understood the risks each time he stepped outside his home, but Aznar didn't intend to throw his life away if he could help it.

Vidal Mendoza, on the other hand...

The Cuban was thirty or forty yards from the house when it happened. A small group of defenders, five or six at most, suddenly appeared around the northwest corner of the house, emerging from the pall of drifting smoke like extras in a stage magician's act. Except, of course, that these performers all had automatic weapons at the ready and they opened up in unison as soon as they had targets clearly in their view.

Aznar hit the turf as the guns went off together, raking the lawn with a spray of bullets at chest height. Vidal Mendoza, for his part, faced the enemy with an inarticulate cry of rage, incredibly advancing on them while his AK-47 chattered nonstop from the hip.

Amazed, Aznar saw his Cuban comrade drop three of the enemy gunners before he started taking hits, the rapid-fire impact of bullets jarring him off stride, making him stagger slightly to his left. Even then, the battle cry stilled in his throat, Mendoza kept firing, chopping down a fourth human target before his magazine was exhausted, the AK's bolt locked open on an empty chamber.

Giving up, Mendoza dropped to his knees, then slumped forward. The Kalashnikov's muzzle speared turf, the weapon somehow twisting in his grasp so that the stock or pistol grip snagged Mendoza's armpit, refusing to let him fall. He looked like something from a sculpted war memorial, hunched over—except for the tremor in his form as more bullets ripped into him, through him from the soldiers he had left alive.

Aznar shot at them from a prone position, one short burst for each, and took them down before they realized there was another adversary yet to be accounted for. Scrambling to his feet and moving out past the Cuban's huddled corpse, Aznar couldn't suppress a smile.

Even in this grim, chaotic world he occupied, some problems still took care of themselves.

BOLAN'S PLAN to search the burning house until he found Alarcon didn't proceed as planned. He was advancing on a doorway facing south, toward the garage and barn—a service entrance, he supposed—when yet another group of armed defenders suddenly emerged, saw Bolan in his midnight garb by firelight, and immediately opened fire on him with everything they had.

The massed fire of half a dozen automatic weapons was enough to drive him back, ducking and running for cover. He found it at the southwest corner of the barn, sliding into relative safety there while bullets chewed up the dirt and woodwork behind him.

Bolan heard commands shouted in Spanish, followed by the sound of footsteps slapping asphalt. They were moving to encircle him. Surround the enemy, cut off retreat and finish him. It was a classic move, and in an adversary's place— if he commanded any soldiers other than himself—Bolan might well have done the same. This was no time for idle speculation, though. He was alone, granted, but he couldn't afford to go on the defensive, not when it could mean his life.

Bolan thrust his M-4/M-203 combo weapon around the corner, not aiming, and lobbed a 40 mm HE round toward the house. He had no reasonable hope of taking anybody down and didn't care. For now, the noise and smoke would be enough.

Before the HE can went off, he was already moving southward along the wall of the barn, turning left at the corner, jogging eastward along the south wall. Bolan paused at the next corner, straining his ears, hearing—or was he just imagining—a sound of cautious footsteps closing on him, somewhere just beyond his line of sight.

There was only one way to find out.

He went around the corner low and fast, almost a waddling duckwalk, with the M-4 carbine seeking targets. What he found, some thirty feet in front of him, were two startled young men in their twenties, each clutching submachine guns so tightly that their tanned knuckles gleamed bone-white.

He killed them where they stood, a raking burst from right to left that dumped them in the dust together, blood mingling as it soaked into the earth. They trembled for a moment, then were still.

The gunfire would bring others, or at least alert them to the Executioner's approximate position. He moved out, reloading the launcher with another HE round as he picked up his pace. Two down from the latest firing squad, with at least four or five remaining to be taken out before he could invade the house.

And after that? What, then?

He blanked the questions from his mind and focused on the mission of survival. There would be no house, no search, if he was lying dead outside.

He found a door unlocked and slipped inside the barn where it was cooler, nearly pitch-dark. Bolan used a pencil flash just long enough to get his bearings and make sure he didn't gore himself on any tools or farm machinery. He found a wooden ladder leading to a loft above and briskly mounted it to try another vantage point.

Moving northward, toward the house, he found the loading bay where bales of hay and other storage items could be hoisted up by means of ropes and pulleys. Peering out, he had a clear view of the yard below, the house beyond and two of his enemies still covering the door that he had meant to enter.

Why? Was someone coming out, or were they simply being cautious?

Bolan decided to give it a moment and see, settling back on his haunches to wait in the dark. Smoke in his nostrils, clinging to his clothes, reminded him that there wasn't much time remaining for his enemies inside the house.

Perhaps, if he could wait for just a little while, a worthy target would present itself.

YAGO SEBASTIANO hesitated in the doorway, listening to gunfire from outside. The sounds were closer now, since Alarcon had sent a man to summon him inside the house and pitch his plan of rescuing the precious horses on their way to flee the battle site. It seemed to Sebastiano that the house couldn't withstand assault much longer and would surely be invaded—if it didn't crumble into flaming wreckage first and kill them all—but he was no less apprehensive about stepping out into the darkened yard.

Sebastiano could see two corpses lying on the pavement, and his own men had scattered, pursuing at least one gunman toward the rear of the barn. The two who remained on the doorstep would make seven altogether headed for the stables. Whether that meant safety in numbers or simply more distraction for any waiting snipers, Sebastiano hoped it would improve his chances for survival.

At least the darkness was a good thing, he hastened to remind himself. With floodlights blazing down, they would have been clear targets as they exited. This way, if someone tried to cut them down, the enemy would need eyes like a cat. The firelight could help a sniper, but smoke was their friend.

The way to do it was a rush, Sebastiano thought. Full speed, but with enough space between runners that a sniper with an automatic weapon couldn't simply rake the line and drop them all. If they were fast enough, lucky enough...

"What's the delay?" Alarcon challenged him, fairly hissing the words. "Why aren't we moving?"

"There is someone in the yard," Sebastiano said.

"And if we wait, there will be more of them," the big man said. "We need to move!"

"Yes, sir." Sebastiano felt as if there should be something he could say, some cautionary words, but he was also anxious to put the estate behind him before it was too late. A few more wasted moments and the enemy might cut them off—not only from the stables, which were no concern of his at all, but from their transportation.

Hissing at the two remaining soldiers he could see, Sebastiano beckoned them back toward the doorway, ordering them to make ready. It was superfluous, perhaps, considering their agitated look, but he would leave nothing to chance. When they were in position, more or less, he randomly selected one of the three soldiers lined up beside him and jerked a thumb toward the yard.

The young man swallowed hard and plunged into the night. Sebastiano followed with Alarcon close on his heels, the last two soldiers bringing up the rear for security. They had covered no more than a half-dozen paces when someone started firing, the rattle of an automatic weapon firing short, controlled bursts. Its sound was more high-pitched than the familiar AK-47, louder than the normal submachine gun.

An M-16, perhaps?

The thought had barely taken shape in Sebastiano's mind when he heard a sharp outcry behind him, glancing back in time to see one of his rearguard soldiers kiss the pavement in a bloody sprawl. Breaking stride, glancing back and upward toward the barn, he saw muzzle-flashes blinking from the open loading bay of the hay loft.

"Goddamn it!"

Unaware that he had spoken aloud, Sebastiano waved his boss past him and turned back to face his enemy, compelled by some strange sense of duty he couldn't resist.

BOLAN WATCHED the dying runner hit facedown and slide for several feet across the asphalt. Drifting smoke was getting in his way, but he could still make out the other seven men, all of them heading for the stables in an flat-out sprint. He recognized Alarcon in profile, had him lined up in his sights, when another member of the flying squad turned back to face him with a weapon raised.

The storm broke before he had time to identify Sebastiano as the shooter, submachine-gun bullets ripping into woodwork, whistling through the open loading bay around him. Bolan threw himself backward, cursing the loss of target acquisition on Alarcon, knowing he had only moments, maybe seconds, before the man slipped through his fingers. If Alarcon and his escorts reached one of the several waiting cars...

Bolan stepped back to the loading bay, raising the carbine's stock to his shoulder before he showed himself, one fluid motion as he stepped around the corner, sighted, squeezed off. The HE round was on its way before Sebastiano could finish reloading his Uzi, striking the pavement between his feet and detonating into a fireball that consumed The Fist's commander where he stood, tearing him apart like a rag doll in a shredder.

It was time to gamble—in this case on Bolan's agility and Alarcon's farm equipment. Slinging the carbine across one shoulder, Bolan leaped up to grab the baling hook fastened to the end of a stout rope that fed through an overhead system of pulleys. Gripping the rope in both hands, the soldier flung himself into space. The line made a sharp snapping sound above and behind him, then started paying out at roughly one-quarter the speed he would have fallen without it, the built-in brake Bolan had hoped for kicking in automatically.

He touched down in a crouch, unslung his main weapon and double-timed after the last of his enemies, just disappearing into the stable. Bolan didn't relish a firefight in the stable, with panicked horses in the line of fire, but he wouldn't let Alarcon slip away.

The game ended here.

Bolan used caution approaching the stables. It stood to reason that his quarry hadn't bypassed the garage and its waiting cars to attempt escape on horseback, so Alarcon had to have something else in mind. Whatever it was, Bolan couldn't have cared less, as long as it didn't prevent a clear shot at the man of the hour. He had marked Alarcon for death at the beginning of this campaign, and he didn't intend to let the robber baron slip through his fingers this late in the game.

The stable's full-time occupants were raising hell by the time Bolan reached the northwest corner of their home, maddened by the nearby sounds of gunfire, the odors of cordite and wood smoke. The horses would be stamping, rearing in their stalls, and from the way it sounded—human voices raised in there, as well as equine—Alarcon's late arrivals were doing little or nothing to improve the situation.

Bolan heard Alarcon snapping at the others, perhaps commanding them to take some action with the horses. Bolan didn't have a clue what that might be, nor did it trouble him. He wanted Alarcon, and if that meant he had to go inside the stable with four other guns as well, so be it.

He found an open door and ducked inside, apparently unnoticed in the chaos of the moment. Half a dozen stalls were open while men grappled horses out and steered them as best they could toward a broad open door at the east end of the stable. The animals were obviously free to run from there, one seizing the opportunity as Bolan entered, the others in their fright resisting unfamiliar hands and orders.

Time to turn up the heat.

Bolan switched the fire-selector switch on his carbine to semiautomatic, sighted quickly on his nearest target, and nailed him with a shot through the left armpit as he flailed hands overhead and shouted something to a rearing steed that sounded very much like "Shoo!" The bullet staggered him and put him down on one knee in a heartbeat, clutching at his wounded side before he toppled forward and the horse sprang over him, clattering away toward the open door and freedom from this madhouse.

Bolan shifted, found another target while the four survivors were reacting to the first report, and shot him in the chest. The dead or dying soldier—still not Alarcon—flopped onto his backside, then slumped forward, forehead striking the straw-littered floor between his splayed legs.

One of the other three, a younger man, released the horse he had been trying to draw from its stall and opened fire with a folding-stock assault rifle, spraying long bursts down the length of the stable in Bolan's direction. The bullets rattled past him in a swarm, then Bolan shot his adversary in the groin and capped it with a head shot as he doubled over, clutching at himself.

Two left, and one of them would be Prospero Alarcon.

He called the Colombian's name and waited for a moment. When the answer came, the sound of shuffling feet was nearly lost beneath the sounds of horses in a panic to escape. Still, Bolan heard it, risked a glance around the corner of the empty stall that sheltered him and saw the last of Alarcon's defenders moving forward, grim determination written on his face.

The man would die because he had been ordered to, and Bolan made it quick and clean with a 5.56 mm tumbler through the forehead. The Executioner's target folded as if his bones had turned to dust at the snap of a finger, going down with a thump of deadweight and a clatter of hardware on the wooden floor.

And that left no one but Alarcon inside the stable with the Executioner.

The man who made a business of manipulating and destroying other lives was in no mood to talk, and Bolan couldn't blame him. He was ready with the M-4 at his shoulder when Alarcon tried mounting one of the Thoroughbreds bareback, tangling fingers in the horse's well-brushed mane.

A clean shot to the shoulder broke his grip and sent him sprawling to the dusty floor. The frightened horse began to dance above him, shod hooves drumming planks, while Alarcon, stunned, raised an arm to protect himself. To scare the horse into leaving Bolan tilted the muzzle of his carbine skyward and triggered half a dozen shots in rapid fire.

The nervous horse went wild, leaping and prancing in circles above Alarcon's huddled form. Hooves met flesh and bone instead of lumber. Alarcon squealed, thrashing out with arms and legs, but his belated self-defense attempts only seemed to madden the animal, causing it to rear and bring its forefeet slashing down like sledgehammers. There was nothing Bolan could do but wait. Before the Thoroughbred broke off and raced into the night, its one-time master lay inert on the floor.

Bolan knew it was too late but went to check him anyway and found no need to waste a mercy round. Unlatching stalls as he retreated toward his point of entry, Bolan let the wooden doors swing open as he passed, leaving the animals to find their own way or remain exactly where they were.

Passing into the darkness that awaited him outside, he wished them well.

Epilogue

"It's still not over, is it?" Regan Kelly asked.

"You may have to accept that there's no ending it," Bolan replied.

They faced each other in a booth for two, inside a small café located near the Bogotá airport. He had three hours yet to kill, before his flight, and Kelly hadn't felt like being on her own.

"We only meant to help," she said, the sorrow in her voice an almost palpable thing. "That's really all we wanted."

"Who's to say you haven't helped?" he asked her, leaning forward with his elbows on the table. "You've been butting heads with the system for nearly two years. There's no doubt that you've made a mark."

"And in the space of a few days you managed to accomplish more alone than all of us achieved together during all those months."

"One treatment doesn't always work for every illness," Bolan said. "Sometimes you need a shock to wake the system up and get things back on track."

"And do you think they are now?" Kelly challenged. "Back on track, I mean?"

He frowned and shook his head. "I wouldn't bet on it. Corruption here is so ingrained, you might be forced to burn the whole thing down and start from scratch."

"More violence, then." The prospect seemed to leave her numb.

"Not necessarily," he said. "And if it comes to that, no one's suggesting you should be a part of it. Somewhere along the line a country's people have to take responsibility for cleaning house themselves."

"Or else they live with the corruption and the violence?" she asked.

"It's not unheard-of," Bolan said. "Even where people vote in droves, their choices aren't the wisest or the best ones every time."

"And that's where you come in."

"I don't change history," Bolan replied, uncertain even as he spoke the words if they were true. "Sometimes I whip the footnotes into shape a little."

"Footnotes," Kelly said. "Like Alarcon, Sebastiano and the rest. Like me. My friends."

"If you want to rank yourself among the dead," he told her, "I suspect there's nothing I can do to talk you out of it. It seems a waste, though, when you've still got so much life ahead of you."

"We've covered this," she said. "Two decent men are dead because of me."

"We've covered it, but you weren't listening. Your friends made choices, and they paid a price. I don't read minds, but something tells me they were thinking of the cause they served, as much as any single person they were trying to protect. You might consider giving them some credit, if you ever take a break from beating up yourself."

"That's easy when you get to walk away."

"What's stopping you?" he asked. "The ICHR can find someone else to take your place. You've got a black eye with the cops here, even with the heat off for the moment, and that's not a healthy way to leave it in a place like this."

"I still have work to do."

"You may be marked," he told her bluntly.

"Then I'll take my chances."

Bolan nodded, recognizing her commitment. He had been there, although granted in a different cause, for different reasons, with a different frame of reference on problem-solving. If she was committed to remaining in Colombia, with all the risks that choice entailed, he reckoned it wasn't his place to try dissuading her. He had completed his work in this place. The rest belonged to others who stayed on.

And she was right, of course. The blows that he had struck in Bogotá and the surrounding countryside wouldn't resolve Colombia's long-running civil war, much less derail the cocaine trade. He had removed some heavy hitters from the game, but Bolan would be first to admit that he had barely scratched the surface of the game itself, much less derailed it or knocked down the stadium where it was played.

The Executioner had still not worked himself out of a job.

"You're staying," Bolan said.

Kelly nodded. "For a little while at least. I can't just run away."

He hoped that she would have the chance, when it was time, and knew before the thought took shape that it wasn't his place to speak the words.

"I hope you make it," Bolan said in place of offering advice.

"I hope we both do," she replied. "Your job's harder than mine."

"It's different," he said. "You pick what works for you."

"I wish—" She stopped herself and sat back from the table. "Never mind," she said at last.

"Okay," he said, and put some money on the table for the waitress. And, with something that wasn't a smile, but close enough, he repeated "Okay."

They rose together, passing through the doorway into sunlight.

James Axler

OUTLANDERS®

PRODIGAL CHALICE

The warriors, who dare to expose the deadly truth of mankind's destiny, discover a new gateway in Central America—one that could lead them deeper into the conspiracy that has doomed Earth. Here they encounter a most unusual baron struggling to control the vast oil resources of the region. Uncertain if this charismatic leader is friend or foe, Kane is lured into a search for an ancient relic of mythic proportions that may promise a better future…or plunge humanity back into the dark ages.

In the Outlands,
the shocking truth is humanity's last hope.

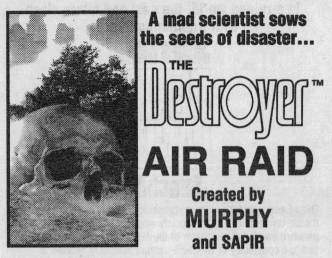

**In a ruined world, the past and future clash
with frightening force...**

JAMES AXLER

DEATH LANDS®

Sunchild

Ryan Cawdor and his warrior companions come face-to-face with
the descendants of a secret society who were convinced that
paradise awaited at the center of the earth. This cult is inexorably
tied to a conspiracy of twentieth-century scientists devoted to
fulfilling a vision of genetic manipulation. In this labyrinthine ville,
some of the descendants of the Illuminated Ones are pursuing the
dream of their legacy—while others are dedicated to its nightmare.

Even in the Deathlands, twisted human beliefs endure....

Available in December 2001 at your favorite retail outlet.